STATE OF ANGER

Virgil Jones: Book 1

THOMAS SCOTT

For information contact:

ThomasScottBooks.com

Linda Heaton - Editor
BluePenEdits.com

Third Edition

VIRGIL JONES SERIES IN ORDER

Updates on future Virgil Jones novels available at:
ThomasScottBooks.com

For Debra
One Love
Always

Anger |'aNGgər|

noun:

A strong feeling of annoyance, displeasure, or hostility

verb:

Fill (someone) with anger; provoke anger in

PROLOGUE

OCTOBER 1987 · INDIANAPOLIS, INDIANA

The cab driver was one of the nine victims—other than the pilot—who actually saw it coming. Unfortunately, he was also the first to die. By the time he did see it there wasn't anything he could do...for himself or anyone else. He didn't see their end, only his own, but he knew they were gone, their clocks, just like his, coming to an end on a final tick or a tock they otherwise would have never bothered to notice, much less count.

The other eight victims stood in the lobby of the Airport Ramada Inn at the Indianapolis International Airport. Six of them were guests waiting to settle their account and check out of the hotel, the other two were hotel employees coming off the night shift. One of the guests had called for a cab even though it was a ridiculously short ride across the street to the airport departure area. Had the weather cooperated this October morning, the hotel guest could have walked to the departure area instead of taking a cab. But weather rarely cooperates, bitch that she often is, so the cabbie made nine.

Nine people have thirty seconds to live.

ONE OF THE HOTEL GUESTS AT THE FRONT OF THE LINE was disputing a charge on his itemized bill. The hotel clerk tried to reverse the charge but failed, the computer telling her she needed authorization from the manager to deduct the proper amount. She tucked a lock of red hair behind her ear and smiled at the man on the other side of the counter and informed him the manager was on the way. The man consulted his watch and smiled back at the pretty redheaded woman, wondering how old she might be. He noticed the name badge on her jacket. Sara. He also noticed the plain silver wedding band on her finger and felt his face flush just a bit as she caught his silent inquiry of her marital status. Just one of those little every day life moments...about to end.

Nine people now have only twenty seconds to live.

From overhead the sound of an aircraft's jet engine is all but ignored by the people in the lobby. It is an airport, after all.

The hotel manager came around the corner and greeted the guest at the front of the line by name. She offered an apology as she entered her approval code into the computer. From the time she appeared, entered the code and reversed the charge, only eighteen seconds had elapsed.

It was coming. The cabbie saw it, and there was nothing he could do.

In two seconds, nine people will die.

THE PILOT, A UNITED STATES AIR FORCE OFFICER WITH the rank of captain, needed his three and three—three takeoffs and three landings within thirty days to stay current. He wasn't due to fly this day, except one of the pilots in the rotation had called off sick, so that bumped the captain up one spot in line. He sat on the corner of the desk in the flight ready room, the way pilots do, and listened to his commander's final instructions before heading out to the flight line at Grissom Air Force Base, in Peru, Indiana.

"We've been having a little trouble with some of the new fuel control units, Captain. Be sure you've got a steady state of fuel flow before you depart. I don't want anything going wrong on a simple three and three."

"Don't worry, Major, I'll keep it right side up."

"See that you do. Call sign today is 'Voodoo.' Designation is Solo, flight of one. Report back to me upon return." The major tossed a casual salute to the captain, then walked away to leave the pilot to his pre-flight routine.

With his flight plan filed, the captain walked out across the tarmac at Grissom Air Force Base and climbed aboard the A-7D Corsair jet. The ground crew members removed the ladder and un-chocked the wheels as the pilot started the jet's massive engine and ran through his pre-taxi checklist. He paid special attention to the fuel flow meter but saw nothing out of the ordinary. He pulled the canopy shut, checked that the latch was secure and then keyed the microphone button on the joystick, his voice calm, detached. "Grissom Clearance, Voodoo Solo, how copy?"

"Five by five, Voodoo Solo. Clearance when ready."

"Go."

"Voodoo Solo, you are cleared back to Grissom AFB via direct Indianapolis, direct Fort Wayne, then direct. Contact ground and have a safe flight."

"Roger that clearance, Grissom AFB via direct Indy, direct Fort Wayne, then direct. So long." The captain switched frequencies, then keyed the microphone again. "Grissom Ground Control, Voodoo Solo, ready for taxi."

"Good morning Voodoo Solo, this is Grissom Ground Control. Taxi to runway 23 via Gulf, then Alpha. Hold short and contact the tower when ready."

"23 via Gulf, then Alpha. Hold short, tower at the end. Voodoo Solo."

The pilot bumped the power lever forward just enough to get the big jet rolling along the apron and performed his pre-flight checks as he taxied. When he approached the end of the runway he stopped short of the hold line, then switched over to the tower frequency. "Grissom Tower, Voodoo Solo, holding short of runway 23 at Alpha, ready for departure."

"Voodoo Solo, Grissom Tower, good morning, sir. Winds are one-eight-zero at one-four, gusting to two-three. Fly runway heading, climb and maintain three thousand feet. Cleared for take off."

"Roger that, Grissom Tower. Any chance for an unrestricted climb to ten?" He knew the after-burners would eat through the fuel, but with both tanks filled to capacity he could afford a little fun, and there was nothing quite like pouring on the power and pointing the nose straight up.

"Voodoo Solo, disregard previous clearance, taxi into position and hold. I'll check with departure. Repeat, position and hold."

"Position and hold. Voodoo Solo." The pilot positioned the jet along the centerline of the runway and ran the engine up to fifty percent power while waiting for the tower controller. The fuel flow held steady. He pushed the throttle to one hundred percent and felt the aircraft strain against its brakes, but the fuel flow looked fine. Maintenance might have been having trouble with the flow control units, but this one appeared to be operating just as it should. When the jet started to slide a bit against the power output the pilot backed the throttle down to twenty-five percent just as the radio chirped in his ear, distracting him from the fuel flow meter that waggled as the engine spooled down to idle.

"Voodoo Solo, Grissom Tower."

"Voodoo Solo, go."

"Voodoo Solo, Grissom Tower, winds are one-eight-zero at one-five now, still gusting to two-three. Fly runway heading, climb and maintain ten thousand feet. Cleared for take off. Enjoy."

"Runway heading to ten, cleared to go. Voodoo Solo." The captain pushed the power lever forward and held the brakes. When the engine reached full power he released the brakes and began his take off roll. Seconds later he was airborne. He raised the gear and leveled off at fifty feet. Once he had the proper speed, he pulled back on the stick and pointed the nose of his aircraft straight up. He was level at ten thousand feet before he reached the opposite end of the runway.

"Voodoo Solo, Grissom Tower. Nicely done, sir. Contact Departure and have a nice day."

He clicked the microphone button twice in rapid succession as an acknowledgement, then switched to the assigned departure frequency. "Voodoo Tracker, this is Voodoo Solo, flight of one, with you level ten, requesting direct Indianapolis."

"Voodoo Solo, this is Voodoo Tracker, good morning, Sir. Radar contact. Maintain ten thousand feet, fly heading one-eight-zero, radar vectors direct Indianapolis."

"Level ten, one-eight-zero on the vector for direct, Voodoo Solo." The captain banked his aircraft to the left until the compass read 180 degrees, then ran through his after takeoff and cruise checklists. His speed was over four hundred knots and he'd be ready for descent at Indy in no time at all. Things happen fast in an A-7D.

As if on cue, the radio chirped in his ear. "Voodoo Solo, Voodoo Tracker, slow to 250 knots, descend and maintain five thousand feet, contact Indianapolis Approach Control on one-one-nine point three. Good day, Sir."

"Two-fifty speed, down to five, approach on one-nineteen three. Voodoo Solo." The pilot pulled the power back to ten percent and dropped the nose, then called Indianapolis Approach Control, who gave him a heading to fly before handing him off to the tower for his touch and go. He would not stop. Instead, he'd just set the wheels down then power back up, take off toward Fort Wayne, and repeat the procedure there before heading back to Grissom AFB.

Still slightly high on the approach, he pulled the power back to idle for just a moment to slow the aircraft before dropping the landing gear. Once he had the proper speed, he pushed the power lever back up to maintain his desired rate of descent.

He was less than half a mile to go on his approach to the end of the runway when the fuel control unit failed and the jet's engine spooled down and died.

Nine people have twenty seconds to live.

WATCH NOW AS OUR CAB DRIVER, THE VERY FIRST TO die, opens the trunk for the bags he'll carry from the lobby. Watch as he happens to look upward, across the street at the bank building and imagine what thoughts must run through his mind as he tries to process what he sees. Watch the way his jaw unhinges and his mouth forms a perfect O so large you could fit three fingers in there and pull him away from the danger of the approaching aircraft if only there were enough time.

The pilot has already ejected and the jet is no longer flying—it is falling. It falls on top of the bank building and bounces upward slightly after this initial impact. It is this upward movement that causes our cab driver to make the O with his mouth. He turns his head toward the hotel, not in denial of what will come, but out of curiosity of what is about to happen. His life does not flash before his eyes, nor does he think with regret of the things not yet accomplished in his life. The last thought his brain processes is no more complicated than the shape his mouth has formed. It is simply "Oh."

See the jet now, its fuel tanks ruptured from the impact with the roof of the bank building. Watch if you dare as it crosses the street and its kinetic energy seeks out the victims in its path. Observe the jagged edge of its broken wing as it decapitates our cab driver with such efficiency that for an instant, even while his head flies toward the lobby his body remains standing erect. Feel the heat as the fireball erupts and follows the twisted hulk of the aircraft into the lobby of the hotel as if the jet's autopilot and navigation systems were set to zero in on a free continental breakfast. See the looks upon the faces of the victims as their clocks come to an end on a final tick or a tock. See it, and feel the flash of pain the way the victims' family members will feel it most every waking moment for the rest of their lives.

Watch the news stories as the days turn to weeks, then watch as the story, sensational as it may have been in the moment, is all but forgotten. It is off the radar, you might say.

But you would be mistaken.

CHAPTER ONE

As far as the Sids were concerned, there really was no other way they could do it. Their target, Franklin Dugan, CEO of Sunrise National Bank in Indianapolis was simply too private, too protected, and too damn stubborn to vary his routine. So in the end they said screw it and did it the hard way.

At forty-two years old, Sidney Wells Sr. had planned, waited, prepared, and dreamed of this moment for half his life. He raised Sid Jr. in the same manner, which is to say he raised her to hate. "Raised her right," he'd say, if anyone ever asked him.

No one ever did.

Morning came, and the light of a cloudless dawn filtered through the windshield of the Sids' van. They were parked a block and a half away on a side street that cornered the property line of the governor's mansion. Sid Jr. was checking the time on the dashboard clock while alternately looking through binoculars at the state police cruiser parked across the street from the mansion. Junior made sure the time on the dash matched her wristwatch. It did. Twelve minutes to go.

"You ready?" Senior said.

"Yeah. Pull around the corner so I can get out without Barney Fife up there seeing me. You sure you're up for what you have to do?"

"I've been waiting for this for almost twenty-five years," Senior said. "I'm more than ready. Just make sure you do your part."

"Don't worry, Daddy-O. I've got the easy part, remember?"

"Yeah, I remember," Senior said. He dropped the transmission into gear and they turned the corner and the van stopped again so Sid Jr. could get out. "You sure the timing's right?"

Junior shut the car door, then leaned down into the open window on the passenger side. "He's never more than a minute off. I'll come in from the south and I should be able to adjust my pace and time it just right. Just make sure you've got the angle on Barney over there. And try not to miss. Missing would be bad."

"I won't miss, for Christ's sake. I never miss," Senior said. Then he said something that both surprised and shamed him, though he couldn't explain why. "I love you, Sidney."

Sidney Jr. smiled and tucked a lock of red hair behind her ear and when she did, Senior thought for a moment he was back in time and looking at his wife more than twenty years ago. Neither one said anything else after that. Junior just turned and jogged away, a fanny pack bouncing lightly on her hip.

INDIANA STATE TROOPER JERRY BURNS SAT IN HIS police cruiser, his radio turned down low, his windows open. He yawned, took the last sip of cold coffee from his thermos and checked his watch. This was the best part of the day for him. The night had been long and boring, but now—just before seven in the morning—he'd be off shift in less than thirty minutes. Better still, in less than five minutes or so, he'd get a gander at the eye candy jogging up the street. She wore the same thing every day...tight black shorts made of spandex or something like that, though he didn't think they called it spandex anymore, a black sports bra, and white Nikes with little ankle socks. Her red hair was cut short and fell against her jaw line and every time Burns watched her jog by he wished he was thirty years younger. Her stomach was flat and firm, her ass was high and tight, and her tits had just the right amount of bounce.

He checked his watch again, and then looked out the window. He saw her come around the corner and jog in place for a minute, checking the time on her watch, like she was taking her pulse, trying to get a read on her heart rate or something. Burns didn't know much about physical fitness anymore, but he knew about heart rates. Age and all.

He watched her jog in place for a few minutes, then surprisingly, she did something she'd not ever done before. She waved at him. Burns sat up a little straighter in his seat and gave her a casual wave back, cool, a little detached. A fucking-A State Trooper, no matter his age.

She tucked a lock of hair behind her ear and started running again. Burns was so preoccupied with bouncing boobs, tight ass cheeks and board-flat stomach muscles he never noticed the cargo van behind him as it braked to a stop and parked at the intersection a half block away.

He did see the governor's neighbor walking down the drive in his robe and slippers. Out to fetch the morning paper, right on time. Like maybe Red and the neighbor had a little sumpin-sumpin going on behind someone's back.

The thought of it sort of pissed him off.

———

RIGHT ON TIME, SIDNEY THOUGHT. SHE PICKED UP THE pace just a bit. The timing would be critical. She got to the end of the drive just as Franklin Dugan did. They smiled at each other and Sidney stopped and bent over to retie her shoe.

"Good morning" Sidney said.

"It certainly is," Dugan replied. "You'll forgive me for saying so, but I've noticed you've become somewhat of a regular, jogging around here in the morning."

"I hope that doesn't bother you," Sidney said, looking up from her shoes.

"No, no, not at all," Dugan said. "Just making conversation with a beautiful young woman." He smiled at her. "Kind of a nice way to start the day."

Sidney finished her shoe and picked up the paper for Dugan. When she stood up she wobbled slightly on her feet, dropped the paper back on the ground and said, "Whoa." She stumbled away from Dugan like she was about to fall and when she did he stepped in close and grabbed her by the arms. "Hey, easy there. I think you stood up too fast."

Sidney smiled and stayed close. "Yeah, you're probably right. But I'm okay. I think I just need a drink of water."

"I'd be happy to get you a glass if you'd like to come up to the house," Dugan said.

"Oh...no, but thanks. I've got a bottle right here in my pack."

Dugan smiled at her. It was the sort of smile that said, *Well, I'm not putting the moves on you or anything like that, even though under the right set of circumstances...* Sid Jr. smiled right back with her best, *Bullshit, you are too and we both know it, circumstances or not* smile. Dugan's face reddened a bit. He bent down to get his paper and when he did, Sid Jr. took half a step sideways and slid her hand into her fanny pack like she was getting a bottle of water.

TROOPER BURNS WATCHED THE ENTIRE EXCHANGE. THE whole thing made him sick. Sure, she was just a fantasy, but she was *his* fantasy. But now the fat cat across the street was ruining everything.

Messing with his mojo.

Burns thought the guy was a banker or something like that. The bankers…they bothered him…getting rich while the rest of the country starved to death. Burns was no bleeding heart leftie, but enough was enough already. How much steak could one guy eat anyway?

He saw the fat cat bend over to collect his newspaper —it had sort of scattered when the redheaded babe dropped it. Burns was secretly hoping she'd bend over and get it. Maybe give him a little ass shot or something. But that didn't happen. Instead, the babe reached into her fanny pack. But she didn't unzip it from the top. She pulled a Velcro flap from the side. She had sort of a stance going, too. Feet planted firmly, knees slightly bent, shoulders square. Burns had an impression forming at the back of his brain and the impression told him that it looked sort of like a shooter's stance. He thought, *huh*.

Then he saw the redheaded babe pull out a gun and thought, *Holy Shit*.

It was the last thought of his career.

And his life.

SID SR. HAD A PERFECT ANGLE. HE WAS IN THE BACK OF the van, a small tinted slider window open just enough for the barrel of his scoped and silenced bolt-action rifle. He kept the cross hairs of the scope tight on the spot just behind the left ear of the cop. Junior was talking to the banker across the street. Their plan was to fire as close together as possible. Didn't want to hit the cop first and have to chase the banker around in a panic, and didn't want to hit the banker first and deal with a trained cop... and his radio.

When Junior reached into her fanny pack, Senior tightened up on the cop. When she had the gun almost all the way clear of her pack Senior saw the cop start to wiggle, the door coming open. It was going to be close, but he had to do it. The cop knew what was happening.

Sid Sr. pulled the trigger.

DUGAN HAD HIS PAPER ALL BUNCHED BACK TOGETHER and started to stand up and when he did he looked across the street. He started to wave at the cop in the squad car, but before he was even half-way straightened up he saw Trooper Jerry Burns' head come apart. The bullet struck with such force and accuracy that Trooper Burns' arm, the same fucking-A State Trooper arm he had used to wave at the beautiful young woman only moments ago raised up as if he were waving once again. Then his body slumped sideways and out of sight into the passenger side of his squad, his age and heart rate no longer an issue.

That was the last thing Franklin Dugan saw before Junior flipped his switch.

SHE POPPED HIM RIGHT IN THE SIDE OF HIS HEAD FROM about a foot and a half with a silenced .22 semi-auto. Dugan dropped on the spot, dead before he hit the ground, the bullet bouncing around inside his head like a ball bearing in a blender. She put two into his chest just to be sure, then bent over to grab her brass. They were hot, but not overly so. Still, when she picked up the third casing—the last one fired—it burned her finger and thumb and she lost her grasp. It hit the pavement just right, did a little flip and a half moon roll, then tinkled down the storm drain between the curb and the street.

The van was rolling up close. She swore silently, took a quick peek into the drain, didn't see anything, swore again, and then jumped into the van. She pulled the door shut and Senior drove them away going no faster than the posted limit, like maybe they were going to church or something. He zigzagged through a few side streets just to be sure and a few minutes later they were on the loop, lost to the world.

Gone, just like that.

CHAPTER TWO

Outside of the two years he served in Iraq One, Virgil Jones had worked in law enforcement his entire adult life. His father, Mason Jones, had been the Marion County sheriff until he retired a few years ago, but Virgil took the state route and became a trooper. He put in the time, got the job done and when the governor of Indiana appointed a black female cop by the name of Cora LaRue as administrator of the newly sanctioned Major Crimes Unit, she hired Virgil as her lead detective. And as a political appointee, Virgil technically outranked even the superintendent of the state police. In theory, he could go anywhere in the state anytime he needed to investigate and arrest criminals who fell under the state's loosely defined rules of Cora's Major Crimes Unit. With scant little oversight, for a guy like Virgil, that was just about perfect. As long as he produced and made a reasonable effort to stay between the lines—blurry that they sometimes were—no one got in his way.

Usually.

The morning was clear and warm, the temperature perfect and Virgil was just about to turn into his parking spot at the state police building behind the courthouse when his cell phone buzzed at him. The caller ID showed the cell phone number of Sandy Small, one of his team members. He grabbed the phone, fumbled it, and then caught it in the tips of his fingers, upside down, almost clipping a parked car in the process. He stopped in the middle of the strect, threw the truck in park, turned the phone over—which by now was on its last ring before it kicked over to voice mail—hit the little green talk button and said "This is Jonesy."

For a moment Virgil thought he'd missed it. It didn't sound like Sandy was there. Just the empty background noise you get over a bad connection. But then, just like that, she was there. He could hear her in the background, and then there was a noise so sharp Virgil winced and pulled the phone away from his ear. It sounded like Sandy was panting, breathing hard, and swearing all at the same time. She kept counting, one through five, over and over.

As a new team member, Sandy had been assigned to the governor's protection detail for the past week as a way to get to know the governor on a more personal level. A better understanding of who she was really working for and all that. Today was her last day with the governor before she started catching cases.

Virgil—who knew how to listen to his gut—had a feeling something was very wrong. He dropped the truck into gear, hit the lights and burped the siren through the intersection. It was just past seven in the morning. Sandy would still be at the governor's mansion. He put the phone on speaker so he could have both hands on the wheel to drive. "Sandy? Sandy, can you hear me?" Virgil shouted into the phone but he didn't get a response. He heard her though...a grunt of effort, then more swearing. He couldn't quite make it out, but it sounded like she was saying 'shit' over and over.

A few seconds later as Virgil slid through a corner and turned north on Meridian Avenue he heard her loud and clear, her voice coming through on the Motorola police radio mounted under the dash of his truck. "Officer down. Shots fired. Officer needs assistance. Governor's Mansion. Repeat...Officer...Down. Officer...needs..." Then nothing.

Virgil dropped the hammer on the truck and blew the intersection. He didn't think about it, he just went, and went hard. A little quick math put him eight minutes out if he didn't kill himself on the way there.

SANDY SMALL HAD A BACHELOR'S DEGREE IN EDUCATION and a Master's degree in psychology. She also ranked as an expert in marksmanship on the shooting range. Translation: She could out think and out shoot just about every cop in the state *and* could also teach anyone how to do it if they wanted to put their ego on the back burner. Most didn't, but that wasn't on her.

She was on the last day of her protection rotation, covering the overnights at the governor's mansion. Her new boss, Virgil, had told her that they'd all had to do it, part of some getting to know the big guy routine, or something. As far as Sandy was concerned, protection was protection, simple as that. Getting to know someone in the process was neither a pro nor a con. It was more of an inconvenience than anything. But no matter...this was the last day and she was almost done.

At seven in the morning she stepped out the back door of the governor's mansion, walked across the deck, down the steps and headed outside. Monday morning, last time of the last day to walk the wall. The governor's mansion was situated on a full acre of property at the northern edge of the city of Indianapolis. An entire acre, Sandy had discovered, covered 43,650 square feet, and in this case, said acre was surrounded by a nine-foot high brick wall on all four sides. At about three feet per walking step around the perimeter, it was safe to say that doing one circuit per hour every eight hours over the last week had been a lot of walking. Good for the heart and lungs.

Not to mention the ass.

She varied her routine—sometimes clockwise, some-times counter-clockwise. She always paused at the gate at the front of the drive though, and waved to the uniformed duty cop who had the overnight street-side patrol before continuing back to the house. This last trip was no different. Jerry Burns, the old coot, whistled at her every time she went by.

Sandy was about fifteen steps from the front entrance —in the middle of pulling her long blond hair into a ponytail—when she heard the sounds, three in all. Or was it four? A *pop*, like a car backfiring. She stopped and listened. Heard another noise, then a short pause, then two more pops. The sound was distinct, especially if you knew what you were listening for—a ratcheting sound almost like the cycling action of a semi-auto. Then she thought, *no, exactly like the cycling action of a semi-auto*. Muffled pops after the ratcheting sound. It took her a few seconds to process, but when she did, Sandy took off full tilt toward the gate.

⁂

BY THE TIME SHE GOT THERE IT WAS OVER. SHE TRIED to push the gate open, then remembered she had to input a code into the box, a wait that made her blood boil. She ran to the street and tried to process what she saw: A white panel van as it turned the corner a half block away. Couldn't get the plate. No more than a glimpse of the vehicle itself. A man across the street on his back, his limbs jutted outward at difficult angles, his paisley robe askew, a leather slipper missing from his foot, a pool of blood that seemed to grow darker the closer she got, glassy eyes staring at nothing. Gone.

A banker, she thought? Where did that come from? She let it go.

A look to her left. The squad car. Windows down. Engine off. Seat empty. Reddish tint on the front windshield.

She ran to the car. Pulled her cell out along the way, and hit Virgil's number from the speed dial. At the first ring she was almost there. At the second ring she looked inside the squad. At the third ring she had the phone pinched between her shoulder and her ear. At the fourth ring she had the door open and pulled the trooper out of his vehicle, her hands wrapped under his armpits. She lost the phone as it clattered to the ground, but she thought she heard Virgil answer.

Sandy pulled hard until she got Burns clear of the vehicle and flat on his back. No pulse. Not breathing. She began CPR, counting with each chest compression, and then pausing to breathe into his lungs. Her hair hung in a ponytail over the front of her shoulder and every time she bent forward to give Burns mouth-to-mouth the ends of her hair landed in the pool of blood next to Jerry's head, like a paintbrush. Eventually she gave up on the counting and began to swear as she compressed his chest...."shit shit shit." Five shits then a breath. Every time she compressed his chest a few drops of blood seeped out of the hole in the side of his head.

When that didn't work, she crawled to the cruiser and

grabbed the microphone and started transmitting. "Officer down. Shots fired. Officer needs assistance. Governor's mansion. Repeat...officer...down. Officer... needs..." Out of breath. She dropped the microphone and started back in on Burns. She tried to remember something personal about him. Wife? Kids? She didn't know. Couldn't think. The microphone she'd just used dangled from the squad car, hung out over the bottom of the doorjamb, smeared with blood. Sandy watched it sway back and forth as she worked on Burns. Somewhere in the back of her mind it registered as one of the saddest things she'd ever seen—the microphone hanging upside down from the door of the squad car.

He was gone—she knew it—but she kept at it anyway. Didn't know what else to do. Heard the sirens. They sounded far away. The blood on her hair painted her shirt as she worked on Jerry.

Five shits, then a breath.

CHAPTER THREE

Virgil was not a believer in God, at least not in the traditional sense. If pressed, he'd admit that he believed in something bigger than life...something bigger than himself, but he'd also be the first to admit it was something he couldn't quite define. He'd been raised Catholic but it hadn't stuck and by the time he'd turned eighteen—more than twenty years ago—he'd never gone back to church at all except for weddings and funerals. *And*, he was hitting the age where he'd begun to notice there were less of the former and more of the latter.

It seemed to Virgil that almost everyone believed all they had to do was talk to God, ask for their prayers to be answered—which really, he thought, amounted to nothing more than asking for *stuff*—and then God, in His wisdom, would either grant the request or not. The whole concept seemed kind of selfish. A little too...feel good. Like comfort food. The idea that groups of people would get together once or twice a week and listen while someone stood on stage and waved a book at them and told them how to live their lives seemed very...republican. Like it didn't matter if you waved the book or waved the flag, in the end it was all pretty much the same. *Praise the Lord and pass the ammunition.*

So. Virgil was a believer of something. What that something might be was just a little hard to pin down. But believer or not, over the last eight minutes since he'd heard Sandy on the radio, he had to admit he'd been talking to someone, asking...*praying,* that she wasn't hurt.

When he finally rolled up to the scene and saw her working on Jerry Burns, saw her physically okay, he felt like his prayers had been answered.

And wasn't that, Virgil thought, a kick in the nut-sack of belief.

HE SLID HIS TRUCK TO A STOP AT THE SOUTH intersection, almost a half-block away. It was as close as he could get. It looked like every cop car in the city had converged on the scene. He flashed his ID to the city cop and ran through. Sandy had moved over and was sitting down on the curb across the street from the trooper, her head down, her hands in her hair. Virgil didn't know who had the overnight duty so he didn't know who the trooper was, but even as he ran he could tell it wasn't good. He looked up and saw two news helicopters circling over-head, and when he crossed the street he saw the fallen trooper was Jerry Burns and that fact made something click in his chest. Jerry had been Virgil's training officer when he joined the state police.

After a few seconds of reflection Virgil walked over to Sandy and squatted in front of her and noticed the blood on her shirt and in her hair. "Jesus, Sandy, are you hurt? Are you hit?"

Sandy shook her head, then leaned into him, her arms around Virgil's neck. He felt her shake and sob into his chest. "I'm...I'm all right. Not hit." She pulled back and rubbed her eyes, then tried to wipe the blood out of her hair. "It's Jerry's blood. It's in my hair. I was trying...I was trying to do CPR."

Virgil looked at her and for just a moment he wanted to scoop her up and take her home. Get her cleaned up. Wanted to take care of her. The blood was everywhere... in her hair, on her shirt, her hands, her face. He tried to wipe some of it from her cheek, but it was useless. He turned toward the EMTs and motioned them over, then turned back to Sandy. "Where's the governor, Sandy?"

She didn't answer right away and he had to ask her again. She pulled her hair away from her face streaking it with more blood in the process. "He's, uh, still inside, I guess. Hasn't left yet."

"Stay here. Do not move. Understand?"

She nodded and Virgil went over and grabbed one of the city cops, a guy named Cauliffer, according to his name-tag. "Officer Cauliffer, my name is Detective Virgil Jones, with the state police."

"Yeah," Cauliffer said. "I know who you are. You're the guy—"

Virgil cut him off. "Listen, Cauliffer, go secure the governor. He's inside his house. Keep him there."

Cauliffer let his face form a question. "Sir?"

"Go, Cauliffer. Keep him in the house. Stay right by his side. I don't care what he's doing, you stay right with him. If he's in there taking his morning dump, I want you standing ready with a roll of toilet paper. You got me?"

"Yes, sir."

"Good. Go. Now."

Cauliffer took off toward the mansion and Virgil went back to Sandy. "What the hell happened?"

Sandy shook her head. "The hell if I know."

"Are you sure you're not hurt?"

"I don't know. I hit my head really hard getting Burns out of the car." She blew a deep breath out of her mouth. "Jesus, Jonesy, half his head is gone. I mean it's Jerry. Who'd have ever thought something like this could happen to Jerry?"

"I know, I know, but listen, it's okay. You did good. Did everything you could. Do you have anything? Anything at all?"

"Nothing really. I saw a white cargo van turning west-bound from the south corner as I came out of the gate. Couldn't get the plate. Couldn't even tell you the make of the van. Chevy, maybe? Or GMC. It had the tall taillights at the top. It was just a glimpse. They were already gone, you know?"

"Okay. But it was a van? You're sure of that?"

"Yeah. White cargo van. Like a delivery van or something."

"Okay. Sit still. I'm going to get the medics to look you over."

"I don't need any of that. Let me work this with you."

"It's not a request, Sandy. They're going to look at you." Virgil stood up. "I'll be right back." He reached for his phone before realizing it was still in the truck. He jogged back down to where he'd parked a few minutes ago and the phone was ringing when he got there. The caller ID showed a blocked number. He hit the button. "Jonesy."

"Uh, Detective Jones? This is Cauliffer, up at the house? The governor's? He gave me your number."

"Yeah, Cauliffer, what is it?"

"Well, you think you could come up here for a minute?"

"Why?"

"It's the governor. He's pretty pissed that I won't let him out of the house."

Virgil could hear the governor in the background and realized Cauliffer was right. He did sound pissed. "All right. Just sit on him for a minute. I'll be right there." Virgil pressed the end button then hit the speed dial for his boss, Cora.

She answered immediately. "What the hell's happening, Jonesy?"

"Ah, we've got a hell of a mess is what's happening. You better get out here. Be nice if you could handle the politics for me."

"Turn around, Slick."

Virgil turned and saw Cora walking toward him. He hit the end button and stuck the phone in his pocket. At fifty-two years old, Cora stood little more than five feet tall, carried about twenty extra pounds, was dark skinned and kept her salt and pepper hair high and tight like a man. She began her career as an Indianapolis Metro patrol cop and the stories of her days on patrol were legendary. She once found herself cornered by three gang-bangers jacked on meth in an abandoned warehouse. When they closed ranks to take her down, she left her gun in its holster and took her nightstick from the chrome loop on her belt and proceeded to offer a free demonstration on the quality of hand-to-hand combat training offered by the Indiana Police Academy. When it was over she shook a cigarette out of her pack, lit up, and stood over them, the ashes from her cigarette scattered around their broken limbs and bloodied faces. She finished her smoke before she called for EMS on the radio. No one messed with Cora LaRue more than once, and only then at their own peril.

She walked up and put her hands on her hips. "Jesus Christ. I heard it's Jerry Burns."

"Yeah," Virgil said. "I don't believe it."

"All right, I'm going to go up and talk to the governor. Get this scene locked down, then come up and join me, will you?"

"You bet."

"Jerry Burns. Who'd have ever thought..."

CHAPTER FOUR

The Sids sat across from each other at their kitchen table; Senior lost in thought, Junior amped from the adrenaline rush.

"I still think we could do them all," Junior said. "I want to do them all."

"We've been over this before. It's too risky."

Junior's hand slapped the table. Hard. "Then what the hell did I drive all the way up there for? Answer that for me, will you? An entire week of surveillance in that God forsaken shit-hole of a town and now you want to just let it go? Who retires to Osceola anyway?"

Senior sucked in his cheeks. Maybe he'd trained his child too well. Or too hard. Sid Jr. could be a handful for sure. Junior wanted it all, and anything less than that would be considered a failure. Sid Sr. shook his head then pointed at the map on the table. "Look, everyone else is either right here in Indy or within fifty miles. He's the only one who's out of the area. You want to blow the whole deal over one guy?"

Junior didn't answer. "You're turning chicken shit on me, aren't you?"

Senior pointed a finger at her. "Chicken shit my ass. Did it look chicken shit to you when that trooper's melon popped? And don't you talk to me that way."

"It was pretty good shootin', I'll give you that," Junior said. "But listen, we may have a little problem."

"What?"

"I lost some brass."

This time it was Senior who slapped the table. "God damn, girl. That could be a problem, right there."

"No, no, listen. I think it's okay. It's not good, but I'm not printed anywhere and neither are you, so if they find it, and they probably won't, what good can it do them?"

"Ah, they'll find it," Senior said. "We killed a cop. There's no way they won't find it."

"I still think it's okay. They don't know to look for it. We fired four shots total, right? Yours, and my three. I picked up two, but the third was hot. That's how I lost it. Slipped right out of my hand and rolled down the storm drain. Unless they pull the grate and look in there..." She let it hang, like she was trying to convince herself. "Besides, you know the cops aren't all that smart to begin with. Hell, half the time they can't find their own ass with a GPS, a flashlight and a how-to video."

"It's not the cops, though, don't you get it? If the cops don't catch us in the act we're probably okay. But those crime scene techs? They scare me. They can figure some shit out."

"Ah, that's a bunch of TV bullshit. We're not printed anywhere, so all they could do is hang us after the fact anyway, and if it comes to that, it won't make much of a difference. It'll be so long and good-bye, know what I mean?"

They bantered back and forth like that for a bit before they got back to work, checking their gear, loading their supplies for the next run, but all the while, somewhere in the recesses of Senior's mind, he heard himself say it wasn't too late to back it down, to toss the whole thing in the shitter and flush it away like a bad memory. But he wasn't really listening to himself, so in the end he never really heard. It was too bad for that cop, no doubt about it, but it really was the only way—the banker had to go.

They still had another one to do later today. By tonight the city would be shocked. By tomorrow they'd be worried. By the end of the week they'd be shit-faced with panic.

And this was just the beginning.

CHAPTER FIVE

A not-so-short walk brought Virgil up to the side entrance of the governor's mansion. He entered without knocking, stepped through a short service hallway, then turned a corner into the kitchen. The governor's chief of staff, Bradley Pearson, was already there along with the governor and Officer Cauliffer. Virgil pulled out a chair and sat down. "Morning Governor," he said by way of a greeting.

"Jonesy," the governor said. "What do we know so far?" Then, without waiting for an answer, "And perhaps we should excuse Officer Cauliflower here."

Cauliffer reddened. "It's, uh, Cauliffer sir."

The governor tipped his head sideways and closed one eye. "Yes, of course. Sorry. Cauliffer. Got it."

When Virgil caught Cauliffer's eyes he gave him a nod that said, 'you're done in here.' Cauliffer gave him a look back that said all at once, 'got it' and 'thank God' then went back outside.

The governor looked at Cora. "Is Sandy out there? Is she hurt?"

Virgil thought, *hmm*. Cora spoke to the governor, but her eyes were on Virgil. "She's fine, Governor. But Trooper Burns is dead, along with your neighbor directly across the street."

The governor's jaw muscles were clenched tight. "Yes, I know. It's all over my Blackberry already." He held his phone up and wiggled it in the air, then tossed it on the counter. Governor Hewitt (Mac) McConnell was ex-military and looked it. Tall, hard and lean with a military buzz cut, slightly gray at the temples, clear blue eyes and a salt and pepper goatee he wore off and on. Today it was on. The gray in his hair and beard contrasted perfectly against his black over black three-piece suit. Pearson, his chief of staff, was the polar opposite. Narrow shoulders, a soft stomach that strained the buttons on his wrinkled shirt, and a polyester suit that looked capable of surviving nuclear devastation. His hair was drugstore bottle black but left gray along the sides. The common consensus held that he was trying for a Mitt Romney look. The reality was he looked more like Pauley Walnuts from the Sopranos.

"Jonesy, ever hear of a guy named Samuel Pate?" Pearson asked.

Samuel Pate was something of a minor celebrity, a televangelist who somehow managed to attain an impressive measure of financial success over a very short period of time despite his lack of education, verifiable credentials, and physical shortcomings. Or perhaps because of them. "Sermon Sam, the Preacher Man? Sure, who hasn't?" Virgil said. "Why do you ask?"

"What do you know about Sunrise Bank? Do you have an account there, or know anyone who works at their institution?"

"That's three questions in a row. Which would you like me to answer? And why does it suddenly feel like I'm the only one in the room who doesn't know what's going on here?"

The governor caught the frustration in Virgil's tone and held up his hand in a peaceful manner before speaking. "You'll have to forgive Bradley, Detective. At times I think he wishes he had chosen a career in law enforcement. Or maybe it's my fault. I often let him ask the difficult questions for me."

"Maybe if we started at the beginning," Cora said.

Pearson let out a heavy sigh, and then started over. "We don't think this attack, these murders...we don't think the governor was targeted. At all. We want to be clear on that. There may be political implications, and we'd like it handled in a manner befitting the office of the Governor of the State of Indiana."

Virgil didn't like Bradley Pearson and knew of few people who did. "I'm not sure what that means, Bradley. And who exactly is Franklin Dugan? The name rings a bell, but I can't quite place it."

"He is, or was rather, the President of Sunrise Bank," the governor said. "He was also one of my closest friends." Pearson had a look on his face. An expression that indicated there was more. The governor noticed, puffed out his cheeks and exhaled loudly through his mouth. "He was also one of my biggest campaign contributors."

"I want you to catch this son of a bitch, Jonesy," the governor said. "Or kill him. Sooner the better. Elections are only nine months away and voters have a memory for this kind of thing."

"Especially if your platform was a reduction in capital crime," Cora added. Sort of dry.

Virgil winced when she said it, but the governor just pointed a finger at her and said, "Exactly." He stood, shot his cuffs and made a circular motion with his hand at Pearson. "Cora will fill you in on the details, Jonesy. I appreciate your efforts. You're sure Sandy's okay?"

"Yes, sir, I think so." He thought, *hmm*, again.

The governor shook his head and looked at no one. Then to Pearson: "Where's officer Cauliflower? Perhaps he can clear us a path out of here so we can get downtown."

TEN SECONDS AFTER THEY LEFT THE ROOM, PEARSON stuck his head back in. "Uh, I just want to be sure we're all on the same page, here. The governor...when he said 'catch him or kill him'...what he was really saying was 'catch him.' Just so we're clear on that, okay?"

———

ONCE PEARSON WAS FINALLY GONE, VIRGIL LOOKED AT Cora and said, "What aren't they saying?"

"You never answered Pearson's question. What do you know about Sunrise Bank?"

"What's to know? They're a bank, just like any other, aren't they?"

Cora pursed her lips. "In many ways, they are. But did you know that there's a bank up in the northern part of the state—I can't remember the name—but they're based out of South Bend. Strictly local, people walk in and out all day and deposit their checks, take out loans, the whole thing. Just a regular local bank, *but*, they also happen to be the third largest specialty financing firm in the entire country. Garbage trucks, rental cars, aircraft for regional air carriers, the works. If it runs or flies, they've got their hand in it."

"Fascinating stuff, Cora, really. But what does that have to do with Sunrise or Dugan?"

"Care to guess where Pate's ministry does their banking?"

"So like the bank up in South Bend, Sunrise does specialty financing?"

"You got it, Jones-man. And it's big business, at least according to the governor. We're talking billions of dollars in outstanding loans to religious institutions all across the country. Big, big stuff."

Virgil thought about that for a few minutes. "If they're doing that much business, what's the tie-in with Pate? He's regional at best. Why has his name come up?"

"Pate just borrowed over five million dollars from Dugan's bank to buy a run down church in Broad Ripple."

"Maybe I'm not quite the detective I think I am, because I still don't see how that would make Pate a suspect."

"Maybe you should go over to Dugan's office and look things over. You'll probably revise your last statement after you do. I've attached his office as part of the crime scene and I sent Rosencrantz and Donatti over there as soon as I heard what happened out here. They've got his office locked down and are personally standing guard outside until you get there. There are only two things on Dugan's desk. One is a copy of Pate's financials and the other is a copy of a Texas Department of Insurance investigator's report. They have an open file on him. He started his ministry there five years ago with the proceeds from an insurance claim that paid out over a million bucks when his Houston church turned to a pile of ash one night. He brought the money here and set up shop all over again. He calls it Grace Community Church, and it's mortgaged to the hilt.

"And the church over in Broad Ripple? The one he just bought? It looks like it's being held together with baling twine. I think they have a congregation of about thirty people, all dirt poor. The building is about to be condemned by the city, the lot can't be worth more than about fifty grand and the victim, Franklin Dugan is the one who approved the loan to Pate. He's also the guy who financed the vast majority of the governor's campaign when he ran for office. Word on the street is ol' Sermon Sam is thinking about making a run at the governor's chair. A quick five million would make a nice campaign starter fund, don't you think? Maybe Dugan was playing both ends against the middle."

Then, as if she hadn't quite made her point, she added, "Politics. It's good stuff, huh? By the way, Rosencrantz says the bank is calling an emergency board meeting. Should be starting anytime now. You might want to stop by at some point. When you get there, ask for Margery Brennan. She's Dugan's secretary, or personal assistant or whatever they're called these days. Keep me in the loop, will you?"

VIRGIL WALKED OUTSIDE AND BACK DOWN TO THE street and saw Sandy at the back of an EMS van getting her blood pressure checked. The two news helicopters still circled overhead, their news feeds streaming live video of the scene, though there wasn't much to be seen from the air. The crime scene technicians had erected two tents with side-flaps, one covering Dugan's body at the end of his drive, the other over the top of Trooper Burns and his squad car. Virgil estimated a total of about fifty uniformed officers on the scene from all three jurisdictions, City, County, and State. Metro Homicide would be in charge of the scene, and Virgil's team, while technically over the Metro Homicide Task Force, would do what they did best: work the fringes, the areas outside of normal investigative procedures.

Virgil got to Sandy just as the paramedics were finishing up. "How are you?"

"I'm okay. Jesus, what a mess, huh?"

"That about says it. So, you've had a little while to think about it. Give me something I can use."

The paramedic interrupted. "If it can wait, I'd like to get her downtown. Her blood pressure is off the charts. I mean way up, and so is her pulse. You said you bumped your head, Miss?"

Sandy shot the medic a look. "It's Detective. And yes, I bumped my head, but it's no big deal. I'm fine."

"Nevertheless, we've got to have you looked at. You may be concussed. The docs will know for sure."

Sandy turned away from the paramedic. "Jonesy, can you do something about this?"

"I sure can. See you at the hospital."

"Jonesy."

"No way, Sandy. You're going. That's a direct order."

"Okay, okay. But listen, before I do, you said you wanted something you could use. I think we've got two shooters, both with silenced weapons. The shots were muffled, like a quiet backfire from a car engine. Not even that loud really. The loudest thing I heard was the ratcheting cycle after the shots. If it wasn't for that, I might not have even thought they were gun shots."

"Why two shooters?"

"It's the sequence. I've been going over it in my head. First I heard a pop, then another pop before I heard the cycle action. Then there were two more pops closer together and two fast ratcheting sounds. So that means one shot from something, a rifle maybe, that doesn't cycle. Something with a bolt action? I'll tell you something else too, the more I think about it, the more I'm convinced that the first pop sounded different—quieter—than the rest. So, two victims, two guns, two shooters...if I'm right."

"Sounds right. But, you know, if you heard it wrong, missed the first ratchet because you weren't listening for it..."

"No, I wondered about that. I don't think I missed it. It was quiet this morning. *I* was quiet. And I was *close*."

"Okay. You can write it up later. Right now you're going in to get checked out."

She raised her eyebrow at him, then let it go. "You think this is about the governor?"

"Have you met Pearson yet?" Virgil said.

"The governor's chief of staff? Yeah, we met a few days ago. Hell of a guy."

"He is. Anyway, McConnell and Pearson made it clear this had nothing to do with them, or at least they don't want it to look like it did."

"And you think different?"

"I like to keep an open mind. The governor asked about you, by the way."

"Yeah?" Sandy said.

"Yeah. Twice. Say, I didn't see Mrs. McConnell up at the house. Where's she?"

Sandy let her eyelids drop a quarter inch. "She's been out of town for the last few days. She's got a sister in Oregon, I think…or something like that."

"I see."

"I don't think you do, Jonesy."

Virgil bit the inside corner of his lower lip, then said, "Get checked out, Small. You did good. Really."

She just stared at him.

VIRGIL LOOKED AROUND UNTIL HE SAW METRO Homicide's lead detective, Ron Miles, speaking with one of the crime scene techs just outside the tent covering Dugan's body. Ron's white hair was mussed out of place and he kept running his hand over it, trying to flatten it to the top of his head. The knees on his pants were covered in dirt and grime.

"Sorry about Burns, Jonesy. Somebody told me he was your training officer?"

"Yeah, he was."

"So, the state getting in on this?"

"Yeah, something like that," Virgil said. "Mac wants us

to take a peek. See if we can get in front of it sort of quick. We'll probably just shadow you guys. See what we can see."

"In other words, we do all the work and you guys get all the credit."

"Nope. You can have the credit. Like I said, we just want to try to get in front of it, if we can."

"Doesn't look like it's going to be easy. We don't have jack-shit on this one."

"Tell me what you've got so far."

"You spoke with Sandy?"

"Just now."

"Okay," Miles said. "Well, there's that, and not much else. Not yet anyway, and most of it's speculation at this point. One of the techs found the slug, or I guess I should say what was left of the slug that took Burns out. It cracked the front window, but didn't penetrate. It rico-cheted off the window and imbedded in the top of the dash. He says it looks like it was probably from a .223, but he says he can't be sure until they get it back to the lab for tests."

"What about Dugan?"

"One to the head, two in the chest. Coroner says he'll get what's left of the slug fragments when he does the post. There's some tattooing on his skull from the powder burns, so it was up close and personal." Miles pulled the tent flap back and they stepped inside. As bad as Burns looked, Dugan was somehow worse. He ended up flat on his back, his arms out at his sides, like a kid ready to make a snow angel. One of his slippers had fallen off his foot and was lying next to his hip. They both looked at Dugan for a full minute then stepped back outside the tent. "Jesus," Virgil said to no one in particular.

"Yeah," Miles said.

"So, what do you think about Sandy's take? Two shooters?"

"I think it works. Dugan was close. Foot, foot and a half. Burns wasn't. So, if Sandy's got the timing right, there must have been two. I mean, how do you shoot from a distance with one weapon and then take another weapon and run over and pop someone up close? Or better yet, why? That doesn't add up."

"What if she heard it wrong?"

Miles flattened his hair with his palm. "Well, I just don't think she did. Plus, I'll tell you something, even if she did hear it wrong and there was only one shooter, what's he gonna do? Take out Dugan up close and then run away with Burns just sitting there? That doesn't work. And neither does taking out Burns first from a distance and then walking up and popping Dugan. So I think she's on the money. Two shooters, two weapons, all at the same time."

They talked it over for a few more minutes running through different variations on the theme, but in the end, Sandy's scenario held up.

"Okay, keep doing what you're doing here," Virgil said. "I'm going to work a specific angle, but I want you to run this by the numbers. Let's not let anything fall through the cracks."

"Like I ever do. You know who's got the best closure rate in Metro, right?"

"Yeah, I know. So do what you do."

"I intend to. So, what's the angle?"

Virgil hesitated for a second. "Uh, it's sort of complicated. Cora's got us looking at something."

Miles looked away for a moment as if studying something off in the distance. "Well, I'll keep you updated with whatever we find," he said.

"Do that," Virgil said as he took one last look around. "I'm heading out. Find us something, Ron. I need a thread to pull on."

"Don't hold your breath, Jonesy. This one feels like we could get our asses kicked." Then, "Is this about McConnell?"

"Have you ever met Bradley Pearson?"

"Isn't he the governor's chief weenie? I heard he's sort of a snake..."

CHAPTER SIX

Virgil drove over to the hospital and walked into the Emergency Department and when he did his gun set off the metal detector at the doorway. He was about to badge the security guard headed his way until he noticed it was a friend of his from the Marion County Sheriff's Department. "Hey Kev. Double dipping these days?" They shook hands.

"Are you kidding me? My oldest daughter is getting married this spring, and the twins start college in a year and a half. If I didn't have to sleep, I'd be triple dipping."

"Amber's getting married?"

Kevin scratched the back of his head. "Yep, she sure is."

"Getting old, Kev."

"Huh, tell me. I don't have much time to think about it though. Too busy trying to make enough money to pay for the wedding."

"Who's the lucky guy?"

The deputy's face lit up. "Ah, she hit the jackpot, man. One of the docs here. Hell of a good kid, just out of med school. Matter of fact, that's how I got this gig."

Sandy came around the corner and walked over to where Virgil and Kevin stood.

"All done?" Virgil said.

"Haven't even started yet," Sandy said. "There was some sort of big wreck out on 465. They're backed up, so I'm just waiting. Supposed to be next." She looked at Kevin and stuck her hand out. "Hi. I'm Sandy Small, the best thing that's ever happened to Virgil and his team."

The deputy laughed and shook her hand. "I'll bet you are. I'm Kevin Campbell. It's a pleasure." Kevin lowered his voice and leaned in toward Sandy. "You know, I wanted a spot on Virgil's team, but they wouldn't have me."

Sandy looked at Virgil. "Why not?"

"Not mean enough," he said.

"Fuck you, not mean enough," Kevin said. "I've forgotten more about mean than you'll ever know." Then to Sandy: "Pardon my French, little lady."

"Fuck your French," Sandy said.

"See," Virgil said. "Mean like that."

Sandy made a pfftt noise with her lips. "You don't know the half of it." Virgil wasn't quite sure what she meant, but before he could say anything a nurse came through the doorway and said, "The doctor will see you now."

KEVIN SAID HIS GOODBYES AND THE NURSE ESCORTED Sandy down the hall. Virgil followed, looking for a waiting area, but before he knew it the three of them ended up behind one of the curtained areas the nurse identified as bed eight. Inside was a wheeled hospital bed with the back raised to a forty-five degree angle, a chair, a stand-up closet and a small stainless steel sink and counter. The nurse reached into the closet next to the bed, handed Sandy a gown, told her she could leave her underwear on, and that the doctor would be right in. She pulled the curtain closed and left Virgil and Sandy standing there, alone. Sandy held the gown and looked at Virgil with an evil grin on her face, but then she gave her index finger a little twirl and said, "No sneaking a look, Jonesy. I mean it."

"How about I just go back out to the waiting room?"

Sandy ignored his question and started to undress. Virgil turned around, but didn't leave. "That guard was something else, huh?" she said.

"Yeah, he was," Virgil was studying the pattern on the curtain, listening to the sounds of the emergency room, watching the feet of the hospital staff and other patients shuffle by the bottom of the curtain. He also listened to Sandy undress. Heard her shoes as she kicked them off, a little static electricity from her shirt as she pulled it over her head, and finally the zipper being lowered on her jeans and the sound of the denim sliding against her skin as she wriggled out of her pants.

"Okay, I'm decent. You can turn around now."

When Virgil looked at her he saw the threadbare hospital gown pulled tight across her front, the fullness of her breasts, her nipples pressing against the thin fabric.

Sandy turned her back toward him and faced the bed, the back of the gown held closed with her hand. She looked over her shoulder and said, "Help a girl out, will you? I couldn't get the ties." She looked forward while letting go of the back of the gown. Virgil watched it fall open and felt himself swallow. He could hear his own heartbeat as he let his eyes follow the shape of her shoulder blades inward toward her spine, then down to her waistline. A small tribal tattoo peeked out of the top of a black thong that rode high on her thin waist, covering almost nothing of what was at least the second best ass Virgil had ever seen in his life.

"Come on, Jonesy. Tie me up. I'm feeling a draft here."

Virgil cleared his throat without meaning to. "Yeah, sorry." He stepped up close to her, and tied the top tie first. The front of her thighs were against the side of the bed and part of the gown was trapped so he had to actually open the bottom part and tug on it a little to release the material. The back of his hand brushed up against her ass and when it did he felt like a schoolboy trying to cop a cheap feel. Virgil was about a foot taller than Sandy, and he fumbled the knot on the first try, the angle awkward.

"Come on Cowboy, you can do it. Just make two

bunny ears and wrap one around the other and pull it through."

"No, no it's not that. It's the angle. I'm taller."

Sandy placed her palms on the edge of the bed and stood on her tiptoes and arched the small of her back. "Better?"

You've no idea, Virgil said to himself.

"What was that?" Sandy said.

When she went up on her toes, Virgil immediately upgraded his assessment from second best to all time best. Without question. He finished the knot. "Nothing. There you go. I'm, uh, going to go wait outside now."

Sandy didn't say anything and Virgil didn't move, and he was just beginning to wonder what would happen if he...but then the curtain was yanked back and a tall, good-looking doctor stepped in the room and smiled. His hair was pure white, but there were no lines on his face. His solid black eye glasses were a sharp contrast to his hair color and it gave him a dramatic flair. He wore traditional green scrubs under a white knee-length lab coat. His clog-style shoes looked like they were made of wood and cork with suede tops. The doctor looked at them and said, "Looks like I got here just in time." He took his pen out of his pocket, tapped it on the clipboard he was holding, then pointed to the ceiling at the corner of the room. They all looked up and saw the security camera. "Two of my nurses just went on break. One of them is getting married in a month. I'm the groom's best man. They said something about it was getting hot in here. So, how can I help you, young lady?"

───────

THIS TIME VIRGIL DID LEAVE THE ROOM, AND A HALF hour later Sandy and the doc emerged as well. The doctor pulled a card from his breast pocket and wrote something on the back then handed it to Sandy, shaking her hand in both of his before walking away. Virgil thought the doc held her hand a little longer than necessary.

A few minutes later they were in Virgil's truck. He started the engine and looked over at Sandy. "What'd the doctor say?"

"He said I was fine, and he meant it, too. He gave me his number. Seemed like a nice guy." She reached into her pocket and pulled out his card, placing it on the console between the seats. "He said if you don't have enough sense to see what you're missing, I should give him a call. What do you think?"

"He was a pretty good looking guy. He sort of had that distinguished doctor thing going for him," Virgil said as he dropped the truck into gear and pulled out onto the street. "Probably makes about a million a year, if that kind of thing matters to you."

"You think I should call him? Or would that be too forward?"

"I should probably get you home," Virgil said, ignoring her question. "You know, doctor's orders, and all."

"Yeah, you're probably right. You didn't answer my question though. What do you think? Should I call him?"

Virgil picked up the card, looked at it for a second, tore it in half and tossed it out the window. "You must have hit your head harder than you thought. You're clearly not thinking straight."

Sandy laughed and watched the card slip away into the wind. Virgil thought it was the best laugh he'd ever heard.

"I memorized the number," Sandy said.

"My ass, you did."

"Already entered it into my cell phone."

"Uh huh."

"I did. Want to see?"

"Want to hand me your phone before I roll the window back up?" Like that, all the way to Sandy's.

Twenty minutes later they were at her place. Virgil walked her to the door and by the time they got there he could see the adrenaline wearing off. There was an awkward moment at the door, then Sandy stood on her toes and kissed him—quick—right on the corner of his lips. "I'll get with you after I rest for a while, okay?"

"How about tomorrow?" Virgil said. Then he pulled her close and hugged her for just a moment before turning around and heading for his truck. When he looked back she was already inside.

CHAPTER SEVEN

When Virgil got back in his truck he saw that he had a message waiting for him on his cell. It was Rosencrantz, telling him Dugan's office was sealed and his computer was already on the way back to the lab for processing. Rosencrantz and Donatti were the other two members of Virgil's team. He'd hired both away from the city, Rosencrantz from Sex, and Donatti from Homicide. Virgil hit the speed dial button and Rosencrantz answered on the third ring. He sounded bored.

"Uh, listen, you guys haven't beaten anyone up or anything, have you?" Virgil said.

"Hey, boss, come on," Rosie said. "Give us a little credit. We're highly trained investigators. Besides, I haven't beaten anyone up for over a week."

"Uh huh."

"If you were thinking about getting something to eat

before coming over, don't bother. When they heard the boss was dead someone made an executive decision and catered in about ten grand worth of food. We've interviewed Dugan's secretary, the entire executive team and their secretaries as well. Everybody except the executive committee is walking around here bumping into each other like a bunch of zombies or something. Nobody has any useful information and there's a ton of food here that's going to go bad if someone doesn't start eating. I'm thinking maybe I should take some home with me. In fact, you know that Crime Scene tech, big Al, the one that weighs in around two eighty or so? I saw him fill four or five evidence bags with Swedish meatballs and bacon-wrapped shrimp before he left. The bottom line is the only real thing I've learned so far is that no one uses the word 'secretary' anymore. They prefer 'executive assistant.' Who knew?"

Virgil thought for a moment then said, "Didn't you go to New Orleans last year?"

"Two years ago, but yeah. I got you that Ragin' Cajun T-shirt, remember?"

"Sure. You flew down, right? How were the stewardesses?"

"Fine I guess. I don't really remember. Why do you ask?"

"Never mind," Virgil said.

Two blocks away from Sandy's, Virgil realized he didn't know where the Sunrise Bank headquarters were located. He pulled over to the curb and tried to Google the address but the signal wasn't strong enough and he didn't have the patience to wait. He called Rosencrantz again.

"What's the address over there. I tried the Google and it wouldn't come up. I don't know where I'm going."

"You know," Rosie said, "I'm not exactly sure. Donatti drove. I was sleeping."

"Well, find someone and ask will you?"

"Don't need to. I'm standing right next to his secretary." Then: "Ouch, hey, that's assault on a police officer. Okay, okay." Rosencrantz cleared his throat. "What I meant to say was, I'm standing right next to his executive assistant. I've got the address. You got a pen?"

City traffic made for a slow drive to the bank. Virgil spoke with his dad on the way over. Virgil and his dad owned a downtown Jamaican bar called Jonesy's. "Listen Pops, I'm going to be tied up tonight, if you've been watching the news."

"Can't miss it," Mason said. "Nothing else on."

Virgil tried to work as many hours as possible at the bar, but when he was on a case, it fell to his father to pick up the slack. "That gonna be okay?"

"Yeah, don't worry about it, Son. I'll see you when I see you."

"I'll probably be in later if I get the chance. Guy's gotta eat."

"A guy sure does," Mason said. "Watch your back now."

"No worries, Pop. No worries at all."

A HALF HOUR LATER AFTER CONSULTING THE LOBBY directory, Virgil took an elevator to the fourteenth floor and found Rosencrantz chatting up an attractive mid-forty-something woman with cat-eye glasses and big hair. She wore a conservative dark gray business suit over a thin white blouse. Donatti was across the hall and stood in front of what must have been Dugan's office, arms crossed, a bored expression on his face. Virgil walked over and Rosencrantz introduced him to Dugan's assistant.

"Ms. Brennan, on behalf of the state of Indiana, let me express my condolences regarding Mr. Dugan."

"Please, call me Margery. And thank you. Why don't we sit?" She didn't wait for an answer, just walked around the corner to a small conference room. Virgil followed her into the room and discovered Rosencrantz was right. Someone had ordered catering...and a lot of it at that. He pulled out a chair, popped a shrimp in his mouth and sat down. The shrimp was good.

Great, in fact...

ONCE THEY WERE SETTLED: "SO, MARGERY, ABOUT MR. Dugan. I'd like to get a little background on him and I'm thinking you're probably the best place to start."

Margery gave a little snort. "I don't think it matters where you start, Detective. I'm quite sure you'll get the same sort of background information from anyone you speak with."

"Meaning?"

"Meaning Franklin Dugan was a son of a bitch."

Well, that's something, Virgil thought.

"Let me guess...not really what you expected to hear, right?"

"Well, I guess not, to tell you the truth."

Margery took a moment before her next statement. "Look, don't get me wrong, Detective. I simply don't know how else to put it. He really was...a son of a bitch, I mean. But everyone knew it. He even referred to *himself* that way. It's just a business thing. We're in a tough business here. People think banks, and then, you know, they think friendly tellers, warm smiles, free toasters with a new account and all that—or maybe not so much anymore, with the economy the way it's been—but our business isn't like that. We're not a regular bank. We deal exclusively with religious institutions. And let me tell you something," Margery bit into a shrimp and shook the tail at him, "These religious guys? I don't care who they are..." She started ticking them off her fingers. "You've got your

Catholics, your Protestants, your Methodists, your Baptists, your Lutherans, not to mention the Scientology nuts—who in my opinion are a whole class of nuts all by their damn self—they're all some very tough hombres when it comes to their money. So if you're going to lend them money—and that's what we do—you'd better be a son of a bitch when you're dealing with these guys or they'll take you to the cleaners." Margery dropped her chin and looked out over the top of her glasses. "All in the name of Jesus Christ mind you, or L. Ron Hubbard or...whatever."

Virgil liked her immediately. He ate a few more shrimp and thought about what she'd said for a minute, then said, "Huh," which made Margery giggle, which made her look about ten years younger. "What?"

"When you said 'huh,' you sounded just like a cop."

"I am a cop."

"You don't look much like a cop. Your hair's pretty long. You look like you should be running a bar, or something."

Virgil's mouth fell open a little, and Margery smiled. "I'm just messing with you a little. I Googled you before you got here. Your bar is sort of famous, you know. I've never been myself, but now I'm thinking I might have to stop by."

"You should. We are sort of famous, in the city, anyway. So, listen—"

"It's Google, by the way. Not *the* Google."

"Excuse me?"

"I could hear you on the phone when you called for the address. You called it *the* Google. There's no *the* in there."

"It kind of feels like we're getting a little side-tracked, Margery."

"That's only because I've already told you everything I know. The people you really want to talk to are in the boardroom. The Executive Committee. They're in an emergency session right now."

"Well, gee, Margery, I haven't even asked you any of the tough questions yet."

"Like what?"

"Well, for starters, why'd you kill Dugan?"

Didn't even faze her. "Oh, honey, I didn't kill Franklin. He might have been a son of a bitch, but he's been my meal ticket for over twenty years."

"So what are you going to do now?"

"You know, to tell you the truth, I think I'm gonna retire and lay on the beach. I've got a fair amount of stock, a 401K, and a husband who died and left me with a pretty fat life insurance settlement. Life's too short to punch someone else's clock. Especially when you get to be my age."

Virgil popped another shrimp in his mouth. "So let's go talk to the board."

"Take me to your leaders, huh?"

"Yeah, something like that." As they walked down the hallway, Virgil said, "Listen, about those shrimp. Where do you get them? They're fantastic..."

"THEY ARE GOOD, AREN'T THEY?" MARGERY SAID. "Believe it or not, they're farm-raised by a couple of guys up in Elkhart. They took over on a foreclosed RV plant a year ago—over a hundred thousand square feet in all—put in a bunch of tanks and heaters and whatnot and started growing shrimp. Or is it raising? Anyway, they're doing something right because they're the best damn shrimp I've ever had. You should get some for your bar."

"I think I might…if you could get me the number. Do they deliver all the way down here?"

"Oh, honey, are you kidding me? They're shipping these little buggers all over the country. I don't know what the growth rate of farm raised shrimp are, but they've got a three month waiting list last time I checked."

"Well, shoot. I was hoping to get some sort of quick. I've got a Jamaican chef and you wouldn't believe what he can do with fresh seafood."

"Get with me before you leave, then. I'll see what I can do about the waiting list. I'm sort of friendly with one of the owners…"

CHAPTER EIGHT

They got to the end of the hall and Margery gave a single knock on a set of mahogany double doors. Virgil followed her in. There were four people at the far end of the room—three men and a woman—all seated in high-backed leather swivel chairs at the end of an enormous, well-polished conference table. The room was windowless and the lights were set at a low level. The man at the head of the table, a tall balding guy with bushy eyebrows and a Jay Leno chin spoke without looking up. "Margery, I was certain I made my position clear. This is an emergency session of the executive committee and we are not to be disturbed. Close the door on the way out and leave it closed. I would prefer not to have to lock it, but if you cannot or will not follow my direction, you will leave me with no other choice."

The room was long, forty feet or so by Virgil's estimation, so he thought he could get away with it. He pulled

Margery close by the elbow, lowered his voice a little and said, "I thought you said Dugan was the son of a bitch."

Margery spoke from the side of her mouth. "I did. And he was. That's James Marriott, absolutely no relation to the hotel Marriott's even though that's what he likes everyone to believe. He's an asshole, but just the regular sort. Whatever you do, don't call him Jim. It's *James*. I'll leave you to introduce yourself." She gave Virgil a pat on the shoulder. "Have fun."

Great. Virgil stood still for a moment to let his eyes adjust to the lighting, then walked the length of the room, pulled out a chair one spot removed from one of the men and sat down. He didn't say a word. Just stared at the people at the table.

"Who the hell are you?" Marriott said.

They were all well dressed. Expensive suits, gold watches, sparkling jewelry, cuff links for the men, diamond earrings for the woman. In front of each of them was a leather-bound note pad with an embossed golden cross overlaid atop of a more subtle—but still visible—shining sun, with the words, Sunrise Bank at the top. Somewhere in the back of his mind Virgil heard himself say, *oh brother*.

"I asked you a question, young man. I don't like to repeat myself. Who the hell are you?"

"My name is Detective Virgil Jones with the Indiana State Police Major Crimes Unit. I'm here to speak with—"

"Well Detective," Marriott said, "We know why you're

here, and believe me, we are happy to oblige you in any way we can, but at the moment, given everything that has happened this morning, tragic as it is, we hope you'll understand that in the immediate we are extremely busy. So thank you very much for stopping by. We'll be in touch at our earliest possible convenience."

It was a pretty good effort, Virgil had to give him that. He thought of what Margery said...*What ever you do, don't call him Jim.* "I understand, and I can even appreciate your position, Jim. But here's the thing—"

"It's James," Marriott said through his teeth. "Not, Jim. *James.*"

"Yes, well, that's fine. James, then. So, as I was saying, the thing is, time is sort of critical for us. The quicker we can—"

"Detective, you're not listening. The loss of Franklin this morning is going to have devastating effects on our company unless we take immediate action. Our stock is already off over fifteen percent since the opening bell an hour ago and our investors need to know—need to be assured—that our company is solid. That's what we are doing now, or rather, that is what we are trying to do. So, once again, thank you for your interest in this matter. A representative of our organization will be in touch with you and your people as soon as possible. Please close the door on your way out, and take your two thugs out there with you. I have notified our security personnel to assist you and your associates to the door. Last time I checked, this is still private property on United States soil and at the moment, you are not welcome here. That will be all, *Detective*. Good day."

Thank you for your interest? "Just out of curiosity, Jimbo, how many of your security staff did you call?"

Marriott's jaw was clenched, and he hissed through his teeth. "I will not tolerate your blatant disrespect of me and this organiza—"

"How many?" Virgil asked again.

"Six," Marriott said, his voice smug. "Two for each of you."

Virgil reached into his pocket and pulled out the papers that Rosencrantz had given him and slid them across the table to Marriott. "That's a search warrant. It allows us access to this building, your offices, your computers, files, and just about anything else we want or need to look at. Your offices are now part of a crime scene in an on-going investigation. I suggest you forget about your stock for a few minutes, Jim, and start assisting us with our investigation."

Marriott ignored the warrant. "Who is your supervisor, young man? I want to speak with them immediately."

"I work for the state, Jim. I already told you that, so maybe you're the one who isn't listening. My boss is Cora LaRue. You've probably never heard of her. A lot of people haven't. But *her* boss is Governor McConnell. I know you've heard of him. In fact, if I'm not mistaken, the governor is a past board member of your institution and currently serves as the lead member of your team of advisors. As I understand it, their job is to advise the board. Do I have that right, Jim?"

"Well—"

"In other words, the governor is going to be advising the board as to who might make the short list for Chairman and CEO to replace Franklin Dugan. I'm guessing you'd like to think you're going to make that list. Maybe even top it. I mean, look at you, you're sitting at the head of the table already. How am I doing so far, *Jimmy?*"

Marriott held up his hands in a placating gesture. "So you've got some stones and you're tough enough to stand up to me. I admire that. So ask your questions. No one here in this room, or in our entire organization for that matter has anything to hide, I assure you."

Before Virgil could respond, the double doors at the far end of the room burst open and Donatti and Rosencrantz marched six uniformed security guards into the room, their hands cuffed behind their backs. Donatti smiled and said, "It's a good thing they all had their own cuffs. I only carry two pair myself..."

IT TOOK A FEW MOMENTS TO GET EVERYONE CALMED down, but once Virgil got Marriott's assurance that they'd all cooperate with him, he told Rosencrantz and Donatti to take the guards out and un-cuff them. Once that was all done, he looked Marriott in the eye and said, "How about we start over?"

The woman seated directly across the table from Virgil looked at Marriott. "Perhaps we should bring Bob in, James. Don't you think?"

Marriott snarled at her. "We don't need Bob for Christ's sake."

"Who's Bob?" Virgil said.

"Bob Brighton. Our in-house counsel," the woman said. "My name is Gloria Birchmier, by the way." She nodded in turn to the other two men at the table. "Dick Hawthorne and Thomas Fallbrook," she said by way of introductions.

Virgil nodded at everyone. "So, lay it out for me. Your organization, I mean. The four of you are the executive committee?"

Gloria answered for the group. "Yes. There are normally five of us. Franklin was the fifth. We have a total of eleven board members. As for the others, two live in Fort Wayne, one in South Bend, and three in Evansville. They are all on their way here of course, but it will be a few hours I imagine."

"Who notified them of Mr. Dugan's murder?"

"We all did," Gloria said. "We have a disaster plan in place. Each of us has assigned duties and responsibilities as defined in the plan. One of those responsibilities in the event of a disaster is immediate notification of the company's board of directors."

"What qualifies as a disaster?"

Hawthorne spoke for the first time. "Well, it's pretty broad. Anything that would affect our operations, like structural damage to our facilities from fire, flood, tornados, things of that sort—to the sudden death or incapacitation of anyone on the executive committee."

"Were any of you unable to reach the other members of the board?"

Fallbrook raised his hand. "I had a little trouble with one of my assigns. Bill Acker. But eventually I got him."

"Home or office?"

"It was at home. He was in the shower."

"So to the best of everyone's knowledge, the board members who were in town this morning are all in this room, and everyone else, everyone who lives out of town were all...well, out of town?" Everyone nodded.

"Yes, I believe that's correct," Gloria said. "Why?"

"Because I'm trying to figure out who killed your boss, Ms. Birchmier."

Gloria put a hand to her throat. "And you think one of us did it?"

Marriott swore under his breath then picked up the phone and punched one of the buttons. "Margery...get Bob Brighton in here. Now."

———

Sunrise Bank's chief legal officer, Bob Brighton, entered the conference room a few minutes later. Brighton was short, not much over five feet tall, and gone to fat. His hair was gray and kinky, he wore a yellow bow tie and his pants were about an inch too short.

"How do you do, Detective?"

"I'm well, thank you, Mr. Brighton. Your executive committee thought it might be best if you sat in for a few of my questions."

"Indeed. Please, proceed."

"He thinks one of us killed Franklin," Gloria said.

Brighton raised his eyebrows at Virgil, a small grin forming at the corner of his mouth.

"That's not exactly accurate," Virgil said.

Gloria pointed a finger at Virgil. "It is too accurate. You said so yourself."

"No, Ms. Birchmier, what I said was that I am trying to figure out who killed Mr. Dugan. You were the one who asked if I thought any of you did it, not me."

"Well, the implication was quite clear, Detective."

Brighton cut in. "Correct me if I'm wrong, Detective, but these types of investigations are usually conducted, mmm, what's the best way to put it? By process of elimination, isn't that correct?"

Virgil nodded. "That's often true. But keep in mind, we also look at the question of 'who benefits?' So let me ask all of you this: with Franklin Dugan now deceased, who gets the big chair? Who is going to be Chairman of the Board and CEO of Sunrise Bank?"

"The board will have to vote on that," Hawthorne said. "But undoubtedly, it would be one of us."

"Okay, so what happens if there's a tie with the vote?"

"Then we would revert to the question of who holds the most stock. It's in the charter."

"So who holds the most stock?" Virgil said, even though he thought he knew the answer.

Marriott rubbed his forehead with the fingertips of both hands. "I do."

VIRGIL HAD EVERYONE EXCEPT MARRIOTT AND Brighton leave the room. When they were gone, Marriott shook his head. "I didn't kill him. Hell, I was up at six and out of the house by six-thirty at the latest. I went to the club, worked out, and then ate a light breakfast in the dining room. Gloria called me on my cell and told me the news. There must have been about ten or twenty people who saw me from the time I walked in the club until I left."

None of Virgil's follow-up questions for Marriott led them anywhere at all, so he pulled at another thread. "I'd like to ask you about Samuel Pate."

Marriott snuffed at the mention of Pate's name. "So ask."

"Well," Virgil said, "What I'd really like is your general, overall impression of the man."

Marriott leaned in, his forearms on the edge of the table. "Detective, we have a rather unique business model here at Sunrise. No other financial institution in the country does what we do. Now, don't misunderstand what

I'm saying—there are plenty of banks out there that lend money to churches and religious institutions all across the U.S. But we are the only one that does it exclusively."

"If you have a point, Mr. Marriott, so far it's lost on me."

"My point is simple, Detective. We are as close as you could come to being called a private bank. We vigorously protect our assets and those of our clients. Confidentiality at our institution is held at the highest regard. I'm quite sure you understand."

"I'm not asking for his financials, Mr. Marriott. I'm asking for your general impression of the man."

Marriott looked at Virgil for a full minute before he spoke. "He doesn't let much get in his way, I'll say that about the man. But that's all I'll say."

FINISHED WITH MARRIOTT, VIRGIL STEPPED OUT OF the conference room and found Rosencrantz and Donatti seated in the reception area, two empty plates of shrimp tails on the coffee table by their knees.

"Get what we needed?" Virgil said.

"Right here boss," Donatti said. "All of Pate's financial history with the bank." He handed him a file folder.

"Okay, I want you guys out at the scene to help with the canvass. Ron should still be there. Widen it out as far as possible. All we've got so far is Sandy's report of a white panel van of some kind. If we can get a plate, or even a partial, we'd have something solid."

The two men stood up and Donatti picked up their plates, looked around for a trashcan, didn't see one, shrugged, and set them back down on the table.

"You know," Rosencrantz said, "If you let that Jamaican chef of yours, what's his name, again?"

"Robert," Virgil said.

"Right, right, Robert. If you get Robert some of this shrimp, and he put some of that jerk sauce on them and sort of sizzled 'em up in a pan, you'd have something right there."

Donatti was nodding. "He's right. That sauce of his is something. You'd pretty much have the crack cocaine of shrimp."

Virgil nodded right along with them. "Yeah, I know. I'm already on it."

BEFORE HE LEFT, VIRGIL FOUND MARGERY AT HER DESK. "I've got something I want to run by you."

"Sure," Margery said. "But wait, before I forget, here's the number of the seafood place in Elkhart. They're expecting your call." She handed him a slip of paper with the info. "They said, and I quote, 'as a favor to me and because you're a new customer, they'll move you to the front of the line.' They've got a truck coming to Indy today. If you could call them soon enough, you'd be all set."

"Hey, that's great. But, uh, I probably won't have time to call them." Virgil pulled one of his cards out of his wallet and handed it to her. "Do me a favor? Call the number on this card and ask for Robert. He's my chef. Tell him I said to order whatever he needs, okay?"

"Sure. That's no problem. You said you wanted to run something by me?"

"I do. Look, I usually don't ask this, but you seem to have your ear to the ground around here and I was sort of hoping you could let me know if you hear of anything that might be, mmm, out of the ordinary."

Margery looked around, like someone might be listening. "Like what?"

"Anything really. Something out of place, someone acting strange, uptight, saying something out of character, something they wouldn't normally do or say. Don't do anything about it, but call me and let me know, will you?"

"Sure, sounds a lot like what I do already." She gave him a little eyebrow wiggle. "And, as long as we're trading favors, how about you do a little something for me?"

"Maybe," Virgil said, a little skeptical. "What is it?"

"Oh don't get all coppish on me."

"No, no. I'm not. What is it?"

"Well, earlier I told you I was thinking about retiring and spending some time on the beach."

"Yeah? Boy I could tell you about some great places in Jamaica. I go every February for a month."

"No, no. I was wondering...your two guys?"

"Yeah?"

"Well, you know...the cute one. Is he attached or anything? I was hoping you could put a word in for me."

Virgil puffed out his cheeks. "Margery, I'll be the first to admit I'm not very religious, and I mean not at all. But with God as my witness, I don't know which one qualifies as the cute one."

Margery huffed a little. "You know...the tall one. What'd you call him? Rosie?"

"He's the cute one?"

Margery gave him a slow blink. Twice. "Oh, honey, are you kidding me? I'd like to buy him a few of those rum punches and get him into a man thong on the beach. You might not ever see him again."

"Ah, Margery, come on..."

"What?"

"I've got to work with the guy. Now every time I look at him..."

CHAPTER NINE

Virgil could feel the day starting to slip away. He had a court appearance scheduled from a previous case in a little over two hours. He thought about calling Sandy—even picked up the phone to do it—but then tossed it back on the passenger seat of the truck. The doctor had told her to get some rest. No sense in bugging her if she was actually doing what she'd been told. His thoughts of Sandy made him think about what she'd said about the governor's wife being out of town...how she'd been there with him at his home, at night, just the two of them...

But the thoughts were nothing more than basic jealousy.

So...Sandy. Virgil had been drawn to her immediately. The feeling was foreign to him. It made him feel like a dopey little schoolboy. A middle-aged dopey schoolboy. Because they were on the same unit and Virgil was her boss, the politics of it could get complicated. There were rules about those sorts of things.

But...maybe screw the politics...*and the rules*.

———

VIRGIL HAD NEVER SEEN SAMUEL PATE'S RESIDENCE, BUT he had a rough idea where his house was located. One of the television stations in town had done a feature story on Pate's home a few months ago and Virgil remembered the story mostly because he was so amazed at the grandiosity on display from someone who'd made their fortune by instilling the fear of God into people who probably could not afford to buy a second-hand bible.

The documents he'd collected from Franklin Dugan's office sat on the seat next to him and Virgil thought he should at least glance at them before he spoke with Pate. He turned into a gas station just off the highway, picked up the papers and began to read. He spent the better part of an hour trying to make sense of what he saw in the documents, but after reading through them three times he discovered he had no more detailed information than what Cora had given him earlier: Samuel Pate was under investigation for insurance fraud out of Texas, he was talking publicly about running for the office of governor of the state of Indiana, and he apparently had a banker who'd been either very generous or foolhardy. Maybe both.

When he finally turned into Pate's drive, Virgil realized the story he'd seen on television a few months back did not do justice to the level of extravagance and excess in the man's life. On TV Pate preached the way to heaven was to give most, if not all of your earthly belongings to God through his ministry, yet it appeared he lived his life as if the very rules he preached somehow didn't apply to him.

The driveway was almost a quarter mile in length and at the far end it split into two lanes. One of the lanes led around the side of the house to a five-car garage, the other to a circular turn-about in front of the three story red-bricked mansion. Virgil parked his truck just past the front door then walked up and rang the bell. When the front door opened he felt a surge of cool, conditioned air brush past, but when he saw the woman on the other side of the threshold who smiled at him and said his name aloud he was left off balance and suddenly at a loss for words.

"Well, Virgil Jones. What on earth are you doing here? Come in, please."

Her accent was manufactured, acquired from her time spent in Texas, the way a person's skin will darken after weeks or months spent outdoors in the summer sun. But Virgil knew she had always spoken with a Midwestern twang, her words contrived and spoken without sincerity.

In high school her name had been Amanda Habern, but her married name now was Pate. Virgil had heard that a number of years ago she and Sermon Sam had married, but at the time Pate was not yet famous and Amanda was just a girl he'd known a long time ago for a very short while. Under any other circumstance he might have been surprised that she recognized or even remembered him, but Virgil and Amanda had a history of a single shared encounter, one which could have been beautiful, or at least just plain old fashion fun, but in the end was neither.

Virgil accepted her invitation and crossed the threshold of the front door and when he did, he found himself suddenly conflicted about the nature of his visit and her eagerness to so willingly invite him into her home. He was in her house as an investigative officer of the state of Indiana and not a casual visitor or long lost high school lover from decades ago. He wondered if the warmth in her eyes and the look of fondness on her face were as manufactured as the accent of her singsong voice. Regardless of the purpose of his visit, he had to admit she was still as easy to look at now as she was twenty years ago. She wore tennis whites, and her shirt was damp with perspiration. When she closed the door the two of them endured one of those clumsy moments old lovers are often faced with when an unexpected chance encounter brings them together. She stepped forward, her arms open to hug him at the same time he put his right arm out to shake her hand. It was awkward and Virgil thought she laughed a little too quickly and perhaps a touch too long. In the end, they went with the handshake.

They looked at each other for a moment before Virgil broke the silence. "It's been a long time, Amanda."

"It has been a long time, hasn't it?" she said. "I just put some coffee on. Why don't you come and join me?"

She placed her hand in the crook of his arm in an effort to lead him through the house, but Virgil held himself steady and refused to go along with her. When she felt the resistance she turned her head and Virgil saw her smile falter. "I'm here in an official capacity, Amanda. I need to speak with Samuel. Perhaps yourself as well, but I'd like to have a word with your husband first."

"Is this about Franklin?" she asked. "Why would you want to talk to Samuel about that?"

Virgil made note of her referral of the victim by his first name, then answered her question. "Yes, it is about Franklin Dugan's murder. I'm investigating on behalf of the state. It's what I do, Amanda. Is your husband home?"

"No, I'm afraid he is not home, *Detective*."

"Where is he?"

"He's at the church. They always tape Sunday's broadcast a few days ahead of time then edit it down for time. I know a lot of people think it's live, but it's not. It's taped. We make no secret about that, you know."

The defensiveness, Virgil thought, was probably a large part of her life in general so he drew no conclusions from the words she spoke or the manner in which they were delivered. "I wouldn't know, Amanda."

"What is that supposed to mean?"

"It doesn't mean anything other than I am not a member of your church, and I don't watch your televised broadcasts. How well did you know Franklin Dugan?"

"Are you asking me that question in an official capacity? Aren't you supposed to read me my rights or something?"

"We only read you your rights if you are under arrest, which you are not. Could you please just answer the question?"

"I could, but I choose not to. My rights are the same whether I'm under arrest or not and in this particular instance, I choose to remain silent. If you have any questions for my husband, or me, I suggest you contact our attorney. Better yet, I'm sure he'll be in touch with you. And your boss." She opened the front door. "It was great seeing you, Jonesy," she said, her manufactured east Texas accent suddenly gone, her voice thick with sarcasm. "Maybe next time we see each other it won't be in an official capacity."

"I seriously doubt it, Amanda. Have your husband call me as soon as he gets home." When Virgil tried to hand her his business card she refused to take it so he laid it on the small receiving table next to the door. As soon as he set it down a gust of wind swirled through the doorway and blew the card onto the floor as if the table were no more willing to accept his contact information than the woman who stood at his side. He stepped out into the sunlight, the sound of the brass door-knocker banging against itself as the door slammed shut behind him.

THERE WERE NO MISCONCEPTIONS IN VIRGIL'S MIND AS to whether or not Amanda Pate would tell her husband to call, so Virgil drove over to the Pate Ministry complex located on the outer edges of a shopping center on the city's west side. The massive brick building situated in the center of the property was so nondescript it looked more like a small hospital or office building than a church. Most of the property had been paved with blacktop and dedi-cated to parking, and when he turned into the entrance of the complex, Virgil saw that the parking lot was completely full. He parked next to the yellow-curbed side-walk in front of the building then set a laminated placard on the dash identifying his truck as an official state vehicle.

A landscaper was spreading fertilizer on the grass. Parts of the sidewalk were covered with the chemical granules and they crunched under Virgil's boots as if he were walking across a crushed shell parking lot, the kind you find in ocean side towns of the deep south. Four sets of double glass doors with reflective tint separated by square brick pillars fronted the building, and when he was less than ten feet away they all opened at once and a throng of people exited the building and made their way to the parking lot. Virgil had to stand aside and wait for the first wave of people to pass before he could get inside the building. The scene reminded him of quitting time at the factory where his grandfather had worked his entire life. His mom or his grandmother would sometimes take him along and they'd sit at the curb or on the trunk of the car and then the steam whistle would blow and the men would pour out of the factory like the inside of the building was on fire and about to explode.

The lobby area of the church was bigger than Virgil expected. Hundreds of people clustered about in small groups, talking or laughing, and some even held hands in a circle, their eyes closed, their heads bowed in prayer as if they had to put in one more request to God before they left the building. There was a café of some sort along the eastern wall of the lobby serving coffee, tea and croissants. Small tables lined a vertical railed enclosure where people sat and talked with one another, their faces full of hope and joy as if perhaps they were the chosen few who were lucky enough to have found their heaven on earth. Next to the café was a bookstore where still more people browsed the aisles while others waited in line to pay for their literary selections. Across the lobby on the opposite wall a large area separated by red-roped stanchions contained a maze of multi-colored tube slides, the kind you see in the children's section of fast food restaurants. Dozens of children ran and happily climbed the ladders then slid down through the tubes, their hair full of static electricity when they popped out the bottom. Virgil turned back around and looked at the doors he'd just entered feeling a little like Alice must have felt when she followed the rabbit down a hole and ended up in a mystical place that made no sense to her at all.

A number of the children and younger adults wore beaded bracelets on their wrists, the ones with WWJD on them and even Virgil knew the letters stood for What Would Jesus Do? He looked around for a few seconds and thought if Jesus were here, he would in all likelihood wait until everyone had safely left the building then burn it to the ground.

He turned in a slow circle, looking for the office area or an information kiosk and that's when he noticed two men approaching. They were both big and ugly. Their biceps bulged hard against their matching sport coats. Though one was slightly taller than the other, they looked almost exactly the same. Shaved heads, thick necks, bulging muscles, and arms that seemed a little too long. Mouth breathers.

The shorter one spoke, like maybe the taller one didn't know how. "Reverend Pate is in his office and is expecting you. Follow us please." The smaller of the two men took two steps forward and motioned for Virgil to follow. The three of them walked through the lobby area and then down a short corridor and into the administrative office area of the complex and found Pate seated at his desk, on the phone. He motioned Virgil in with an exaggerated circular arm movement then pointed to a chair in front of his desk, then into the phone he said, "Yes, yes he's here now. I'll call you later."

After seeing the size of the lobby and its carnival-like atmosphere, Virgil was surprised that Pate's office was no bigger than his own. It was decorated in muted tones, a contrast so stark from the rest of the building Virgil was almost more amazed by its utilitarian form and function than he was of the lobby just down the hall.

Samuel Pate looked like a televangelist, the way some people carry the look of their profession, like an airline pilot or a doctor. His hair was pure white and he wore it combed straight back, each strand held perfectly in place by some type of product that left a reflective sheen so thick it looked like a translucent helmet. When Pate finished the phone call he smiled. His eyes held a certain light that looked both welcoming and mischievous at the same time, as if maybe the way to heaven might just be through a lesser-known back door. He wore a starched pink shirt with a white collar and tie, and the armpits of his shirt were soaked through with perspiration, although the size and shape of the stains were so uniform it looked like they may have come from a make-up artist's spray bottle instead of his own sweat glands.

Pate stood, but before he did he affixed the metal bands of arm crutches around his forearms, grasped the handles, then pulled himself out of his chair. He came around to the front of his desk, pointed to the chair with the end of one of the crutches and said, "Welcome Detective. Please, have a seat."

They shook hands and when Pate squeezed his fingers harder and longer than necessary, Virgil said, "That's an impressive grip, Mr. Pate. Please release my hand."

Pate chuckled as if caught in a polite fib, the kind one might tell to save someone from an unnecessary embarrassment. "I prefer Reverend, if you please," he said. "And

I hope you'll forgive me. I've spent years moving around with the aid of these crutches. It tends to build up one's musculature, wouldn't you agree? I often forget my own strength. How exactly may I help you, Detective? My wife said you wanted to speak with me about Franklin's unfortunate passing."

Virgil noticed two things right away: Like his wife, Pate had referred to the victim by his first name, which was indicative of a certain level of familiarity beyond a business relationship, and two, he had referred to Dugan's murder as an 'unfortunate passing.' Virgil decided to go for some shock value.

"The victim was shot to death in his own driveway, Reverend. The top of his head was blown off and you could use what's left of his skull for a gravy boat. I'd hardly call that an unfortunate passing."

Pate ignored the statement in its entirety and said, "There is a war going on out there, Detective. I witness it every day. The book of Revelation speaks of what is to come and the fate that will befall those who choose to ignore the word of God. The script is already written, the players already cast. The outcome for those who follow the teachings of the bible is a foregone conclusion. The only real question left to ponder, the only real way to fight the war, is to ask yourself, where do you stand in the eyes of the Lord, Detective? Do you stand in the light of God, or in the darkness like those who would murder a man in his own home? You come to my office with intentions of questioning me over something I know nothing about regarding a man I knew as a professional, a friend, and a member of this church. I find your behavior and your demeanor not only questionable but repulsive."

Virgil pointed a finger at him. "Save the shuck for the misinformed you preach to on TV, Reverend. I'm not here to be your witness. When was the last time you saw Franklin Dugan?"

When Pate answered the fire had gone out of his voice and his eyes seemed dull. "I saw him last week, at the taping of the show. He was here, as he always was."

"When was the last time you were at his home?"

"I have never been to his home, Detective. Ever. Let me ask you something, if I may. Franklin was one of our biggest benefactors. Why in the world would I or anyone from this church for that matter want to see him harmed?"

"That's a fine question, sir. It's also one that I don't have the answer to. But here's an even better one: Why do you think, Reverend, that the man who was personally responsible for the approval of a five million dollar loan to your church was murdered just days after you got the money? Better yet, how is it sir, that you were able to obtain that kind of credit using an all but condemned building as collateral? Is any of this starting to make sense to you, Reverend? Would you care to enlighten me as to the nature of the investigation currently being conducted by the Texas Department of Insurance regarding your former ministry in Houston?"

Virgil thought Pate might try to defend himself, but

he didn't. "My wife told me of her past relationship with you when you were schoolmates. She's an interesting woman, is she not? We're having a viewing party this Saturday, here at our facility. We watch the broadcast with a select few members of the congregation to try to get a feel for how well our message will be received the next day. She's asked me to invite you to attend. Would ten a.m. work for you, Detective?"

WHEN HE LEFT THE PATE MINISTRY COMPLEX VIRGIL realized he had more questions than answers. As he headed downtown for a court appearance on a previous case he spoke with both Rosencrantz and Donatti to get a feel for any information they might have gathered from their canvass of the double murder. Rosie's voice crackled over a bad cell signal. "Found a paperboy who says he might have seen the van. He's just a kid. Sort of a punk, little bit of smart-ass in fact. Or hell, maybe he's completely normal and I'm just getting old. Either way, he didn't see anything of value. No plate, no make. Says he forgot one of the houses along his route and had to double back. That's when he saw the van. But there's nothing there."

"You sure?"

"Positive, Jones-man. On the plus side, techs found some brass."

"No shit?"

"I shit thee not."

"Prints?"

"Yep. Says it's probably a thumb from pressing a shell into the clip."

"All right, that's something. Let's get it going through NCIC."

"Already on it."

"Okay. What else?"

"Just spec if you want it."

"Let's have it," Virgil said.

"If you go with the theory that the banker, Dugan, was the target, they probably shot Burns first then Dugan."

"What makes you say that?"

"I talked with Becky back at the shop and she pulled everything, and I mean everything that Burns had been involved with for the past three years. It's all basic, no bullshit kind of stuff. Hell Jonesy, he's been on third shift protection for the last two years and there's been nothing going on there. He hasn't even written a traffic ticket in over thirty-six months. No one's got any reason to be pissed at Jerry, so that leaves the banker, right?"

"Yeah, probably."

"Plus," Rosencrantz went on, "Somebody's always pissed at their banker about something. I mean hell, just last week I was at my bank—"

"Stay with me here, Rosie."

"Yeah, yeah, sorry. Anyway, I know Jerry was close to retirement, but he was still sharp, you know? I don't know if you noticed or not, but crime scene said his weapon was still holstered."

Virgil thought about that for a few seconds. Rosie's theory could fit. So too could about ten others. "All right, stay on the canvass and let me know what you get."

"You got it Jonesy. Are you headed over here?"

"No, I've got this court thing. I'm just pulling in now. Probably be here the rest of the day. Meet me tonight at the bar and we'll cover everything there." Virgil killed the phone, parked the truck and headed into court. He was fifteen minutes late. If the court was on schedule, the judge would not be pleased.

CHAPTER TEN

From the moment of birth, the hunger of death feeds from an army of life. Day by day it creeps ever closer, a silent, merciless hunter, its endurance without end, its clemency non-existent. It chews on the mind, feeds on the body, digests the spirit, and regurgitates the soul. It is the single, inescapable, inevitable end of everyone, and no one knew that better than Rhonda Rhodes.

Rhonda worked six days a week as a home hospice nurse where she currently served twelve patients, all of them in their final battle with the Big C. It was a gut-wrenching way to make a living, but Rhonda knew, just knew, down to what she called her ever-lasting soul, that what she did for a living was the reason she was ever set down on God's green earth.

Rhonda and her ever-lasting husband, Tom, had been married for twenty-seven years. Tom was a career fireman for the city of Indianapolis who'd retired three months ago and the spare time was eating him alive. He wanted Rhonda to retire as well, but Rhonda was a hospice nurse when they met, and, as she so often told anyone who asked, 'probably will be till the day I die.'

Her days tended to start late and run later, a sore spot for Tom that just didn't want to heal. "The Big C works on its own schedule," she told him. Tom was on his hands and knees in the middle of their driveway, pulling the weeds out of the cracks in the aging cement, the sleeves of his t-shirt damp with sweat.

"Won't be long and we're gonna have to replace the drive," he said to her without turning around. She stood just behind him in the driveway, ready to leave for work. Rhonda still wore the traditional nurse's uniform—white skirt and blouse, white hose, and white leather shoes. It may have been a throwback from years past, but she refused to dress in those silly scrubs everyone else was wearing these days. It seemed every week one of the other nurses was going on about this new print or that new design. Somewhere along the way nursing had become secondary to making a fashion statement, and a bad one at that, Rhonda thought. She'd keep her whites, thank you very much. Besides, she thought the patients seemed to appreciate her attire. More than a few had said so over the years, and if it worked for them, bless their ever-lasting hearts, it worked for her.

"The Wimberley's down the street had theirs done a couple of weeks ago," Tom said. Rhonda realized she'd drifted a bit. Tom was talking about something the Wimberley's had bought. A new car? "Got a deal from Bill. You remember Bill? From over at the three-two?"

"I'm sorry dear, what was that? The Wimberley's bought a car from Bill?"

Tom dug at a particularly stout weed that did not want to give way and when it finally came loose, he scraped his knuckles across the jagged edge of a crack in the cement and tore the skin off the tops of three fingers. He yelled loud enough that the next-door neighbor's dog began to bark. Tom stuck the back of his fingers in his mouth, sucked off the blood, and then pressed them into the side of his jeans. "No, they didn't buy a car from Bill. He poured their new drive for them."

"Let me see your hand," she said.

"Are you listening to me?" Tom said. "I'm trying to tell you we need a new driveway." His knees popped when he stood.

"Tom, you're bleeding. Let me see."

"I'm fine. It's nothing. You going to work?"

"Yes. I've got four patients today. One of them is new, that little girl I was telling you about last night, God bless her. She's first, and I'll probably be there for most of the ever-lasting day, then I've got follow-ups on the other three. We can have leftover's or I can stop and get us something on the way home."

Tom pulled his hand from the side of his pants and inspected his knuckles. "Either way," he said. Then he softened his voice. "It wasn't so bad when we were both working, but I miss you, Rhonda. You're hardly ever here with me."

"I miss you too darling, I do. But my patients need me." Rhonda watched the blood fill the cracks in the broken skin of Tom's fingers and saw that her husband needed her too. "Tom, really, let me see your hand. I've got bandages in the trunk. Let me patch that up for you."

"Go on to work, Rhonda," he said. "I'm fine. I think I'll live."

Tom was right.

He lived.

THE SIDS BATTED THE IDEA BACK AND FORTH—THIS WAS a week ago—right before what they called Go Time. Junior wanted to be creative. Senior wanted to be practical. Junior argued that creativity could be useful and work to their advantage. If they varied their methods enough, the cops would be running around chasing their tails and probably wouldn't put two and two together right away, if ever. It would give them all the cover they'd need.

Senior argued that creativity could, and probably would lead to mistakes and missed opportunities. "Besides," he'd said, "With this many killings, you're talking about a lot of creativity. Be better if we keep it simple. We've got the guns and the silencers, and the van is ready. Let's just take our shots and be done with it."

"The silencers are pretty cool," Junior said. "Gotta love Indiana...legal silencers and all."

"That might end up changing," Senior said.

"Yeah, probably will," Junior said. "Too late now though."

So they'd settled on the practical, and in the here and now it put them across the street from Beans Coffee shop with Junior at the wheel and Senior at the trigger. They watched as Rhonda Rhodes pulled to the curb and walked inside, the glare of Rhonda's stark white nurse's uniform almost too bright for Senior's scope. He had to squint to keep from being temporarily blinded by the whiteness of the damned thing. He followed her track into the store, but didn't pull the trigger. He'd catch her on the way out. That was the plan.

Go time, baby.

RHONDA RHODES PARKED IN FRONT OF HER FAVORITE stop off, Beans Coffee Shop, gathered her paperwork, then walked inside and took a seat at a table by the window. Beans was usually busy during the morning rush, but later in the day slowed just enough that Rhonda could sit in peace for thirty minutes or so and tend to her paperwork. The dying, bless their ever-lasting hearts, created a lot of paper.

Beans was unique not for their quaint name, but because instead of counter service, they employed actual wait staff who would come to your table and take your order. Plus, their prices were right—two bucks a cup with free refills—unlike those newer fancy places that were popping up on every blessed corner that made you wait in line for a paper cup with different sizes, the names of which no one ever really understood. Her favorite waiter approached the table with his usual smile in place.

"Good morning, Rhonda," the waiter said. "Get you your usual?"

"Yes, please," she said as she spread her paperwork across the table. "I've got quite the schedule today."

"I'll bet you do a lot of good for a lot of people," he said. Rhonda felt like he meant it.

"I do what I can. I'll probably be doing this until the day I die."

"Well, our coffee will keep you going until then, that's for sure. Be right back."

The waiter returned a few minutes later with a large mug full of brew and a muffin wrapped in cellophane. "Muffin's on the house today, Rhonda. Enjoy."

She smiled and said thank you, but the waiter remained in place. "Mind if I ask you something, Rhonda?"

"Sure."

"How do you do it? I mean, don't get me wrong, I'm glad you do, you and others like you, but to serve the dying like that, day after day, I just don't think I could do it, you know?"

Rhonda set her pen down, took a sip of coffee and

looked the young man in the eyes. "Everyone in here is dying. The difference is, some know it, and others don't. The ones I serve, the ones with the Big C, they know it. I just help them during the final part of their lives. I'll tell you this though, the suffering I've seen...sometimes it's almost too much. I pray to the lord every night that when my time comes I go quickly. I sometimes think I'd rather take a bullet than to suffer through even half of what I've seen."

The waiter glanced at his other tables. One of his other customers held a cup in the air, eyebrows raised. "Hey, I better get back to work. I wouldn't worry, Rhonda. The work you're doing, you'll probably live forever."

"I hope you're right," she said.

Thirty minutes later, when Rhonda Rhodes stepped out of the coffee shop, the Sids got busy. Junior already had the engine running—nothing screamed get-away vehicle like an engine start after a gunshot, silenced or not. Senior had been lying on his back on the floor of the van, the rifle held at port arms. When Junior said "Good to go," Senior sat up and put the business end of the barrel through the custom hole in the side of the van, just under the windows in the back. He squinted through the scope, drew a bead on his target, exhaled, and squeezed the trigger. When he did, the silenced bullet smashed through Rhonda Rhodes' sternum and chewed through her chest organs like the Big C on speed.

The waiter had gone behind the counter to put Rhonda's cash in the till and brew another pot of house blend. He turned around and saw Rhonda walk out the door then down the sidewalk toward her car. When the bullet hit her chest it lifted her from the pavement and tossed her back, her arms and legs flying forward. The waiter would later tell the police it looked like—at least for a moment—that her body hung in the air in the shape of a big C, and wasn't that ironic because that's what she always called it, the big C. But the cops didn't care about irony so the waiter decided he'd keep his mouth shut regarding the comment to Rhonda about her living forever, because as anyone will tell you, with the cops, you just never really know.

So, as it went, the waiter was wrong, but Rhonda's prayers were answered. She went quick, dead before she hit the ever-lasting pavement. The hole in her chest left a red stain on her throwback whites that looked like a rose petal on a blanket of snow in the middle of an otherwise fine summer day.

CHAPTER ELEVEN

They were behind on the docket and Virgil waited at the courthouse for three agonizing hours. His cell phone was set on silent but he felt the vibration and pulled the phone out and checked the screen. A text from Ron Miles. After he read the message, Virgil leaned forward across the bar and tapped the prosecutor on the shoulder. "I've got a situation. I need to leave."

"You're joking, right? We've got a situation right here. It's your testimony that's gonna keep this prick locked up. You want to blow that?"

"It can't be helped. I'm in the middle of this thing and I've got to go."

The prosecutor turned in his chair and looked at Virgil. "Listen, I know we're behind schedule here, but the defense is just about to wrap it up, then we'll be able to get you on the stand and out of here. If you'll just wait for a few more—"

The judge tapped her gavel, leaned forward from the bench and spoke into her microphone. She sort of whispered into the device, her tone mocking Virgil's attempt not to disturb the proceedings. "Gentlemen, is there something you'd like to share with the court?"

The prosecutor turned his attention forward. "No, your Honor. I'm sorry for the—"

Virgil stood and looked at the Judge. "Your Honor, may I approach the bench?"

The prosecutor turned and spoke through his teeth. "What the hell are you doing? Do you want to be held in contempt? Sit down." The judge raised her eyebrows.

"Urgent matter, your Honor."

She seemed to consider it for a moment. "Step up. This better be good Detective."

Virgil crossed the bar with the prosecutor on his heels and walked up to the bench. "I appreciate the court's indulgence your Honor." The judge made a circular, 'get on with it' motion with her hand. "Judge, an urgent situation has come to my attention. I'm sure you've heard about the murders earlier today of one of our state troopers, along with one of our city's more prominent citizens, Franklin Dugan."

The judge leaned forward and looked out over the tops of her glasses. Judge Andrea Moore was the senior judge in the superior court system and was not known for her leniency. "Yes, Detective, I have heard. But what does that have to do with me, my court, or this case?"

"Nothing at all your Honor."

"Then why are we speaking, Detective?"

The conversation already wasn't going exactly as Virgil had hoped. "Your Honor, there's been another murder, just a few blocks away from here as a matter of fact. My—"

"Are you psychic, Detective?"

"Beg your pardon, your Honor?"

"I think you heard me. I said are you psychic? You know we do not allow electronic devices of any kind in the courtroom. So, either you're psychic, or you're breaking the law in my courtroom. Which is it, Detective?"

Virgil opened his mouth to answer, thought better of what he wanted to say and instead chewed on the inside of his cheek for a moment.

The judge leaned back, smacked her gavel against the sound block and said, "The court will be in recess for five minutes. Detective, I'll see you in chambers. Now."

Thirty seconds later Judge Moore sat at her desk with Virgil standing on the other side. "You're killing me here, Jonesy. I'm already over three hours behind. What the hell is going on?"

"I need to leave, Andrea. There's been another shooting, and that makes three today."

"Oh come on, Jonesy. This is Indy. We have shootings almost everyday. What makes this such an emergency?"

She reached for a pitcher of water and poured two glasses. "Water?"

"No, thanks. Listen, we're not sure, at least not yet, that this latest one is connected. But the crime scene techs are saying—and initial witness statements back it up —that it was a high-powered sniper rifle. It was silenced. Broad daylight, woman goes down right on the sidewalk, shot in the chest, and no one heard a thing. What are the chances?"

"It sounds to me like you've got plenty of people on the scene right now."

Virgil took a deep breath. "Judge…" He paused, then started over. "Andrea, do you remember last year when you came to me about that little high speed chase your son was involved in?"

"It was hardly a high speed chase. He was a passenger in the vehicle and he says he did everything in his power to convince the driver to stop the car."

"Uh huh. Took him over four miles to do it though."

"Make your point, Jonesy."

"My point is, you brought that to me, and I took care of it for you, did I not?"

"Really? You've got this one bit of juice with me and this is how you want to spend it?"

No, I don't. "I guess I'll have to."

"Yeah, I guess you will. Use the side door. I'll handle the lawyers."

"Are you going to reschedule for a later date on the docket?"

"Are you kidding? No way. The prosecutor doesn't really need you and the ink isn't even dry on the public defender's Bar exam. The defendant isn't going anywhere except back to a cell."

Virgil shook his head. "So I wasted my juice, huh?"

"Yep. Isn't it fun though? I hate it when someone has something on me. Anyway, we're square now. Go catch your shooter, sharp stuff. I don't like it when people shoot up my city."

"It may be your courtroom, Andrea, but it's my city," Virgil said as he reached for the door handle. "Stop in at the bar sometime, I'll buy you a beer." The judge made a go away motion with the back of her hand, so Virgil went away.

TEN MINUTES LATER HE ROLLED UP TO THE SCENE, spotted Ron Miles and went that way.

"Jonesy...what a mess. I'm trying not to get ahead of myself here, but this is too coincidental, don't you think?" He pressed on without waiting for an answer. "First Burns, and that banker guy, Dugan, and now this." He turned and pointed at the victim lying on the sidewalk. Virgil followed his motion and then looked inside the plate glass windows of the coffee shop. Three uniforms and two plain clothes were inside talking to the customers.

"Tell me what's what, Ron."

"Okay. Victim's name is Rhonda Rhodes. ID on her person confirms. Looks like she was a hospice nurse according to documents in her possession and initial statements from the coffee shop's employees. She's a regular here. Five or six days a week, again according to the employees. Married, husband is a retired fireman."

"He have an alibi?"

"Yeah, a good one too. He was just down the street from his residence speaking with one of his neighbors, guy named Wimberley about replacing their driveway."

"Has he been notified yet?"

"Yep. He's here now," Miles said, then pointed to the back of the EMS van. "Getting his vitals checked by EMS. He's wrecked."

"All right, go on."

Miles took his notebook out, flipped through a few pages for a second, then continued. "Victim pulls up, parks right at the curb, goes inside, sits down to have a cup of joe and do her paperwork. Guy that waited on her says she was here for about twenty, twenty-five minutes tops, drank her coffee while working on her paper, then gathered everything up, paid the bill and left. The waiter says he was putting her money in the register as she walked out. Says he saw her get hit. Said the impact of the round lifted her up and sent her flying backwards. Didn't hear a thing. He said it was like watching a movie scene with the sound turned off or something."

"Okay, keep him here. I'm going to want to talk to him."

"You got it, Jonesy."

"Any other witnesses?"

"Nope. At least not yet."

"All right. Keep the uniforms talking to people. Let's go speak to the husband."

Tom Rhodes sat in the back of the EMS unit, his forearms resting across his thighs, his head down. Virgil nodded at the paramedics and asked them if he could have a few minutes. They climbed out and Virgil and Ron sat on the bench opposite Rhodes. Miles spoke first. "Mr. Rhodes, this is Detective Jones. He'd like to speak with you for a moment, ask a few questions if you're up for it."

Tom Rhodes did not, Virgil thought, look up for it. "Mr. Rhodes, I'm sorry for your loss, sir. I know you're going to think the timing is lousy, but the sooner we can get the information we need, the better our chances are of catching whoever did this to your wife."

Tom Rhodes looked up and shook his head. "You don't look like a cop. You damn sure don't look like a detective."

Virgil gave him a sympathetic grin. "Yeah, I get that a lot. Sometimes that's the whole point though. Not to look like a cop."

"I guess. I really wouldn't know."

"I understand you're a retired fireman?"

"That's right."

"I want you to know that I have a tremendous amount of respect for you guys and what you do."

He nodded, looked at nothing. "It's been my experience that people who make that kind of statement are people who've had a traumatic experience with fire."

Virgil nodded at him. "You're right. I was just a kid, but it changed me. Tell you the truth, I always sort of thought I might end up in your line of work."

"Why didn't you?"

"Ah, you know, my dad was a cop. Marion County Sheriff until he retired."

He processed that information for a few seconds, then said, "Jones. You said your name was Jones? Is Mason Jones your old man?"

"That's right. Do you know him?"

"No, not really. Just enough to recognize him if we were on scene together. Hey, always voted for him though."

"I'm sure he appreciated that, sir. Listen, I've got some questions, but tell me about your day so far, with your wife."

He put a little gravel in his voice. "Well it's been just splendid, Detective." Then he caught himself and raised a hand in apology.

"What I mean, Mr. Rhodes—"

"Call me Tom, okay."

"Okay. What I mean, Tom, is that I'd like you to tell me about your day with your wife up to the point she left for work."

He shook his head and chewed the bottom of his lip. "There's nothing to tell. It was a normal day. We got up, had breakfast and went about our day. Then a little later, hell just a little while ago, she left for work. I know she likes to stop off here for coffee before getting to it. I think it helps her—or helped her I guess I should say—to clear her head, know what I mean?"

"I think I do. Anything out of the ordinary, today in particular?"

"No, nothing."

"Was she acting strange, like maybe something was bothering her?"

"No, absolutely not. If anything it was the other way around."

"What do you mean?"

"I mean it was me. I was the one who was acting strange. Well, hell, that's not right. I wasn't acting strange. I was sort of pissed off if you want to know the truth of it."

"Why? Were the two of you arguing?"

"No. Probably would have turned into one if she hadn't left for work when she did. It's been a bit of a sore spot lately, ever since I retired. I'm stuck at home with nothing to do except busy work, while she's out doing real work. We'd talked about retiring together. Maybe do a little traveling, but that never worked out."

"Why not?"

"Well, I guess because she just couldn't give it up. Her work."

"I understand she was a hospice nurse?"

"That's right."

"Okay. So you two had an argument right before she left?"

"That's not what I said, Detective. You're putting words into my mouth. I said it probably would have turned into an argument."

Virgil looked at the bandage on his hand. "What happened to your hand?"

"I scraped the ever-lasting shit out of my knuckles pulling weeds from the cracks in the drive. That's what I was doing when she left."

"What about her patients, Tom?"

"What about them?"

"She was in a difficult line of work," Virgil said. "She cares for people at a time when there's nothing left for them to do but try to die with a little dignity."

"Sounds like you've had some experience with that too."

Virgil didn't answer.

"Well, I'm sorry for your loss, Detective, whenever it may have been. But to tell you the truth, I never knew much about her patients."

"Why's that?"

"Because of those damn HIPPA laws. Rhonda took her job very seriously. She never spoke about individual patients with anything more than very vague generalities. And even then, never by name. And if I'm being honest with you, I didn't want to hear it anyway. The whole damned thing depressed the ever-lasting shit out of me. I guess that says something about me, huh?"

"Is there any chance, Tom, that this could be one of her patient's family members? Someone mad at Rhonda because their loved one died?"

"I don't know. Doesn't sound right to me. Doesn't feel right. Everyone I've ever talked with thinks hospice workers walk on water. I guess it could be possible, hell, anything's possible, right? But I don't think so."

Virgil scratched the back of his head and thought, *what the hell.* "Where do you bank, Tom?"

"Firefighter's Credit Union. Why?"

"What about church? Did you or your wife attend anywhere?"

"I was raised Catholic, but I let it slip. Same with Rhonda. Does that mean anything?"

Virgil didn't answer and instead looked at Ron with an anything else? look on his face. Miles shook his head.

"She's really gone?" Rhodes said, his voice suddenly small, like a child.

"Tom, look," Ron said. "Why don't you go on home. You've got a tough few days ahead of you. Gather your family around you and let them help you. You don't want to be here right now. When they move her body, it's, well...it's just something you don't want to see."

"Where are they going to take her?"

"They'll take her to the hospital," Virgil said. "There will be an autopsy and after that they'll send her to the funeral home of your choice. But Detective Miles is right. Go home. Let us do our job. We'll figure this thing out."

"All she wanted to do was help people. Why would someone do this?"

And Virgil thought, *how do you answer a question like that?*

VIRGIL FOLLOWED RON INTO THE COFFEE SHOP AND got introduced to the waiter who served Rhonda.

"How about we sit down for a few minutes? I've got a few questions."

"I've already answered just about every cop in the city, so far," he said.

"Well, not everyone," Virgil said. "It looks like you were the last one to speak with her before she died. I just want to ask you a few things. Sometimes witnesses know something they don't even think they know and it can be something that might not mean anything to you but can make all the difference in the world to us. Have a seat." Virgil pointed him to a table in the corner. No other patrons were in the cafe. The smell of burnt coffee hung in the air.

After the three of them were seated, the waiter started right in without prompting. "You know what's weird?" he said. "I don't really feel anything. I mean, I've known Rhonda for a long time. Well, that's not quite right. I don't really know her at all. What I mean is, I've been serving her for a long time. We'd talk, you know? Nothing substantial, not really. Just the casual 'how you doing' kind of chitchat bullshit that customers and waiters have." He shook his head. "Jesus. I've never seen anyone get shot before. Aren't I supposed to feel something? I feel like I should be upset. I mean more upset than I am. Is something wrong with me? Am I in shock or something? Is this what shock feels like?" He sat with his elbows on the table, the heels of his hands pressed into his forehead. His fingers worked their way into his hairline and pulled his hair back taut. It gave him a haunted, almost effeminate look. "You may very well be in shock," Ron said. "Do you feel like you require medical attention?"

He let go of his hair and forehead. "No, no, I'm good. Besides, I don't have any insurance."

"Just take us through it, from the time she walked in the door until you saw her get hit. Take your time. Don't leave anything out," Virgil said.

"I don't know what to tell you. I mean, there just isn't anything to say. She came in, same time as she always did, sat at the same table she always sits at, unless someone else is sitting there, except they weren't, so she did." He pointed to the table in the opposite corner of the cafe. "That table right there."

"All right, that's good," Virgil said. "Go on."

"Well, like I said, there really isn't anything to say. She sat down, spread out her paperwork and started doing whatever it is she did with it. The paperwork, I mean. I asked her if she wanted her usual. She said yes, so I brought her a cup of our house blend and a muffin. The muffin was on me. It wasn't part of her usual. I just wanted to give her a muffin, you know? We made nice for a few minutes and I got back to work. Before she left I asked her if she wanted anything else. She says 'no I've got to run. See you tomorrow though.' I said something like 'you bet' or whatever and then she walked out and I just happened to glance up from behind the counter and I saw her flying backward through the air. She hung there for a second, hell not even that long I guess, because you know how everything seems like it's going in slow-motion? Well, anyway she hung there for a second in the shape of a big C with her arms and legs flying forward and her body going backwards. It's kind of ironic if you think about it, because that's what she always called cancer. The big C."

"And you didn't hear any gunfire?" Virgil said.

The waiter shook his head. "Nope. It looked like she got hit by a huge gust of wind or something. It was unreal. I didn't know what the hell was happening."

"What about a car backfiring? Did you hear anything like that? Some kind of noise that may have been a gunshot but in the moment it just didn't register?"

The waiter thought about it, but shook his head. "Huh uh."

"What did you do next?"

"What do you mean?"

Virgil tried not to let his impatience show. "I mean, what was the very next thing you did? Did you call 911?"

"No."

"Did you run outside to help the victim?"

"No."

"Why not?"

"I guess, I...well, what I mean is, I just sort of froze. Besides, we're not supposed to leave the cash drawer unattended."

"I see," Virgil said, even though he didn't. "How much money was in the drawer?"

"I don't keep an exact accounting."

"If you had to guess," the impatience in Virgil's voice now obvious.

"Well if I had to guess, there might be, I don't know, seventy or eighty bucks in there or something like that."

Virgil leaned across the table. "So a woman, a hospice nurse, comes into your coffee shop nearly every day of the week, sits at the same table, orders the same thing, then one day leaves and gets shot to death right in front of your eyes and the only thing you could think to do was guard the seventy or eighty bucks in the cash drawer?"

"Hey, man, come on. That's a little harsh. I didn't shoot her."

"No, but you sure didn't do much to help her after she was shot."

"Look, guys, I'm sorry about Rhonda. I really am. She seemed nice. She did good work. She was a consistent tipper. But that's all I know. Maybe I didn't do the right thing. Maybe I panicked, or froze or whatthehellever. But I didn't do anything wrong. There were about ten other people in here who were already dialing 911 and I know about as much emergency first aid as a cocker spaniel.

Besides, even from behind the counter you could tell she was dead before she hit the pavement. You could just see it. So, what, I'm supposed to lose my job over something I couldn't do anything about?" He stood up and started to walk away, then turned back. "You guys ever ask yourselves why no one ever wants to talk to the cops?"

CHAPTER TWELVE

Virgil's house sat on one of the last remaining gravel roads in the county, just off of highway 37 south of 465, the loop that circles Indianapolis. He owned ten acres of land, the back third wooded with a pond between the edge of the woods and the house. The suburban sprawl was creeping closer year by year, but the long drive at the front and the woods at the back assured his privacy.

He tossed his mail on the table next to the door, checked the answering machine—no messages—and turned the shower on to steam the bathroom. Thirty minutes later he was back in the truck and headed downtown to the bar.

The bar Virgil and his dad owned was popular and drew a consistent crowd. He turned into the back, parked his truck at the far end of the lot and walked in through the back kitchen area. The aroma of burgers and chicken halves sizzling over an open broiler reminded him that he'd not yet had anything to eat throughout the entire day, other than a few shrimp.

Robert, their Jamaican cook, saw him walk in. He flipped a burger on a bun then brushed the surface with homemade jerk sauce, tossed on a slice of red onion and handed it to Virgil, a skeptical look on his face. "Dat shrimp, mon, it be comin' by later tomorrow."

"Was supposed to be today," Virgil said.

"Yeah, mon. But the truck already left. So tomorrow. Hope it good. Day say day raise it in a swimmin' pool or someting like dat. But it your money, no?" Virgil took the plate, clapped him on the back and walked into the darkened atmosphere of the bar.

The patron area of the bar was long and narrow with high-back mahogany booths along one wall and the bar itself along the opposite wall with an aisle-way between the two sides. A large mirror ran the entire length behind the bar and gave the illusion of extra space. Small stained-glass light fixtures hung low over the booths. The effect was an intimate atmosphere that often conflicted with the mood of the customers. A blue neon sign above the bar mirror advertised *Warm Beer & Lousy Food*. A small elevated stage at the back between the kitchen entrance and the restrooms provided just enough room for the Reggae house band that played from midweek through the weekend. The lunch hour during the week was usually busy with downtown suits, and the weekend nights had been standing room only since opening day over three years ago.

Virgil knew the city of Indianapolis offered hundreds of small bars where you could eat and drink your fill, but to his knowledge their little bar was the only one that offered the true taste and atmosphere of a small island nation that had held a place in his heart for most of his adult life.

Three years ago during one of his visits to Jamaica, while driving through the Hanover Parish, Virgil experienced one of those rare moments that can change your life for the better if you weren't too preoccupied to notice and let it happen. One of the tires of the rental car he was driving picked up a nail and he pulled over in front of a ramshackle, multi-colored hut fashioned from scrap metal and drift wood at the edge of a town called Lucea which sat at the half way point between the resort towns of Montego Bay and Negril. A handsome, well-dressed bald man approached and asked if he could help, his voice carrying across the gravel lot with the musical lilt of his native land. "What you do, you?" he said. "Dat tire no good now, mon. Come inside. Have a drink and someting to eat. We fix you right up." He held out his balled hand and Virgil bumped fists with him and when they did, the Jamaican man said, "Respect, mon, respect."

Virgil said, "respect," and then before he knew it, three and a half hours had sailed by, he was full from too much Jerk chicken, a little drunk from too many Red

Stripes, but his tire was fixed and he had made two new friends.

But the story didn't end there. The owner of the establishment, the man who came out to greet Virgil was named Delroy Rouche. He served the drinks and befriended his customers while his partner, Robert Whyte, handled the cooking, and apparently, tire changing. During their conversation Virgil learned they both longed to live in the United States. He listened politely to their stories, gave them his business card and got back in his rental. Three weeks later after cutting through the red tape, Delroy helped Virgil and his father set up the bar and Robert took over the kitchen. They both flew back to Jamaica twice a year for a week at a time to their homeland, and every time they did Virgil found himself a little panicked at the thought of ever losing them.

He took a stool at the mid-point of the bar and sat down with his burger and watched his father at the far end laughing with an attractive, middle-aged female customer. A row of clean beer mugs lined the drip trough on the tended side of the bar and when Delroy saw Virgil he turned one over, set it under the tap and pulled him a Red Stripe draft. Virgil's father, Mason, walked down to greet him as well.

"Hey Pops. How's it going?"

"Going fine, Son. Just fine." He glanced back down the bar at the woman who was watching him in the mirror. "How's the governor's main man?"

Virgil sipped his beer and watched as Mason pulled

two shot glasses from under the bar and filled each with an ounce of over-proof rum. "I'm squeakin' by," Virgil said, his eyes drifting to the woman in the mirror. "Who's that?"

"That's Carol, from County Dispatch. She's going to help wait tables around here, mostly on the weekends. She answered the ad. Starts tomorrow."

Virgil felt a kernel of anger pop inside his chest. He fought to contain it, but there was a bite in his tone. "Known her long?" He regretted the words as soon as he said them, but Mason didn't take the bait. Instead, he thought for a moment as he wiped the bar. "You're a grown man, Son."

"Point being?"

"Point being," Mason said, "I was a grown man before you were ever born. I live my life, my way. Might not be your way, and that's all right. But it's mine."

Virgil looked at himself in the mirror and when he did, he saw his father's face in his own. Found himself wondering about who he saw staring back. He'd always been comfortable with himself, but at forty-one years old it was getting harder and harder not to notice the strands of gray at the temples or the lines in his face around his green eyes growing more prevalent with the passage of time. A faint scar ran the length of his jaw on the left side of his face, a result of a boyhood injury. It wasn't nearly as noticeable as he sometimes thought it was, but it flashed with white whenever he smiled. He'd been told on more than one occasion that his smile was a little scary. He looked at his father. "I just miss her, that's all."

"You think I don't?" Mason replied, a little bite of his own. "Not a day goes by, hell, not a minute goes by, I don't think of her." He was quiet for a moment, and when he spoke again, his voice was softer. "I can remember walking in the park with her. We'd see an old couple, not old like me, hell, I'm only sixty-eight, but I mean old, eighties, nineties even, holding hands. Your mom, she'd smile and say 'see that, Mason? That'll be us some day.' Well, that day isn't ever going to come for me, Virgil. Not ever. That part of my life is over now. I don't know what you'd have me do, but I know what your mother would want. She'd have me honor the time we did have together by getting up and getting on with my life. So that's what I'm doing."

Hc picked up the shot glasses and held one out for his son. They had toasted Virgil's mother once a year for the last eleven years. "She's gone Virgil, but she's not forgotten. Not for a minute. I love her and I always will. But I'm done toasting the past. So here's to you and me, and whatever waits down the line." Mason drained his shot glass and set it down hard on the bar and walked away, leaving Virgil there alone, staring at himself in the mirror.

A few minutes later he got up and put his rum behind the bar then moved down next to Carol. They watched each other in the mirror for a few seconds, and then Virgil turned on his stool and said, "I'm Mason's son, Virgil.

Everyone calls me Jonesy. You must be Carol." He smiled when he said it though he really didn't intend to.

———

As the night went on Virgil worked the bar with his father but neither one of them had much to say to the other about their shared loss. They had a decent crowd and the band brought the house down with their original Reggae tunes. With two hours to go until closing, Mason took off his apron and walked over to Virgil and ruffled the hair on top of his head like he was still a little boy. "See you tomorrow, Son."

Virgil watched him and Carol as they walked out the door, then took his shot glass of rum from the drip tray where he'd left it earlier in the evening, held it up for a second and then drank it down. "See you tomorrow, Dad."

Delroy walked over, patted him twice on the chest then put his arm around Virgil's shoulder and said, "Your father...he loves you, no?" He then went back to work, singing along with the band, his voice carrying across the bar.

———

Half an hour later Miles, Donatti, and Rosencrantz walked in and took a table in the back. Virgil drew two pitchers of Red Stripe, placed them on a tray with four frosted mugs and joined them at the table. "What have we got so far? Ron?"

Ron took a long pull of beer, let a small belch escape the corner of his mouth, and said "to put it as professionally as possible, we ain't got dick."

They all sat with that for a moment. "He's right," Donatti said. "We got nothing on the canvass from this morning out at Dugan's. The houses are all too isolated, and hell, Jonesy, you know that crowd. They're good people and all, but when you've got that kind of jack, unless you're at one of those fancy social functions, everyone keeps to themselves. And besides, it was early enough that most of the husbands were gone, the wives weren't up and the help hadn't arrived. All in all, I'd say that whoever did this had it pretty well planned out."

"What about the print off of the shell casing?"

"Didn't get a hit. Who ever it was, they've never been printed."

"So," Miles said. "I stand by my original statement. We ain't got shit."

"You said 'dick' the first time," Rosencrantz said.

Miles looked out over the top of his glasses. "I'm pretty sure I said 'shit.'"

"No, no," Donatti said. "He's right, you said 'dick.' I heard it."

"Yep," Rosie said. "I think you've got dick on the brain. Is there something you'd like to talk about?" He wiggled his eyebrows at Miles.

Put four cops around a pitcher of beer, Virgil thought,

and this is what you get. "Maybe we could stick to what's important here? Rosie, do you have anything at all?"

"Yeah, your sign's wrong. The food's good. And the beer is ice-cold too."

"Tell me again why I hired you."

"My superior investigative skills."

Virgil stood from the table. "Work it out, guys. We need leads and I want a plan of action by tomorrow morning before the governor and the press start breathing down our necks."

As he walked away he heard Rosie tell Miles again that he was positive he'd said 'dick.'

TWENTY MINUTES LATER VIRGIL WAS READY TO PACK IT in for the night. He told Delroy he hoped to see him tomorrow, but wasn't sure he'd make it.

'Dat irie, mon. Everyting come in its own time, no?"

"I guess so, yeah."

"Your father, he worries about you."

"Is that right?"

"Yeah, mon. Of course dat's right. He wants you here, run the bar wid him. Safer for you here, you know what I mean?"

"He's never said anything like that to me, Delroy."

Delroy laughed. "Yeah mon, you two a couple of talkers, you are."

"I don't get it," Virgil said.

"Hey, what do I know? Probably not my bidness anyway, mon." He nodded over Virgil's shoulder toward the front entrance of the bar. "Dat probably not my bidness either, but here come your woman."

Virgil turned and looked around just as Sandy slid onto a stool next to him. She wore a loose blue halter dress that hung almost to the middle of her thighs and a pair of platform sandals.

"Delroy," Sandy said, her hand over her heart, "that voice of yours melts me every time I hear it." Then to Virgil: "Buy a girl a drink?"

Virgil leaned over the bar and drew two Red Stripes from the tap, and touched eyes with Sandy in the mirror. He set the mugs down and took a seat beside her. "You don't look too worse for wear. How're you holding up?"

Instead of answering, Sandy took three long drinks from her mug and set the half-empty glass back down on the bar. Then she turned her head and saw the rest of the investigative team at the table in back. She looked back at Virgil, picked up his mug and started toward the back.

"Hey, where are you going?"

She stopped and turned back. "Gonna see what's shaking back there. I love working for you, Jonesy. Have I told you that yet? But I'm either in or I'm out, know what I mean?"

Virgil thought her eyes were made of liquid blue. "Sandy, it's not that."

"It's not what?"

"Well, it's not...well, hell, I don't know. I guess I just sort of thought—"

Sandy moved toward him and leaned in close, her mouth right next to his ear. "I know what you thought, Jonesy." She kissed him on the cheek, then leaned away. "I'll see you tomorrow, okay?" Then, almost as an after thought, "You look pretty good your own damn self."

Virgil watched her walk to the back of the bar. So did everyone else in the room.

———

HE MOVED BEHIND THE BAR AND PULLED DELROY ASIDE. "A minute ago you said something."

"What's that, mon? Delroy always saying one ting or another, no?"

"When Sandy came in. You said, 'here comes your woman.'"

Delroy laughed and shook his head. "I also say it probably not my bidness."

"Yeah, you did. But she's not my woman. She just works for me."

"Yeah, mon. Dat's all right. You keep telling yourself dat."

"I'm not sure what you mean."

Delroy put his hand on Virgil's shoulder. "I'm just a happy-go-lucky Jamaican bartender. What do I know?"

Virgil scratched the back of his head. "I don't understand."

"Hah. I tink you do. I grew up wid my family, you know? We live right by the beach. When I was little, after school get out, I'd run and play in the water. Sometimes when I do I see a fish and tink to myself, 'there go a fish.' Simple as dat, mon. Plain as day, no?"

"But what did you mean about Sandy?"

"Delroy mean what he say. I say 'here come your woman, then it mean here come your woman.'"

Virgil caught the twinkle in Delroy's eyes. "But you said *my* woman."

"Uh huh. Dat's true."

"Is there something I should know, Delroy?"

"Yeah, mon. There sure is. Maybe I draw you a map. You and that one," he tipped his head toward Sandy, "you were meant to be together. It written all over the both of you, plain as day. Just like the fish, no?" Delroy made a swimming motion in the air with his hand and grinned at him the whole time.

When Virgil turned and looked at the table in the back he saw Sandy looking at him. He thought about going over and joining them, but then someone else walked in the front door and he discovered his evening was far from over.

CHAPTER THIRTEEN

In the dim light of the bar Virgil couldn't immediately tell who it was, but it didn't take long before he recognized the familiar stride and the attitude that went with it. The house band was playing an unfamiliar tune and the bass drum thumped through Virgil's chest until it was no longer a drum beat, but an explosion from over a decade ago when their HUMVEE was stopped in the sand and he was out in the dark with only his .45 and a pair of faulty night vision goggles in territory unknown to a young soldier from the heartland whose orders were to kill on sight, no questions asked. One of his men, Murton Wheeler, had asked to stop the vehicle so he could relieve himself, and when he didn't come back, Virgil went looking for him. He found him about thirty yards from the HUMVEE, sipping on a flask filled with whiskey while simultaneously urinating on the body of a dead Iraqi Republican Guard. When the armor-piercing round hit their vehicle, the explosion knocked them both to the ground and the smell of phosphorus hung in the air as the three remaining men inside the troop carrier burned to death before they could escape the twisted wreckage. It was the second time in Virgil's life that he had almost burned to death and those thoughts hung in front of his vision until he heard a voice pulling him back.

"Hey, Jonesy, you okay? How about a double Jack with a beer back?"

Virgil blinked the vision away and looked at the man on the opposite side of the bar. Murton Wheeler stared at him as Virgil took a glass from the shelf under the bar and filled it with tap water and set it on a coaster. "This is on the house. You won't be drinking here, Murt. Not tonight. Probably not ever. Are we clear on that, soldier?"

Murton sipped the water, his eyes locked on Virgil's, then set the glass gently on the bar. "It was a long time ago, Jonesy."

"Not long enough, Murt. Heard you were in Westville. Assault or something like that, wasn't it?"

Murton ignored the question as the jab it was and instead looked back over his shoulder at the front door. When he spoke again, his voice was soft but his eyes were rimmed in anger. "Look, Loot, I've got some information you should have. I give you what I think you ought to know, and I'm outta here."

"You're taking liberties you do not have when you call

me Loot. Everyone calls me Jonesy. You can call me Sir, or Detective Jones. Are you getting the picture here, Murt?"

Murton snapped to attention, saluted and said, "Yes, Sir."

Virgil wanted to drop him where he stood, but instead lowered his voice and said, "Knock that shit off. What exactly is it you want, Murton?"

But before he could answer, the front door opened again and two men walked in together and scanned the bar, obviously looking for someone, but they made a mistake when they looked at the tables and booths before they looked at the bar, and that gave Murton the time he needed. He reached for his glass and lobbed it overhand toward the opposite wall. As a diversion, it was very effective. The glass arched through the air end over end like a poorly punted football and before it landed he placed both hands along the brass railing in front of the bar, swung his legs up and vaulted over the top like a gymnast mounting a pommel horse. When the two men turned toward the sound of the glass shattering against the wall, Murton looked at Virgil, winked and said, "Gotta boogie, Jones-man. These boys are a little upset with me right now. I left your tip under the coaster. Keep your powder dry." He picked up a cardboard case of empty beer bottles from the floor in front of the freezer and placed it on his shoulder, blocking the view of his face as he walked toward the back of the bar and through the doorway that led to the kitchen.

The two men gazed at Virgil for a beat before they

started toward the back. Virgil moved with them, along the length of the bar, his hideaway .25 caliber semi-auto in his left hand, behind his back and out of sight. It was then that he recognized that they were the same two men who had escorted him back to Samuel Pate's office earlier in the day. He held up his right hand as a signal for the two men to stop and said, "Sorry fellas, employees only past this point."

The shorter of the two tried to sidestep him and squeeze past into the kitchen, but Virgil matched his maneuver and kept him in his place. "The band's really cranking it out tonight, aren't they?" Virgil said. "I guess you didn't hear me before. Employees only past this point."

The commotion caused by Murton tossing his glass against the far wall as a diversion had subsided, but Virgil noticed Rosencrantz and Donatti watching him and when they saw the two men try to get by him, they separated and approached from different directions. Virgil slipped his gun into his back pocket and crossed his arms in front of his chest. It was now three against two. Rosencrantz stepped up close behind the two men and said, "How's it going, Jonesy? Think we could get another pitcher over at our table?"

Virgil looked at him and said, "Right away, Rosie. These guys were just leaving, but they're having a little trouble distinguishing the front from the back. Help them out, will you?"

The two men turned and looked at Rosencrantz and

Donatti, then back at Virgil, who let them have the last word. "Tell Wheeler to get in touch next time you see him," the tall one said. "Like I said, we need to talk with him."

Rosencrantz and Donatti muscled the two men out the front door and came back inside a few minutes later. Donatti walked behind the bar and ran his knuckles under the tap for a few minutes. Rosencrantz stood there and smiled.

"What happened?"

"Not much," Rosencrantz said. "My guy didn't want to fight. The other one tried to throw a sucker punch at Ed. He missed. But then his ball sack decided it wanted to launch itself at Ed's knee, and when that didn't work he tried throwing his jaw as hard as he could into Ed's fist. Twice. Sort of an unconventional style if you ask me. I think those guys might have been dropped on their heads as infants."

"Where are they?"

Donatti grabbed a dishtowel and wiped his hands dry. "We helped them to their car and sent them on their way. It was either that or take them downtown. The paperwork's a drag."

"Yeah, we'd be up all night," Rosencrantz said.

"Do me a favor, will you?" Virgil said.

"I think we just did," Rosencrantz said.

"Uh huh. Run a sheet for me tomorrow morning on a guy named Murton Wheeler. Let me know what you get."

"No problem, Jonesy," Donatti said.

Rosencrantz grabbed a handful of peanuts from a dish on top of the bar and tossed them in his mouth. "Hey, I was serious a minute ago. Can we get another pitcher of beer?"

Virgil had a waitress take another pitcher over to their table and tear up the ticket she had going, then remembered what Murton had said about his tip being under the drink coaster. When he moved the coaster he discovered a safe-deposit box key, the words *do not duplicate* stamped on one side, and Sunrise Bank on the other.

He thought, *huh*.

AN HOUR LATER HE WAS HOME. IT WAS LATE AND HE thought about going to bed, but he needed to unwind a little first. He grabbed a beer before going outside where he propped his butt in a chair and his feet on the upper rail of his back deck. The night was clear and calm and when Virgil looked up at the stars it made him think of his mom, gone now an entire year.

His beer wasn't even half gone when the doorbell rang. He checked the time again, saw that it was just after midnight then pulled the .25 auto from his pocket for the second time of the evening and went to the door. When he saw who was there Virgil felt his knees get a little weak.

"I'm not wearing a watch," Sandy said, "But I'm pretty sure it's tomorrow."

Virgil tried to smile in a cool sort of way, fairly certain he ended up looking like a schoolboy with an aw shucks kind of look on his face, though he did manage to get a grip on himself and invite her inside. When he flipped on a few lights he heard Sandy take in a breath.

"My god, Jonesy. This is beautiful."

Virgil had designed the house himself, going through three different builders in the process before he found one who got it just right. Double doors led from the foyer into the great room with a massive fireplace made entirely of fieldstone he'd collected from the building site. The floors and walls were all wood, a mixture of natural pine, cherry, oak, and maple, blended together in a way that gave the interior a colorful, natural look.

"Thanks. It was a lot of work at first. Took over two years to build from the time I bought the site. Sometimes it seems like a little more work than I'd like, but then every year when summer rolls around and you can sit out back on the deck at night it all seems worth it. In fact, that's what I was doing just now, sitting on the deck, finishing my beer. Want one?"

"Sure."

He handed her a beer, then leaned against the counter and watched her wander around the great room for a minute taking it all in. When she circled her way back she tilted her head to the side and just looked at him. Virgil started to think about it, but then just as quick he stopped thinking and pulled her close and pressed his body into her. He felt her press back. As he started to move his lips toward hers, Sandy pulled back and said, "Jonesy, is that a gun in your pocket or are you just happy to see me."

He laughed. "Yes to both." Virgil took the gun from his pocket and set it on the counter and when he did, Sandy started to laugh too.

"What?"

"Oh, I don't know," Sandy said. "It's so...little. I guess I imagined it would be bigger."

"Hey...."

SANDY: "LISTEN, DO YOU MIND IF I FRESHEN UP A little. I love your bar and everything, but I sort of smell like barbecue sauce or something."

"Don't let Robert hear you say that. It's called jerk sauce, and it's his specialty."

Sandy cocked an eyebrow at him. "You've got the hottest woman in the county standing in your house after midnight and you're worried about what your cook thinks?"

Virgil felt himself redden. "No, no. I'm just saying..."

Before he could go on, Sandy stood on her toes and kissed him on the cheek. "Where's the bathroom?"

AFTER HE WALKED HER TO THE MASTER BATHROOM AND showed her where the towels were, she gave him a little girly wave then closed the door. Virgil heard the lock click and thought, *hmm*. He decided that it was some kind of signal so he left the bedroom and went back out to the deck.

She had a little tease in her, he thought. He wondered if she wanted him to tease back. He thought about trying it out, even played some scenarios around in his head, but he got lost in the thought long enough that he didn't hear her when she came up from behind and wrapped her arms around his waist.

"I thought you'd be waiting for me in the bedroom."

She was wearing one of Virgil's white dress shirts. Her hair was still wet, slicked back from her forehead. Little drops of water had dripped from her hair and they left dark spots on the shoulders of the shirt. She had the sleeves rolled up to her elbows, and only one button halfway down holding it closed. "I thought maybe...I mean, I wasn't sure..."

"You think too much, Jonesy." She reached up and unbuttoned the shirt, slinked her shoulders back and let the shirt slide to the floor. She took a half step back and said, "Are you sure now?"

Virgil discovered he was sure.

Quite sure.

SIDNEY WELLS, JR. SAT ON HER FRONT PORCH, A cigarette at the corner of her mouth. Her eyes moved back and forth between the little pile of ash at her feet and the street corner a half block away. She saw the head-lights sweep through the turn, then extinguish as the car pulled up and stopped in front of the house. Amanda Pate climbed out, tugged a bit at her skirt, then walked up and sat down next to Junior. "The hell you been?" Junior said. "You're over an hour late."

Amanda picked up the pack of cigarettes next to Junior, shook one out and lit up. "Samuel was up late. I had to wait until he took his sleeping pills. I told you it might be a while." She took a long drag and held her smoke for a few seconds before blowing it out the corner of her mouth. "So, anyway, I'm here now, aren't I?"

"Yeah, you are," Junior said. "And I still think it's a bad idea. We agreed we were going to lay low until this was over. That was the plan, anyway. So what's so important that you had to come slumming down here after midnight?"

Amanda lifted her ass off the porch a little and tugged at her skirt some more. "I'm just nervous," she said. "It threw me a little when the cops came to my house today. And it wasn't just any cop. It was Virgil Jones. I know him, Sid. Or knew him, anyway. I went to high school with him."

Junior snorted. "Uh huh. What was that, twenty years ago?"

"That's not the point."

"So what is?"

"The point is what I just said. I know him, or knew him anyway. We had a thing. It was a one-time thing, but I never forgot it, or him. I've sort of followed him his whole career."

"So?"

"So get on the Internet and look him up. He's good. That's what I've been trying to tell you. He *does not* mess around. He works for the governor for Christ's sake. And so on day one when he shows up at my front door asking questions, yeah, I'm nervous."

"What did you say?"

Amanda flicked her cigarette into the weeds next to the porch. "I didn't say anything. He wanted to speak with Samuel and me about Dugan, but Samuel was at the church."

"That it?" Junior said.

"Yeah, except he went to the church and spoke with Samuel."

"Tell me about that."

"I can't," Amanda said. "Samuel didn't say anything about it."

"So don't worry about it then. We knew going in that they were going to look at Samuel. We want them to, remember? So just relax. It's all good."

"But so soon, Sid? I mean, the first day? And now this cop, I'm telling you baby, he's bad news."

Junior thought about that for a few minutes. "So maybe we move on the cop."

"You think?"

"I don't see why not," Junior said. "Might give us a little misdirection. Let me talk to the old man about it."

"Oh, god, he's not here is he?"

"Yeah, so?"

"He doesn't like me. Doesn't like us."

"He doesn't like anyone, Amanda. I can handle him. Don't get your panties in a wad over it, okay?"

Amanda spread her legs open far enough that her knee touched Junior's. "I can't. I'm not wearing any panties."

Junior ran her hand up the inside of Amanda's thigh, and felt the moisture, and warmth. Amanda tipped her head back and let out a little moan. "Maybe we should go inside."

Junior leaned over and kissed her hard, then said, "We'll have to be quiet this time."

"I can do quiet," Amanda said. "Might be a fun change."

———

WHEN THEY WERE FINISHED THEY STAYED IN BED FOR A few minutes, neither of them saying much of anything. Sandy gave him three quick kisses, one on the lips, one on the chest, and one on his pecker. "Don't go anywhere, handsome. I'll be right back."

Virgil told her he wouldn't and watched her walk to the bathroom, her ass moving with just the right amount of jiggle. The jiggle factor was important. Too much was never a good thing, and too little meant you didn't have anything to work with. He had his hands behind his head and listened to the sounds coming from the bathroom... the toilet flush, the water running in the sink, the dowel on the holder creaking just a bit as she hung a towel...and then the familiar stealthy squeak of the mirrored medicine cabinet door.

And Virgil thought, *ah...a snooper*.

She came back out, took a running start and jumped on the bed right next to him. Virgil instinctively covered his crotch in case she missed the landing. "Relax, big guy. I won't hurt you."

"Mmm, we'll see," he said. "What were you doing in there?"

"Girl stuff. Don't you worry about it. Maybe a little poking around, too."

He rolled onto his side to face her. She was on her back and moonlight spilled in from the bedroom window and bled across the swell of her breasts. "Find anything incriminating?"

"Yes, as a matter of fact I did," she said as she sat back up. She swung her legs to the opposite side of the bed, away from him. "It's good and bad."

He propped himself up on one arm, reached over and placed his hand on her back. "What is it?"

"Well, the bad news is I found a prescription bottle of unidentifiable pills, with no label on the bottle."

"Yeah? That's easily explainable. What's the good news?"

Sandy reached down to the floor and pulled something out of her purse, then turned back toward him, an evil grin on her face. "The good news is, I have handcuffs," she said, as she twirled the cuffs around her index finger. "And I know how to use them."

AN HOUR LATER THEY WERE EXHAUSTED, BUT WIDE-awake, so they moved from the bedroom out to the sofa in front of the fireplace. Virgil pressed a button on a remote and the gas logs in the fireplace lit up automatically, the glow of the flames dancing across the room. He watched Sandy stare at the fire, then she looked toward his office, squeezed Virgil's hand and said, "Tell me about the turn-out helmet."

Virgil blinked in surprise, then let go of her hand and walked over to his office. A fireman's helmet sat on the credenza behind the desk. It was still stained with soot, the eye shield cracked diagonally across its entire length. He picked up the helmet and carried it to the sofa and handed it to her. "Hell of a story from a long time ago."

"Would you tell me about it?"

Virgil nodded. "I will, but I'd like to ask you something first."

Sandy held the helmet in her lap and traced the outline of the crest above the visor. Her fingers trembled like they were charged with an electrical current. "Okay."

"You called it a turn-out helmet. That's a term firemen use."

"My father was a fireman," Sandy said, staring at the flames. Her movements were almost imperceptible, but she was rocking back and forth on the sofa, the helmet in her arms. "Tell me your story, Jonesy."

Virgil thought that he must have held that helmet a thousand times over the years, and would probably hold it a thousand more before he died. It was part of who he was, part of why he was still alive today. "One of the worst days of my life," he said.

Sandy nodded, still looking at the fire, but she didn't speak, so Virgil told her the story. Told her about the time when he was just a boy, only five years old, and what happened that fateful day on his birthday.

His mother had wanted carpet in the kitchen. It seemed like such an extravagant thing at the time, but his parents could afford it and everyone agreed just how nice it would be to have wall-to-wall carpeting in the kitchen of all places. At first, Mason had tried to talk Virgil's mom into maybe just an area rug or two, but her mind was set. The day the carpet was installed, the trucks pulled into the driveway and the men all got out wearing identical green cover-all's, as if their matching uniforms could somehow make up for their inadequacies of procedural forethought.

"I went inside to play, to smell my cake baking in the oven, and to look at my presents that were wrapped and sitting on the table in the family room. I was walking through the kitchen—god, it was hot in there, I remember that—it was the middle of August, no air conditioning, and the oven was on. I stood and watched as two of the workmen began to pour the glue on the floor to hold the carpet in place. No one ever thought about the pilot light on the stove.

"The glue was flammable. As it turns out, the stuff was so volatile it wasn't even legal in all fifty states. What I remember most about the explosion is the way everything went white. So white that things almost looked transparent, like some of the films you can watch of atomic bomb blasts. That white. And quiet. No loud bang or anything like that. Just the white.

"And then I couldn't move. I'm not sure how long I was out, though it couldn't have been that long. I was in the garage. The explosion had blown me through the screen door and a pile of rubble had landed on top of me. I wasn't hurt too bad, except for the cut on my face, but I couldn't move because I was trapped under the debris. I tried to call out to someone, but the blast had knocked the wind out of me and I couldn't catch my breath. I'll tell you something, I was five years old, I could smell the smoke and feel the heat and I thought I was dying, Sandy. That's not the kind of thing that's easy to forget.

"I heard my mom screaming my name, but I couldn't call back to her. I remember I kept thinking *the sirens are coming, the sirens are coming*. Not the firemen, just the sirens, and I remember thinking I wanted my mom to just please shut up so I could hear the sirens, and then I did hear them, that long, slow wail as they wound their way toward me, the smoke so thick I had to keep my eyes pinched shut."

Virgil paused for a moment to collect his thoughts. Sandy still had the helmet, but she'd turned it over and held it crown down in her lap, her hands caressing the age-old sweat stains of the liner inside the hard shell. Tears were running down her cheeks and they dripped into the inside of the helmet with little plops that sounded like rain falling on top of snowpack at winter's end.

"And they pulled you out." She said it softly, no louder than a whisper, her words thick and lonesome, but it was what she said next that made Virgil wonder about the workings of fate and the mystery of things unknown. "It took two of them to get you out," she said. "They always go in as a team. The debris was deep and heavy and they had to be careful when they were pulling it off so it didn't collapse down and crush you. The other firemen were pouring water in to keep the flames back and when they finally got to you it was just before the rest of the garage collapsed."

Virgil looked at her, his voice a shadow of itself. "Yes, but how—"

She placed her hand on his forearm to quiet him. "One of the firemen had to pick up a rafter that was directly over you. It landed just inches from your head. He picked it up, straining against its weight, the heat of the flames no longer being held back by the water. They were losing the fight, but you were almost free. And then, when he had the rafter up high enough, the other fireman picked you up and carried you out. It was only a dozen steps or so to safety. The one holding the rafter let it drop, but when he did it shifted and came down on top of him, crushing his legs. He couldn't move and seconds later there was another explosion when the gas main went. But you and the other fireman made it out."

Virgil couldn't speak. When he tried to swallow he discovered his throat was as dry as scattered ash. When he opened his mouth to say something—he wasn't sure what—his teeth clicked together like marbles being rattled around in a glass jar. He finally just nodded, letting her know she was right.

She took her hand from his arm and unsnapped the liner inside the helmet. Written in permanent marker on the inside of the hard shell was a name: S.C.A. Small. "S.C. stands for Station Chief," she said. "The A. stands for Andrew. Station Chief Andy Small was my father, Jonesy. He died in that explosion while saving your life."

Virgil took the helmet from her lap and pulled her close, his arms tight around her shuddering body. There were no words to say in the moment, the heat from the fire unmatched by the shame and responsibility he felt. He had just made love to a woman whose father had died to save him, and while Virgil had lived, it was at the expense of Sandy's life-long sorrow.

Virgil thought, *how do I ever reconcile that?*

CHAPTER FOURTEEN

The Sids. Up early. And grumpy. There was a schedule to keep, and now, it was time again.

This one was a coincidence. The Sids knew this. They had talked about it like everything else, tossed it around for a while like a game of Hot Potato. Junior thought it might be a problem, though by her own admission she couldn't explain why, just that it might. Senior pointed out that wasn't much of an argument, and even though it pissed her off, she knew he was right. "Besides," he had said, "One way or another we're going to do her. Might as well create a little misdirection while we're at it." Junior thought about it, and the more she did, the cooler the potato got. "Yeah, I can see that," she finally said, and so for the Sids, the coincidence of another nurse was just that.

For Elle Richardson, third-shift nurse supervisor on

the maternity ward at Methodist Hospital, it was anything but.

Elle Richardson thought she had about the best gosh-danged job in the entire hospital. No one really liked hospitals, she knew, but Elle (Ells to her husband Eugene and her close friends) thought they were about the best place on earth. Sure there were a lot of sick and dying, (nine gosh-danged floors of them if you were counting) but her floor was where life was delivered, where little bundles of hope and happiness slid out of the gate (Ells always giggled to herself when she thought of it that way) and were swaddled up in loving arms, the balance between life and death maintained for another day, or at least her eight hours of the ten-till-six. Like most of her clothing (including her mouse pad and coffee cups) Ells was reminded on a daily basis that Life is Good.

Her shift had been a busy one, that was for sure. Three singles and a double, (Ells sometimes thought her version of hospital speak sounded an awful lot like ordering at the drive-thru....either that or the scorecard of a little-league baseball game) all before her late morning break. But the rest of her shift remained quiet (all gates temporarily closed for business, ha, ha) and when the big hand was on the twelve and the little hand was on the six, Ells scrunched her shoulders at her co-workers, squinted her eyes, and gave them a tootle-do before she scooted down the hall and out to her car.

Gosh almighty, she felt happy. Her life was everything she had always hoped it would be, and more. Her husband, Eugene (Genes to her, Gene to his friends) was a police officer for the city of Indianapolis, and even though he was a cop and she was a nurse, Ells always thought she and Gene worked hand in hand to help bring goodness and life to the city where they lived. They were, Ells thought, a match made in heaven. It even said so on the matchbook covers at their wedding reception.

Gene worked the third shift as well, except his went ninety minutes longer than hers, but the good news was (and there's always good news if people would just take their gosh-dang time and look for it) today marked the beginning of Gene's weekend. Plus, now that Ells was a shift supervisor, she could make her own schedule so she and Hubby had the same two days off each week. Could life be any better? Ells thought not.

Problem was, Ells was wrong. She just didn't know it yet.

———

THE SIDS IN THEIR VAN. JUNIOR HAD THE DRIVER'S seat, Senior in the back, low and out of sight. They had everything planned nine ways from Sunday, but it didn't take long for Senior to realize they'd forgotten at least one thing—something for him to lie on. The floor of the van was ribbed and it was pressing into his spine like nobody's business. The harder he tried to get comfortable, the worse it got. "How much longer?" he grumbled.

Junior looked at her watch. "How the hell should I know? Just give it a few more minutes."

"Few more minutes my ass. If I lay here any longer I'm gonna be paralyzed. I'm sitting up."

"Better not. Don't want to be seen."

"To hell with that. I'm getting up. Besides, the windows are tinted. No one saw me last time, did they? No one is going to see me now. We need a pad or some pillows or something back here to lie on. What the hell are you laughing at?"

"I was just thinking that after this, they'll probably change the name of this place." Before Senior could say anything, Junior stopped laughing and started the van. "Here she comes. Get ready."

———

ELLE PULLED INTO THE SAFEWAY GROCERY AND PARKED her car between a rust colored pickemup (that's what Daddy always called them, pickemup trucks...gosh she missed him, fifteen years gone now if you could believe that) and a cute little lime green VW Beetle-bug, (dang, she wanted one of those sooo bad) one of the newer models that came with a flower holder, complete with a Daisy that stuck out of the column. She forced herself to look away from the Bug when she walked by. She wanted to stop and look, but time was short. Genes would be home soon and she wanted her shopping out of the way so she could sit with her hubby and tell him all about her shift. The prospect of regaling Genes of the fine work she did today (three singles and a double!) made her feel so good it caused her to put a little extra scoot in her step. She even grabbed a stray cart that had rolled away from the corral and gave it a shove back where it belonged. A good deed for a good day. Jake and Rocket were right. Life is Good. So very, very gosh-danged good.

SENIOR LOOKED OUT THE WINDOW. "WE'RE GONNA have to move. I don't have an angle."

"You sure?"

"Yeah, this isn't going to work. Move over a few rows. We'll get her on the way out."

Junior backed out of their spot and moved the van a couple of rows over. "Take a quick peek. This should be better."

Senior did, and it was. Elle caught a break.

A short one, anyway.

TWENTY MINUTES LATER, NOW SERIOUSLY BEHIND schedule, Elle pushed her cart toward her car. The Bug was gone, (thank gosh for small favors—she might have spent a few extra minutes looking it over—minutes she didn't have) but the rust colored pickemup was still there. Somebody taking their sweet ol', she thought. That was another thing Daddy always used to say. He had all kinds of words and sayings. They were his *isms*. Elle sighed. *Love you, Daddy*.

————————

SENIOR WATCHED THROUGH THE SCOPE AS THE WOMAN loaded the groceries into her trunk. They were parked four rows over and one spot further away from the store, close for the scope's powerful optics. He clicked off the safety and kept the crosshairs centered on the space between her eyes. From Senior's perspective it looked like she was about a half an inch away. He could make out every feature, every flaw on her face.

Bitch needed to tweeze.

————————

ELLE PUT THE LAST SACK IN THE TRUNK AND SHUT THE lid. She stood still for a moment—something was bothering her, but she couldn't for the life of her figure out what it was. Genes had always told her to listen to her gut. That, and situational awareness. Good gosh he was big on situational awareness. He had practically drilled it into her over the years.

And that was the last thought Elle ever had in her Life is Good life. The bullet caught her in the center of her brow, right where she needed to tweeze. It snapped her head backwards and blew out the back of her skull just like it did to JFK on the day she was born. The force of the bullet knocked her backwards, her arms pin-wheeling merrily along after her. When her legs realized they were no longer receiving signals from her brain they collapsed under her and what was left of the back of her head made contact with the basket section of an empty shopping cart. The cart flipped forward and came down on top of her and wouldn't you know it, the next person out of the store, the one who found her lying under the cart like a discarded doll and stroller in someone's back yard was just some guy taking his sweet ol' back to his pickemup. When he saw Elle's body he dropped his bags and spun around, twice. A white van turned a corner at the edge of the lot and was lost to the early morning traffic. Mr. Pickemup never saw it.

HIS CELL PHONE RANG AND VIRGIL TRIED TO SLIDE away from Sandy, but when he did she held tight to his arm. He listened to the ringing, four, five, six times, then a little half ring, cut down by voice mail. A minute or so later, the phone rang again.

"I should probably get that," Virgil said. "Could be something happening."

Sandy untangled herself, sat up and then leaned forward, her forearms resting on her thighs. She turned her head and looked back over her shoulder. "Could be something happening *here*, Jonesy." A little edge in her voice.

He stood, looked toward the kitchen where his cell phone was, then back at Sandy. He took a step toward the other room, but when the ringing stopped, so did Virgil. Sandy was right. Something was happening and it was right here. He sat down on the bed next to her. "Whatever it is, it can wait."

"I'm not talking about the sex, you know," she said.

"Hey, give a guy a little credit, will you?" Virgil took in a deep breath then puffed his cheeks as he let it out. Then he said the only thing he knew to say on the heels of the most complex discovery he'd ever made. "I'm sorry."

They sat there for a few minutes with that and when Sandy raised her head and looked at him, he started to say something else but ended up repeating himself. "I'm sorry, Sandy. I'm so very sorry."

"You don't have to apologize, Jonesy. It wasn't your fault."

"Wasn't it?"

"No. It wasn't. You were a victim of something that happened a long time ago, just like I was. In a different way, but a victim just the same. I accept your apology, but know this: I don't ever want to hear you say those words again with regard to the fire. I can't build the rest of my life on an apology."

"What did you just say?"

"Tell me you don't feel it. Tell me we don't belong together. Tell me you have some logical, even mystical explanation as to how we came together thirty years later as friends, co-workers, and now as lovers." She reached out and took Virgil's hands in her own. "What I'm asking you, Virgil, is to tell me it means something. Tell me I've found what I've been looking for since I was five years old. Tell me you haven't been searching for something all these years without really knowing what it is, either. Tell me that what we did last night, what we just had isn't the reason I lost my childhood, it's the reward. Tell me that the part of me I thought I lost didn't die in that fire with my father, but has been waiting for this one single moment where it's safe to say that this is who I am, this is where I'm supposed to be, that this is my life, right here, right now, with you. Tell me that my father not only gave you the gift of saving your life, but in some mysterious way that gift belongs to me too. Tell me I'm wrong, Virgil."

"I can't."

"Tell me."

"I can't."

Sandy leaned forward and kissed him. "Tell me."

When he looked at her face Virgil felt something inside let go in a way he'd never experienced. It was in that moment that he discovered something he'd known all along. "I love you."

When Sandy crawled into his lap and wrapped her arms around him she sounded childlike, but her words were those of a woman and lover undivided, freed from something by a gift Virgil knew only he could give.

"Tell me."

"I love you."

"Tell me..."

"I WAS THERE YOU KNOW," VIRGIL SAID, THE RINGING of his phone now forgotten. They were back on the couch, her feet tucked in Virgil's lap. "At your dad's funeral. My mom and me. My dad didn't go. He said he was sick, but I don't think he was. It wasn't a happy time for us. It feels sort of ridiculous to say that now—it was just a house—but I'll tell you, we lost something that day —as a family—and we never got it back.

"But I remember the funeral. The sea of red trucks that stretched for block after block from the cemetery. All the firemen in their dress uniforms. The flag over your dad's coffin. The way they folded the damn thing and handed it to your mom like, like..."

"Like it was some sort of substitute," Sandy said. "Like that flag would somehow put food on the table, or keep my mom safe, or tuck me in bed at night. I wasn't very old, but I remember thinking it was a joke. I remember thinking it might make everyone else feel good, except for the ones who really mattered."

"We don't have to talk about this right now, you know. It's sort of a lot to process."

"It'll always be with us. It's part of who we are."

"I want to say I remember seeing you there, and I

think maybe I do, but it might just be wishful thinking, you know, like when you want to remember something so bad you end up making part of it up and then that becomes the reality. I remember the line of trucks, I remember your mom, and I remember the sadness. I remember thinking for the longest time how I wished it had been me who died that day. I remember thinking about how there wouldn't be all those fire trucks at the cemetery, how there wouldn't be as many people, how there wouldn't be a flag over my coffin.

"I've got to tell you, I didn't want to go. But my mom made me. She didn't say it, but she made it clear that your dad had died trying to save me, and it was our duty to go."

"Oh, Virgil, that's terrible."

"You know, it wasn't really," he said. "She didn't put the weight on me. She didn't have to. She just helped me see that it was the right thing to do. Boy, I can remember her and my dad fighting about it. They fought for weeks after that. Not about me going, but the fact that he didn't."

"Why do you think he didn't go?"

"He never told me. He was drinking pretty hard back then, but I think the real reason was he felt responsible for your father's death."

"Why?"

"I don't know. You have to understand, I might not know what I'm talking about here. It's not something my dad and I talk about very often, but I think he feels like if he could have gotten me out, then your dad would still be alive."

"But you know that's not true. It took two men to get you out."

"Yeah, try telling that to him."

"I will."

"Yeah, well, good luck with that. He's not exactly the easiest guy in the world to talk to sometimes."

"So says the son."

Virgil looked at her, a reply forming, when the phone rang again. Sandy dug her feet into his lap for a second, then swung them off and went to the kitchen. She answered the phone like it was the most natural thing in the world, spoke into the receiver for a moment, then handed it to Virgil, a hint of a smile sneaking across the corner of her mouth. "It's your dad."

"How do you know that?"

"Caller ID," she said. Then with playfulness in her voice Virgil was grateful to hear, she added, "*Detective*."

Virgil laughed at himself and took the phone. "Morning, Pops. What's up?"

"Hey Virg. Your boss is looking for you. She tried here out of desperation. Said she couldn't reach you. Anyway, sounds like something big might be happening with your case. She wants you to call her right away. Say, who's that just answered your phone?"

CHAPTER FIFTEEN

Virgil dialed Cora's number then put the phone on speaker so Sandy could hear the conversation. When she answered her words were clipped and the frustration in her voice was evident. "Know where the Safeway off Morris Street is?"

"What's going on, Cora?"

"Woman named Elle Richardson is dead. Shot in the middle of her forehead. Ron Miles is already there and says the crime scene crew thinks it's the same shooter. If you're not doing anything you might want to swing by. And by the way, Pate's lawyer is raising holy hell with the governor as we speak so you may have touched a nerve somewhere. Things are happening, Slick. You might want to get in the game."

"We'll get right over there," Virgil said, then wished he'd been more careful with his choice of words.

"Is there something you'd like to tell me?" Her voice

seemed to relax a little, but as was often the case with Cora, she didn't wait for an answer. "Your phone sounds sort of funny. Do you have me on speaker or something? Hey, one other thing, I've got everyone else's paperwork from yesterday's mess outside the governor's place, but I'm still waiting on Small's. Tell her to get it to me, will you? Or did I just do that?"

———

FIFTEEN MINUTES LATER THEY WERE DRESSED AND IN the truck, the bubble light flashing on the dashboard. When they pulled up to the crime scene, TV was there, along with a few print people. When they got out of the truck, the cameras turned their way. Virgil looked at Sandy and said, "I hate it when the news beats me to the crime scene."

"Well, they don't really have a life," Sandy said.

A very tall and skinny female reporter and her cameraman caught them just before they ducked under the crime scene tape. "Detective Jones, what can you tell me about this latest murder? Our information is that the victim was a nurse, just like one of yesterday's victims. Do the nurses of our city need to be concerned, Detective? Is it the work of the killer you've been hunting in connection with the death of Franklin Dugan?"

Hunting. Good word.

Virgil's opinion of the press went like this: They had a job to do like anyone else. It had always been his experience that as a detective, if you treated the press with dignity and respect, they in turn, would reciprocate in kind, thereby establishing a mutually beneficial relationship between all concerned parties.

They ducked under the crime scene tape. "No comment," Virgil said.

The reporter put a pout on her lips. "Come on Jonesy..."

"Not now, Karen." He looked at Sandy. "Go find Miles, will you? I'll be right there."

Sandy looked at him, a quiz on her face. "Sure. What's up?"

"I'll be right there."

"DID YOU KNOW I'D BE HERE, KAREN, OR DID YOU JUST get lucky?"

"I'm certain I don't know what you're talking about," Karen said.

Virgil thought she was trying to look surprised, but with all the plastic surgery she'd had in an attempt to maintain the appearance of a twenty-two year old, it was hard to tell. He stood there for a moment and watched her try to blink.

"Who's the cutie?"

He wanted to ignore her and walk away, but negative intimacy is a powerful force and when he turned back around to say something to Karen, he saw the taxi. It slowed in the street behind them and when it did the passenger in the rear of the cab turned his head away at the last second. Virgil's eyes followed the cab, darted to Karen for a second, then back to the cab that was already turning the corner at the end of the block. When he looked over at Karen again he could not think of one single thing he ever liked about her, but he also was not afraid to admit that probably said more about him than it did her. He watched the cab turn the corner, stuffed his hands in his pockets and headed to where the victim was, all the while questioning his past preference in women.

Something about the cab, though.

―――――――

SANDY WAS LEANING OVER THE BODY WHEN HE WALKED up. "Just like Cora said, Jonesy. Caught her right between the eyes."

Virgil looked at the victim's body. A pool of blood had formed under her head. Groceries were scattered everywhere. "I see that. Where's Miles?"

Sandy stood, then turned to face him. "You okay, Jonesy? What was that back there?"

Virgil was trying to process too many things at once; the discovery he and Sandy had made together just hours ago, their love making, another shooting victim, the cab that just went by. It was a lot of information. "What?"

"Who was that?"

"I don't know. Just someone in a cab. It was weird.

How many people have you ever seen that look away from a bunch of cop cars?"

Sandy frowned, tilted her head. "What cab? What are you talking about? I'm talking about the woman. Who was that?"

"Oh, that," Virgil said. "Uh, her name is Karen Connor."

Sandy chewed on the inside of her lip. "Well, I don't like her. She seems kinda...brassy."

Virgil puffed his cheeks, then blew out a breath. "Let me tell you."

"Oh, you will, boss man, you will."

"Well...as long as we're on the subject, I guess I should tell you something."

"Yes..."

"You know, just so it's out there."

"What?" Sandy asked, a note of skepticism in her voice.

He didn't know if it would matter to her or not. "You see, the thing is..."

"*WHAT? YOU WERE MARRIED TO HER?*"

"Well, yeah, but the key word here is *was*. As in *I was married to her, but now I'm not*."

"You never told me you were married."

"I'm not."

"But you were," she said.

"Right. But I'm not now."

"You didn't tell me."

"You didn't ask. Besides, I thought you would have detected it, *Detective*." Virgil watched her expression and picked up a hint of jealousy. Just a whiff. The fun kind though. He hoped. "It was a mistake. I was just waiting for the right woman to come along."

Just then, an overweight bald man in a cheap suit walked over, eating a double cheeseburger. He held the burger with three fingers, the other two pinching the cardboard container underneath the sandwich as a drip tray, an unused napkin in his other hand. He'd caught the end of their conversation. "Hope that wasn't her."

Sandy said, "Excuse me?"

The fat man took another bite of his cheeseburger, chewed three times, pushed the rest of the sandwich in his mouth like a wad of chewing tobacco, and spoke with his cheeks puffed full of food. He pointed the empty box at Virgil, but spoke to Sandy. "He said he was waiting for the right woman to come along. I was just commenting that I hoped it wasn't this one here." Then to Virgil: "How's it going, Jones-man? Crime Scene been here yet?"

WALLY WRIGHT, DEPUTY CORONER OF MARION County, placed his napkin in the empty box and then shoved the box into his suit pocket. Ron Miles walked up behind him, and the four of them, Virgil, Sandy, Wally, and Ron all adjusted into a little circle. Miles spoke to Wally first. "Took you long enough."

"Yeah well. Traffic. What can you do?"

Miles wrinkled his nose, sniffing the air. "You said you were going to bring me something to eat."

"Didn't have time to stop." Wally took a few steps over toward the body, looked down, then back toward the group. "Are you all done here? Where are your crime scene people? I've got work to do."

Miles shook his head. "Wally...we've been waiting on *you* for a preliminary assessment."

Wally took in a deep breath, belched, and then let out an exasperated sigh. He squatted down next to the body and when he did the bottom of his jacket rode up on his waist and revealed his ass crack. A mole rode high between his cheeks, and the entire thing looked like a hairy, upside down exclamation point. His left hand pulled something out of his pocket, then went to his mouth. He stood, visibly swallowing as he did. "GSW to the head. Probably dead before she hit the ground. Maybe I should have been a cop. Okay if I get the gurney now?" He walked away, not waiting for an answer.

Miles looked at Virgil. "Was that a French fry he pulled out of his pocket? He said he was going to bring me something to eat."

Sandy looked at Ron. "Did you get a chance to

look at the security tapes?"

Miles shook his head. "Not yet."

"Want me to take a look?" she asked Virgil.

"Yeah. See what you can see. I'll be there in a few minutes."

After Sandy walked away, Ron said, "You getting any of that?"

"Course he is," Wally said as he pushed a gurney in front of them. "It might as well be tattooed on his forehead. I really should have been a cop. You guys are something, you know that?"

TEN MINUTES LATER SANDY WAS BACK, HER FACE GRAY and the corners of her mouth turned down. "What's the matter?" Virgil said. "Are you okay?"

She held up a CD. "Got the shot on tape, Jonesy. It's bad."

"What does it show?"

"Everything. Everything except what we need that is. Picture isn't good enough to get the plate. Not even close. I don't know, maybe the lab can do something with it, but I doubt it."

"Okay. Send it back to the shop with Crime Scene and see what they can do. I'm going to have Rosencrantz and Donatti come out here. We need to figure this thing out."

"All right. What are you doing?" Sandy asked.

"I'm going to church."

CHAPTER SIXTEEN

Virgil found the broken down church in Broad Ripple easily enough. Cora had indicated that the building looked like it was being held together with bailing twine and when Virgil arrived he had to admit that her assessment wasn't very far off the mark.

The building was originally constructed well over a hundred years ago and although it was larger than a small country chapel, the resemblance was unmistakable. The entire structure was made up of red brick and clapboard, the latter having long ago lost its protective coat of top paint, the boards now rotted and sagging at their joints. The nail holes wept reddish brown and the stains in the vertical tracks of the wood looked like blood. A traditional steeple sat on top of the main entrance to the church. An iron cross stood like a spire and leaned slightly askew, held in place with guy-wires attached to its base.

The wires were pulled taut and were pinched against sagging gutters at the roof's edge, then attached to steel bands that encompassed the perimeter of the structure. Virgil parked his truck a safe distance from the structure and walked inside, his gaze held to the steeple until he was at the front steps of the building.

When he opened the door and stepped inside he heard the sound of children laughing and jumping about from the second story as well as a pipe organ being played from the chapel area. The notes bellowed through the church with a laborious effort that sounded painful and redemptive all at the same time. Then, when the music stopped, the church suddenly felt empty, even though the children could still be heard.

A woman turned the corner, looked at him and smiled in a sad sort of way. Then something happened that left Virgil momentarily unable to speak and caused a slew of questions to form in his mind at once, none of which he was prepared to ask, let alone comprehend the answers. The woman stepped forward, extended her hand and said, "Hello. My name is Amy Frechette. You're the police officer, aren't you? From the state? Murton's told me all about you, but I'd recognize you any day from all the pictures he's shown me. I'm terribly worried about Murton. Do you know where he is?"

———

THEY WALKED INTO THE CHAPEL AND SAT NEXT TO

each other in the first pew. Virgil had little if any preconceived notions of what a female pastor may look like, but if he had, Amy Frechette would fit the bill with perfection. He guessed her age a little younger than his own, perhaps thirty-five or so. She wore a matching plain brown skirt and blazer over a white turtleneck sweater.

"I haven't seen him in over a week. I don't know what's going on." Her voice was strong but the skin under her chin trembled when she spoke. "You're the best friend he's got, Detective."

"I wouldn't be too sure about that."

Her unexpected smile caught him off guard, but then the light went out of her expression, replaced by something dark and defensive. "You've not been kind to him," she said. "He thinks of you as a brother."

"I'm here on another matter, Ms. Frechette. But if you don't mind me asking, how do you know Murton, and by extension, his relationship with me?"

She shook her head and chuckled, then turned in the pew to face him. "How do I know about your relationship? I guess Murton hasn't been exaggerating when he speaks of your feelings for him. We've been living together for over a year, Detective. I guess I somehow thought you knew that."

"No, I'm afraid I didn't. In fact, I think there are a number of things I don't know about Murton these days."

"What in the world is that supposed to mean?" she said.

"What do you know about a man by the name of Franklin Dugan?"

"Who?"

"I am investigating a series of murders. One of the victims was a man named Franklin Dugan. He was the President of Sunrise Bank. Murt is either trying to insert himself into the investigation for reasons I can't begin to understand, or he's trying to extricate himself from it. I can't tell which. Or maybe he's guilty of something again, and he's—"

"What? What do you mean guilty of something again?" she said, the anger in her voice evident.

"If you've lived with him for over a year, then I assume you know of his record. He spent some time at Westville for assault. He beat a man, almost to death."

She pointed her finger at him. "Murton carries images around in his head from the war that leave him little room for peace. The man he beat was a drug dealer who tried to steal from him. I make no excuses for his past behavior, Detective, but I don't delude myself into thinking it was something it was not. He's paid his debt to society. Why not leave him be?"

Virgil decided to try a different direction. "Tell me about Samuel Pate."

"What about him?"

"You sold him your church. Why?"

She pinched her lips together and shook her head the way a grade school teacher might if she were addressing the slow student at the back of the classroom. "First of all, Detective, you don't sell a church. No one does. You might sell a building that once housed a church, but the church is never for sale. As far as the sale you're speaking of, it was more of a merger."

"A merger?"

"That's right. The Pate Ministry wants to branch out. They've brought me on board as one of their staff ministers. The building we're sitting in is scheduled for demolition in a few months. In time, it will be replaced with a modern ministry center designed for the children of our community."

"So you're going to be an employee of Pate's?"

"I already am," she said.

"What about the money?"

"What money?" she said. "What on earth are you talking about?"

"Franklin Dugan and Sunrise Bank handled the financing of your so-called merger. It was a multi-million dollar deal. Shortly after the paperwork was completed, Franklin Dugan was murdered at his home. He was shot to death, Ms. Frechette, and your boyfriend, Murton, has shown up out of nowhere and inserted himself into my investigation. He has a record for almost beating someone to death. By your own admission he's a tormented war veteran. Do you see where I'm going with this?"

She swallowed then clenched her hands together. It took her a few moments to speak. "He's been working security for the Pates," she said. "This deal has been in the works for over a year now. That's how we met."

WHEN VIRGIL GOT BACK OUT TO THE SAFEWAY, HE SAW the manager of the store arguing with Donatti, who stood in front of him, his hands spread, palms up, in a what-can-you-do? gesture. He joined Virgil a minute later.

"What's going on?" Virgil asked.

"Man wants to open his store. We should probably let him. Body's gone, Crime Scene is done, and the witnesses have all been processed."

"So why don't you let him open?"

Donatti popped a stick of gum into his mouth and tossed the wrapper on the ground. "Because he's been a dick, or at the very least, sort of dickish all day long."

Virgil picked up the wrapper and rolled it between his fingers. "Besides," Donatti continued, "that would be what us underlings refer to as an executive decision."

Sandy walked up. "He's right, we're not authorized to make those kinds of decisions."

Virgil looked at Donatti. "Let him open."

"You got it, boss."

To Sandy: "Where's Rosie?"

"He left a little while ago. He said something about some follow up questions for someone at the bank. Margery, I think he said."

Virgil shook his head.

Sandy looked at him, her head tilted. "What?"

"Ah, nothing. I'll tell you later."

"That seems to be a habit of yours."

"Listen, I'd like for you to go back to the shop, take everyone's notes and get them into the computer. The victims, their families, their co-workers, friends, neighbors, witness statements...all of it. This is all connected somehow. You're the one with the psychology degree. See if you can psychologize some sense out of it all."

"I don't think that's a real word. In fact, I'm sure of it."

Virgil gave her his best fake smile. "I know. I was trying to be charming."

"Keep trying. See you tonight?"

He leaned in close, smelled her hair and whispered in her ear. "Count on it. I'll let you psychologize me."

"Like we've got enough time for that."

"Hey..."

VIRGIL HAD A THOUGHT AND PUNCHED ROSENCRANTZ'S number into his phone. "Still at the bank?"

"Did Small rat me out?"

"No. I'm psychic. Are you still there or not?"

"Yeah. What's up?"

"Let me talk to Margery for a minute, will you?"

"She's in the can, freshening up. We're uh, going to have a late lunch. Wait a minute, here she comes."

"Have her pull up the records for their safe deposit boxes. See if one of them belongs to Murton Wheeler."

Rosencrantz repeated the instructions to Margery, and Virgil could hear a keyboard clacking in the background.

A few seconds later: "No Murton Wheeler listed."

"How about anyone with the last name of Wheeler?"

More clacking. "No Wheeler's listed at all."

After thinking for a moment, Virgil said, "Try Samuel Pate.

"Sorry Jonesy. No Pate listed either."

Virgil was about to hang up when he thought of one more thing. "Ask her if she can identify a safe deposit box by the code stamped on the key."

"She says the keys are code stamped to match the boxes. If you have a key she can match it to the box, then check the box against the owner to get a name."

Virgil gave him the code and waited again. When Rosencrantz came back on the line his voice sounded flat, like he was talking on the other side of a glass wall. "What the hell is going on, Jonesy?"

"What do you mean?"

"That key code you gave me belongs to a box currently shown as rented to you. You know those signature cards they make you sign so they know it's your box? I'm looking at yours as we speak. It sure looks like your signature, man."

WHEN VIRGIL ARRIVED AT SUNRISE BANK, Rosencrantz was waiting for him at the entrance to the executive offices. He stood with his back against a marble-tiled wall, a half-eaten apple in his hand. When he saw Virgil he pulled the signature card out of his breast pocket and handed it to him without saying anything. Virgil studied the card for a moment. "What do you think?"

Rosencrantz took another bite of the apple and thoroughly chewed, then swallowed before he answered. "I think you messed up what promised to be a very interesting lunch."

"That's not exactly what I meant."

"No shit. So let's go see what's in the box, Sherlock," he said.

Virgil felt the focus drain out of his eyes. "As long as we're on the same page, then." He took the apple from Rosie and took a bite before he gave it back. "After you."

THEY WENT AND FOUND MARGERY AND SHE TOOK THEM to an account manager named Beth, a heavy breasted, dark haired woman who reminded Virgil of his first grade teacher. Beth took them downstairs to the safe deposit box area and Virgil had to sign the signature card to demonstrate that the box was his, even though it wasn't. When she compared the signatures she looked at the card, then back at Virgil. "You say you never rented this box?" she said.

"That's right."

"Well, that is weird, isn't it? I mean, your signature matches perfectly. I'm probably breaking some rule by allowing you access to this box, but you guys are the good guys, right? And with what's happened to Franklin, I don't think anyone would object, do you?"

Virgil took the bank's master key from Beth's hand and inserted it into the top lock on the box, turned it and heard the tumblers ratchet into place. He then took the key Murton had left at the bar and placed it in the lower lock, but before he turned it, Rosencrantz's hand clamped around his wrist like a pair of vise grips.

"Tell me again where you got the key," he said.

"From Murton Wheeler. He's the one I asked you guys to run the sheet on."

"Yeah, I just put that together," he said. "This is the guy that almost got your bacon fried outside Kuwait, right?"

"Something like that," Virgil said. "He also saved my life. I took some shrapnel. He pumped me full of morphine and blood expander until the medics arrived. I would have bled to death. You can let go of my wrist now."

"I will, but don't turn that key."

"Why not?"

"What was Wheeler's specialty in your unit?"

"He was a demolitions expert. It was his job to blow the Iraqi ammo dumps," Virgil said. He felt himself swallow before letting go of the key as carefully as he could.

The three of them stood there and stared at the box in the wall. Beth put a hand to her throat and whispered, "Oh my God."

Virgil turned and looked at Rosencrantz. "Clear this building and get the bomb squad down here."

THEY SOON DISCOVERED THAT YOU DO NOT CLEAR AN operating bank during business hours as quickly as you would like, no matter the reason. The bank's in-house security had to be notified, the main vault locked down, the teller drawers locked, the computers had to be shut down, and all of that took almost thirty minutes. Virgil wondered what they would do if a fire broke out. When he asked the bank's security chief that very question he looked at Virgil with an expression that seemed to indicate he might not be operating at full speed. "We'd get the hell out," he said. Virgil stared at him until he shook his head and walked away.

When the bomb squad technicians arrived, Virgil and Rosie showed them the safe deposit box, then walked across the street and waited inside a coffee shop. Virgil bought two large cups of coffee from a purple haired teenage boy who had enough piercings on his face to set off an airport metal detector. A college textbook entitled *Ethical Issues of Molecular Nanotechnology* sat on the counter next to the cash register. He saw Virgil looking at the book and said, "Yeah, it's pretty heavy stuff, man. Did you know that it won't be long before they'll have computers so small you'll need a microscope to see them? They'll put them inside little capsules you can swallow that'll cure cancer and all kinds of shit. Isn't that something? Say, you want cream or sugar for your joe?"

Virgil wasn't sure which question to answer, so he handed him a ten-dollar bill and told him to keep the change. When he sat down, Rosencrantz said "I almost forgot. Your boy Wheeler? He came up blank."

"You must have missed something then. He'd be on record with the V.A. Plus, he was busted for assault. He did time in Westville."

Rosie shook his head. "I think you misunderstood what I said. Everybody's got something, right? A traffic ticket, a divorce settlement, a beef with the IRS, whatever. I wasn't saying he comes up with no record. I'm saying he doesn't come up at all. We checked Federal, State, local, the service, everything. There's nothing there, Jonesy. He doesn't exist. Not on paper anyway. You know how hard that is these days?"

"Yeah. It's impossible."

An hour later the bomb squad technician walked out the front door of the bank and waved them over, but just as they crossed the street and were about to enter the building a black Crown Victoria slid to a stop behind them, it's front tire bouncing off the curb. A young man who looked like he had just graduated from college got out of the car and approached the front entrance of the bank. He wore a dark blue suit under a lightweight tan trench coat and his hair looked as if it had been cut just this morning. He walked over to where Virgil and Rosie were standing and identified himself as Agent Gibson with the FBI.

"Is one of you Detective Donatti?" he asked.

Rosencrantz looked at Agent Gibson, then said, "I think what you meant to say was '*Are* one of you Detective Donatti?' You see, grammatically speaking, when asking—"

Virgil cut him off before he went any further. "I'm Detective Jones with the Indiana State Police. Donatti works for me. How may I help you?"

Agent Gibson peeled his eyes off of Rosencrantz. "A request was put in earlier today for information regarding Murton Wheeler. It had Donatti's name attached. Wheeler is part of an ongoing federal investigation. We'd like to know why."

"You're federal agents and you're asking us why Wheeler is part of an ongoing federal investigation?" Rosencrantz said.

"No," Agent Gibson said, a look of exasperation on his face. "We'd like to know why you're looking for information on Wheeler."

"That's not what you said. You said—"

"Rosie, why don't you wait by the box with the bomb tech?" Virgil said. "I'll be right there."

"Sure thing, Jonesy," he said. But before he walked away he turned and winked at Gibson then gave him a big smile and two thumbs up. "Keep up the great work, dude.

I sleep better at night knowing you're out there doing your job. I really do."

After Rosencrantz walked away Virgil looked at Agent Gibson and tried a little diplomacy. "I'll be honest with you, Murton Wheeler was a boyhood friend of mine. We grew up together and even served in the first Gulf war with each other. It has been a number of years since we've seen each other until just last night. He walked into a bar I own, gave me a key to a safe deposit box inside this bank then disappeared out the back. In addition, two men I'd never seen before until that very same day were following him. I don't know what else I can tell you. Why are you looking for him?"

"I didn't say we were looking for him. I said he's part of an ongoing investigation."

"What exactly do you want with him then?"

"I'm afraid I'm not at liberty to say."

So much for diplomacy. "Look, Agent Gibson, I'm in the middle of a murder investigation. The CEO of this financial institution was murdered yesterday, and we've had several other shootings that I now believe are somehow connected. Murton Wheeler ties in to it somehow. Anything you can give me would be a big help."

"Murder is not a federal offense, Detective, so I'm afraid I can't help you."

"Have a nice day, then," Virgil said, and turned to walk away.

"We're not done here, Detective," Agent Gibson said.

"Yes we are," Virgil said without turning around. But

after a few steps he stopped and turned. "I don't know what's going on with Wheeler. We were friends for a long time before he dropped out of my life. But I'll tell you this, federal agent or not, you better watch your back. Murton is not someone you want for an enemy. I can probably help you, if you'll let me." But it's hard to get over on a federal agent and Gibson had already lost interest in anything else Virgil had to say.

BACK INSIDE, ROSENCRANTZ AND THE BOMB TECH WERE looking at X-rays of the inside of the safe deposit box. "It's either a folded piece of paper, or an envelope or two. Won't be able to tell until we turn the key." When neither Virgil nor Rosencrantz said anything, the tech shrugged his shoulders, turned the key and opened the door. Inside the box were two letter-sized envelopes, one with Virgil's name hand written on the front. The tech picked up the envelope, ran the scanner over it, rolled his eyes before handing it over, and then said, "You got a case number for my report?"

"I'll send one over when I get back to the office," Virgil said.

"Good enough. Tell that Jamaican cook of yours I like my sauce extra hot, will you? I'll be in tonight for supper. Man, that's good stuff."

After the bomb tech walked out Virgil asked Rosen-crantz why he was so hard on the FBI agent. "Ah, those guys flat piss me off sometimes. They strut around like their shit doesn't stink and every time you ask them for something they tell you they're not at liberty to say, but what they're really saying is we're just small time. Those guys wouldn't piss on you if you were on fire."

"Anything else?"

"Yeah, maybe. I applied twice to be an agent. They turned me down both times. You think it might be my attitude?"

"I don't see how that could be."

THE FIRST ENVELOPE CONTAINED A COPY OF A BIRTH certificate for a female named Sidney Wells, Jr., born in May of 1987. Virgil double-checked the spelling of the first name, then the sex of the child. It was either a mistake or the parents had opted to use the male spelling for the name of their daughter. The mother's name was listed as Sara Wells. The line for the father's name was blank. Virgil had no idea what any of it meant. He put the birth certificate aside and opened the other envelope.

What he saw made him squint and blink back the sting in his eyes, as if he still stood in the heat of the desert over twenty years ago, an arid wind filling the corners of his eyes with grains of sand from a place he could not seem to cleanse from his soul.

THE ENVELOPE CONTAINED TWO ITEMS. ONE WAS A picture of Virgil's mother lying in her hospital bed. She was propped up by pillows and blankets that held her upright, her lack of strength and fatigue evident, even though she was smiling. The side effects from the steroids her oncologists had prescribed had taken a toll on her body, her face puffy and swollen, but the light in her eyes remained strong even on her deathbed. What gave Virgil pause though, and caused his hands to tremble was the man who sat next to her on the edge of the bed, one arm around her shoulders, the other holding her hand in his.

Murton Wheeler.

Somewhere in the depths of Virgil's consciousness he heard Rosencrantz say his name.

"It's personal, Rosie. Would you excuse me, please?" When Rosencrantz left the room, Virgil sat down at one of the small cubicles and set the photograph on the table. The letter was from his mother, in her own hand, written less than a week before she died. It read,

My dear Virgil,

This is a fine picture of Murton and me, isn't it? I thought you might like to keep it. When you and Murton became friends it was a friendship that changed our family for the better. After his own mother died, I watched you boys play and grow together over the years and I began to think of you as brothers, and myself as a substitute for the mother he never had the opportunity to fully know or love.

Murton was a fine child and from what I gather, he has

turned into a fine man as well. I believe it's time to let the past go, Virgil. You have chosen to punish Murton for what happened, but I thank him. I thank him for asking you to stop that horrible night in the desert. I thank him for wandering off and getting lost in the dark. But mostly, I thank him for keeping you alive while your body bled from the inside. It's time for you to forgive yourself and Murton for what happened over there, and quite frankly, I think you should thank him too. I have.

I hope throughout the years my love for you was as evident as it could be. I hope you're lucky enough to eventually find someone to share your life with. Don't be afraid of marriage. There is a woman out there waiting for you and all you have to do is be open enough to recognize it when she finds you. Have children if you can, and someday when they're grown and gone and you find yourself older and in the twilight of your life, find this letter and read it again. My hope is it will offer you an understanding not previously possible. I consider it an honor to be able to live on through you and I'm proud to say I am your mother. I love you Virgil, my sweet darling boy.

Love,

Mom

P.S. Don't forget to duck if someone shoots at you. Ha ha.

LATER THAT NIGHT VIRGIL WORKED BEHIND THE BAR

with Delroy. But the events of the last two days had left him in a fog and he was mostly in the way. Everyone has their limits, even Delroy. Finally, after he'd made half a dozen drinks in a row the wrong way, Delroy pulled him aside and asked him what was wrong. Virgil told him about his case, from the beginning when he'd first learned of Franklin Dugan's murder, to speaking briefly with an old high school flame and her peculiar and mercurial husband, his encounter with Sandy, seeing Murton, and most of all, the letter and photograph that allowed his mother to speak to him from the grave as if the elements of time, space, and mortality held no sway in her existence even though she had passed a year ago.

"Let me see dat picture, you," he said. When Virgil handed him the picture, Delroy studied it for a long time before he spoke. "My mother's name was Hazel," he said. "She stood 'bout five feet tall, her, no more of dat, mon. She work her whole life, mostly laundry for the rich people live in the hills high above the road dat look out over the bay water. One day Robert and me went wid her to carry the buckets. We were both only fourteen. When dat truck swerved to miss the goats in the road it headed right toward us. She shoved Robert and me into the ditch but dat truck, mon, it struck her dead. She land right next to us. I never forget it. I never had no picture of my mother. No letter, either. But I'll tell you this, if I did, I do what it say to do, mon. Your mother, she don't live here," he said as he tapped his finger at the side of Virgil's head. "She don't live in no picture, either." Then he placed his palm flat upon Virgil's chest over his heart and said, "She live in here, just like your grandfather do. Go home now. There's nothing here for you. Not tonight, no."

"How did you ever become so wise, Delroy?"

Delroy just laughed and went back to work and Virgil thought: *Bottom line? If you find yourself in need, seek out the advice of a Jamaican bartender.*

CHAPTER SEVENTEEN

The next morning on his way to work, with little forethought, Virgil turned into the entrance of the cemetery where his mother was buried. He wound his way around the perimeter road and parked his truck on the service pathway next to her burial plot. A black Crown Victoria sat on the road a few yards ahead of him, its parking lights on, the engine idling. Virgil got out of his truck and walked over to his mother's gravesite. What he saw when he got there stopped him in his tracks.

Murton Wheeler stood by the grave, a single flower clutched in his right hand. Virgil gave it a moment, then walked up behind him as Murton placed the flower on top of her tombstone. "I always loved your mom, Jonesy. You know that, don't you? She was the mom I never had. Remember how she cried when we got back from sand-land? She hugged me like I was her own then kissed me on both cheeks and once on the lips, just like she did with you."

"I remember her crying even harder when you disappeared. You broke her heart, Murt."

A morning wind blew hard through the cemetery and the flower Murt had placed on top of her tombstone fell off the back. He retrieved it, this time placing it on the ground in front of her marker and used his fingers to half bury the stem in the ground to hold it in place. When he stood, he looked at Virgil and said, "There are things you don't know, Jonesy. Sometimes things go a certain way and you end up someplace you never knew existed and you see things that are hard to forget."

"What the hell are you talking about, Murton?"

"I'm talking about trying to figure some things out, that's all." He turned a full circle and looked across the cemetery. "Did you know I was here the day you buried your mom? You didn't, did you? I can tell by the look on your face. I wanted to talk to you then, but I knew how that would turn out."

"Maybe not," Virgil said, though he thought Murton was probably right. "Who were those men looking for you last night at the bar? Why did you leave?"

"You talked to Pate at his church, didn't you?" he said. "I know you did because I saw you there."

Before Virgil could respond, the corner of his mother's tombstone seemed to fragment, the granite exploding outward just as a distant gunshot echoed through the trees. Murton pushed Virgil to the ground where he landed face first in the grass. By the time he'd cleared his eyes of dirt and debris, Murton was already at his car. Virgil started to run after him, but then simply stopped and watched him go. There were no other shots fired, and the shooter was nowhere in sight.

* * *

THE DAMAGE TO THE TOMBSTONE WAS MINIMAL. In fact, Virgil thought, given the nature of the design, no one would probably notice the chipped piece missing from the corner unless they were specifically looking for it. A casual glance would reveal what looked like nothing more than a clean spot, as if someone had started to clean away a year's worth of grime then given up. Nevertheless, he would have to file a report of the gunshot, both with his department and the city. He stopped at the cemetery office building, more as a courtesy than anything else and informed the lone worker of the incident. When he showed him his badge and informed him of the incident that had just occurred, the attendant seemed completely underwhelmed by the entire situation.

"Did you happen to notice a black Crown Victoria enter the grounds before I arrived?"

"I didn't see you arrive, so I don't know if it was before or after," he said.

"I think you've misinterpreted my question. I'm not asking if you saw the car before or after, I'm asking if you saw it at all."

He rolled his eyes the way young people do when forced to participate in a conversation they want no part of. "There's a form you can fill out if you want to report any type of vandalism to a grave site," he said. "But the cemetery is only responsible for the grounds. Any damage to the marker is your own responsibility. It says so in your contract. I saw the Crown Vic a few minutes ago when it left. If they're friends of yours the next time you see them you might want to mention the speed limit around here is five miles per hour. But you're a cop right? I guess you'd know that already."

Virgil looked at him without saying anything, and after a few seconds of silence the attendant asked if he wanted the form or not. Virgil told him no and walked out the door.

WHEN VIRGIL GOT TO HIS OFFICE THERE WAS A NOTE from Cora taped to the door with instructions to see her when he got in. He opened the door, tossed his jacket on the chair and started back out, but his desk phone rang so he turned around and picked up the receiver.

Bradley Pearson, the governor's aide. "Do you mind explaining to me what in the hell is going on over there?"

"Hello, Bradley. I'm not sure I understand the nature of your question."

"Then try this. The governor does not appreciate

agents from the FBI questioning him in a public setting about a case that you're supposed to be handling for him."

Pearson had a way of making something sound completely different than it actually was. His choice of words and the manner in which he spoke suggested Virgil was, at the very least, doing a personal favor for the governor, and at most, covering something up for him and his office. "Let me see if I can clear something up for you, Bradley. I work for the state. I am not *handling* anything for the governor. The agent you're talking about is named Gibson, right? He rolled on a bomb threat that turned up bust yesterday and tried to tell me I was interfering with a federal investigation. If he complained to the governor, that's your problem, not mine. Anything else?"

"Yeah, Jonesy, there is something else. Who the hell is Murton Wheeler?"

Virgil almost answered, but he instead hung the phone up gently and walked over to Cora's office. It was only ten thirty in the morning.

WHEN HE WALKED IN SHE HAD BRADLEY PEARSON ON speaker, and he was shouting into the phone about how Virgil had just hung up on him. Cora let him go on for a few minutes, waving Virgil into one of the chairs in front of her desk. When his rant got old and repetitive, Cora interrupted him and said, "Listen to me you pathetic little piss-pot, the governor and I go back further than you and he ever will. Much further. In fact, I knew him when you were still in diapers, so hear me when I say this. If you ever call up one of my people and question their tactics, loyalties, or methods of operation again, I will personally see to it that the next political position you hold will be cleaning out the congressional toilets. If you don't think I've got the juice to pull it off then pick up the phone and call me back." Then for the second time in less than five minutes someone hung up on Bradley Pearson.

If you have a boss like Cora LaRue, Virgil thought, going to work in the morning wasn't too difficult at all.

She puffed out her cheeks, then said, "So Jones-man, where are we? I can take care of Pearson, but sooner or later the governor himself is going to come calling."

Virgil sat down and spent the next thirty minutes explaining his relationship with Murton, how they were raised together, how they fought together in the war, their falling out, his recent visit to the bar and cemetery, the interviews with Amanda and Samuel Pate, and his talk with Amy Frechette. Thirty minutes later, after he'd finished, she asked the most basic of questions. "So what now?"

"I hate to say it."

"Well, at least we're on the same page then. Boyhood friends or not, Jonesy, you've got to follow this wherever it leads you. Get warrants for Wheeler. One to search his residence and one for his arrest."

"You asked me to look into Pate, Cora. I've had one brief conversation with him. For reasons I can't readily explain, they've invited me to a gathering at their church this Saturday. I think I might go and see what I can see, though it's probably a waste of time."

"Maybe, maybe not. You know how these things work. Get the warrants cut on Wheeler anyway."

"I just don't think Murton is involved in the way it seems."

"It's not a request, Jonesy. Get it done."

Virgil wanted to argue, but he knew she was right.

Sorry, Mom, he thought.

VIRGIL FILLED OUT THE APPROPRIATE FORMS FOR THE warrants, walked them over to the prosecutor's office, then spent the better part of the day with Sandy reviewing the case notes that had been put together on the murders of Franklin Dugan, Jerry Burns, Rhonda Rhodes, and Elle Richardson. But he had a difficult time concentrating, his thoughts bouncing back and forth between his growing feelings for Sandy and his sudden rekindled loyalty to his lifelong friend, Murton Wheeler, whom Virgil felt he was about to betray. He picked up the phone and called Cora in her office. "Got a second?"

"Sure. What's up?"

"I'll be right there."

Virgil walked into her office and laid it out. "This morning you asked me to get warrants for Murton

Wheeler. On the surface I think that's sound procedure, but there's something else at play here."

She was tapping her pen against the blotter on her desk. "Like what?"

"Murton Wheeler worked for Pate. His girlfriend, Amy Frechette, is now one of the pastors of Grace Community Church. Pate borrowed over five million dollars from Dugan's bank to buy an all but condemned building. Amy Frechette says she doesn't know where Wheeler is. The two goons who followed him into the bar the other night work for Pate. Did you read my report on the shots fired at the cemetery?"

"Yeah?"

"Who do you think was doing the shooting?"

"My guess would be the two who tried to brace you at your bar about Wheeler. Pate's guys," she said. She tapped the pen harder and faster on her blotter.

"Mine too." Virgil looked at the pen and the little ink marks it made on the desk pad. "Would you mind not doing that, please?"

She lowered her chin and raised her eyebrows at him. Virgil looked down for a moment, then raised his hands, palms out. An apology. "So if Wheeler, who works or worked for Pate is responsible for the murder of Franklin Dugan, why would he seek me out at the bar? When I saw him at the cemetery he hadn't followed me, he was already there."

"So you're saying you don't want to pick him up or search his last known residence?"

"No. I'm not saying that at all," Virgil said, but he let his eyes fall away from hers when he spoke.

"Like it or not, Jonesy, Wheeler's a part of this."

"Whether or not I like it has nothing to do with it, Cora."

"You're right about that," she said. "But you don't have to convince me."

"Meaning what, exactly?"

"Wheeler is, or was, a friend. You two have a history together. You can't serve a personal agenda and the state at the same time, Jonesy."

"There is no personal agenda," Virgil said, but he regretted the lie as soon as the words were out of his mouth.

"So what was in the safe deposit box then? I didn't see that in your report." When Virgil didn't answer her question, she tried another. "So what is it, exactly, that you want to do?"

Virgil told her and when he finished she gave her pen a little rat-a-tat-tat on the blotter, winked at him and said, "So let's walk over and talk to the D.A. It should be fun. Did you know he used to teach a criminal law course at Notre Dame? I'm sure we won't have any trouble convincing him."

PRESTON ELLIOTT, THE PROSECUTING ATTORNEY FOR Marion county, was a hands-on administrator who still worked his own caseload, put in more hours than anyone else in his office, and held one of the highest conviction rates in the history of the county. He stood five feet, four inches tall and had an attitude consistent with someone who carried a short man complex around in his hip pocket. He took his job seriously and his scotch neat.

When they walked into his office he greeted them from behind his desk without standing up. His shirt-sleeves were rolled up past his elbows and Virgil saw him peek at his watch as he motioned them to the chairs in front of his desk. Twenty minutes later they'd laid it out for him.

"It's not enough. Surely you know that. Cora, you told him, right? It's not enough."

"It's where the answers are," Virgil said. "But Pate's not talking. If we can get a look at his books—"

Elliott interrupted him. "Have you served the warrant on this Wheeler fellow yet?"

"Not yet."

"So let me see if I've got this straight," he said. "Wheeler has served time in Westville for assault. Franklin Dugan, who wrote the note on a five million dollar deal is shot to death in his driveway. Nobody knows where Wheeler is, not even his girlfriend, who coinciden-tally is the pastor of the church that was bought by Pate with the money he borrowed from the dead banker. Do I have that right?"

"Yes, but—"

Elliott held up a finger. "Let me finish," he said. He

was pacing back and forth now behind his desk, as if he were in the courtroom giving a summation to a jury. "Wheeler worked for Pate, but again, no one knows where Wheeler is, save the run-ins you've had with him. So for reasons you've yet to explain, you want to sit on the arrest and search warrants of a convicted felon and instead want another warrant so you can toss the offices of one of the city's most famous, and I might add, influential people?"

"Murton Wheeler didn't have motive," Virgil said. "Why would he want to kill Dugan?"

"That's a great question, Jonesy," Elliott said. "Why don't you use the warrant, pick him up and ask him?"

"I intend to, Preston. But I'm telling you right now, this all leads back to Pate. Murton Wheeler might be a player somehow, but Pate is the one we should be looking at."

"What proof do you have?"

"He's under investigation by the Texas Department of Insurance for Fraud out of Houston. His last church burned to the ground," Cora said.

"Yes. And that would be a matter for the State of Texas, and maybe, just maybe, a matter for the FBI, depending of course on which way the federal winds are blowing at the moment," he said, his voice impatient and thick with sarcasm. "Either way, it's just a tad bit out of our jurisdiction, Cora. The fact of the matter is, neither of you can offer any proof whatsoever of Samuel Pate's involvement in the murder of Franklin Dugan. As an officer of the court I appreciate your efforts, but this office has certain standards we like to follow and we cannot infringe upon the rights of our citizens based solely on supposition or minimalistic circumstantial evidence. Get me something concrete and I'll sign off on a warrant. Until then, I suggest you round up Wheeler and work your case from that angle. If he's not involved he's got nothing to fear. But he might have the exact information we need to move on Pate. One step at a time, Jonesy." After a moment he looked at Cora and said, "Are you free for dinner tonight?"

LATE THAT NIGHT THE PHONE NEXT TO VIRGIL'S BED rang just as he was about to fall asleep.

"You've got your warrant for Pate. One for the office and one for the house."

"What? Cora? Say that again, will you please?"

"I said you've got your warrants for Pate."

Virgil thought her words were slightly over-enunciated yet slurred and it reminded him of his days on patrol when he'd stop an intoxicated driver then listen as they tried to talk their way out of a trip to jail. "Uh, that's great, Cora. How did you pull that off?"

"Don't ask," she said, then giggled like a young girl. "Let's just say my powers of persuasion are still as good as they ever were."

Among other things, Virgil thought.

"What was that?" she said.

"I didn't say anything. I think the connection is bad. Thanks for going to bat for me."

"Anytime," she said. "Hey, did you ever see that Far Side cartoon? The one where the couple is in the delivery room at the hospital? The father is standing next to the bed and the doctor is holding their new baby boy right after he comes out of the chute. The father looks at his wife and says, 'Look honey, it's a boy. Let's name him Preston.'" She howled with laughter, then hung up on him.

Out of the chute?

Virgil looked at the caller ID. It read Elliott, Preston. It was just after one-thirty in the morning.

CHAPTER EIGHTEEN

The next morning, Saturday at ten o'clock, Virgil and Sandy were to meet at the Pate Ministries complex. When he turned in, Virgil saw her state car. She'd beat him there. He looked at his watch and discovered he was about ten minutes late. He had a search warrant for the complex tucked inside his jacket pocket. The lobby of the church had been converted from the wide-open space Virgil had witnessed on his last visit to a smaller, more intimate setting, the latter being achieved by erecting a three-sided red pipe and drape system, the kind you see at trade shows and conventions. At the front of the enclosure an electrically operated viewing screen had been lowered from its ceiling mount and the image being displayed prior to the screening of tomorrow's broadcast was a closed circuit view of the enclosed area where Virgil now stood. There were about twenty to twenty-five people scattered about the area, some seated in padded folding chairs that were set out in four rows of twelve across the width of the enclosure. Others either stood or were seated in various places at the round four-top tables that were covered with white linen cloths and set with dishes and flatware.

Virgil watched himself enter the area on the closed circuit system and almost tripped on the leg of a chair as he did. A buffet was set up on the left side of the room and the wait staff were busy as they placed stainless steel chafing dishes into their holders. A faint wax-like aroma filled the room from the cans of chafing dish fuel that burned with blue flames under the containers.

Samuel and Amanda Pate stood at the front of the room next to the lowered view screen. Samuel had his back to Virgil, the armbands of his crutches clamped tightly around his suit sleeves. Amanda glanced his way, though her eyes skipped across him as if he were not there.

Virgil and Sandy saw each other at the same time, first on the screen, then in real life as she turned around in her chair and looked back. She leaned over and whispered something to a handsome man seated next to her, then stood and walked between the chairs to the end of the row. She wore a cream colored sweater dress with matching knit stockings that were just slightly longer than the bottom of her dress. When she walked the tops of her stockings peeked out from under the bottom of her dress.

"Hey, Jonesy," she said, her hand now on Virgil's arm. "How are you?"

But before he could say anything, Amanda was at his side and she slipped her left hand into the crook of his arm, the words she spoke pointed directed at Sandy. "Virgil and I go way back. I'm Amanda Pate, Samuel's wife. You're one of Virgil's people, aren't you?"

Her actions were vintage Amanda, Virgil thought.

But it didn't play with Sandy. She tilted her head slightly and said, "Something like that."

"Well," Amanda said with mock sincerity, "I love your little outfit. It's so, so...."

"Yes?" Sandy said, her eyes blinking more than usual. "It's so what, exactly?"

"Well dear, it's so, um, edgy I think is the word I'm looking for. Yes, that's it. It's so edgy I think I might be a little jealous. You've managed to capture just about every man's attention here this morning. For example, that man you were seated next to just a moment ago. Do you know who that is?"

"It's your party," Sandy said. "Don't you?"

"Of course I know, dear. I was just wondering if you did. He's a very successful bond trader. Single too. In fact, don't look, but he's watching you right now. Would you like me to formally introduce the two of you?"

"We've already met, thank you," Sandy said. "Speaking of attention, I think your husband is trying to get yours. By the way, I can't wait to see the show. I've heard it's a hoot." Then to Virgil: "Detective Jones, could I speak with you for a moment?"

Amanda peeled her eyes from Sandy and walked away

without saying anything more. Once she was gone Virgil looked at Sandy and said, "hoot?"

She ignored him and waved at the bond trader.

―――――――

"WHAT WAS THAT ALL ABOUT?" SHE FINALLY SAID.

"That," Virgil said, "was a master manipulator in action."

"No kidding." Then, a few seconds later, "What time are they coming?" She was still making eyes with the trader.

"In about thirty seconds. Donatti's running this squad. Rosie's at the Pate's residence. Once they're in, I want you to keep an eye on Amanda."

"You got it, boss" she said, her head turned upward. Virgil wanted to kiss her right then and there, and in fact would have except a number of things happened almost simultaneously. Samuel Pate picked up a spoon and tapped it against the side of a water goblet and said, "Excuse me everyone, if you'll take a seat please, we're ready to—"

At the exact same time, Donatti and ten uniformed state troopers came through the front doors of the lobby. Donatti shouted, "Police! Search warrant! Nobody move. Everyone stay right where you are and keep your hands where I can see them."

Virgil started moving toward Pate. The bond trader who had been flirting with Sandy saw Virgil coming, stood up to get out of the way and tripped backwards over the row of chairs behind him. Amanda tried to duck behind the drapery out of sight, but Sandy wrapped her arms around her and tackled her to the ground. The drapery and support rods got tangled up in their struggle and fell over the buffet table, then the table and everything on it crashed to the ground as well. People were screaming and trying to get away from the commotion by the buffet and Donatti was still yelling for no one to move. Virgil pointed a finger at Samuel Pate, told him not to move, then ran over to where Sandy was still struggling with Amanda. He yanked the drapery free from the top of them both, then held her down while Sandy got up.

Virgil had his foot stationed in the middle of Amanda's back to hold her in place. Samuel Pate walked across the room knocking chairs aside with his crutches as he approached. "What in God's name is going on here?" he said, his voice coarse with anger. "Will you take your foot off of my wife's back please? Why are the police here?"

"Step back please, Reverend," Virgil said. "I'll speak with you in a moment."

But Pate refused to listen amid the chaos of the events as they unfolded around him. He stepped closer and put his crutch against Virgil's hip, forcing him to remove his foot from Amanda's back or lose his balance. "Step away from my wife, Detective. I insist you tell me—"

Virgil grabbed the still extended crutch and pinched it under his arm, then swept Pate's legs out from under him. Pate was face down on the ground before he knew what had happened. Virgil yanked the crutch from his right arm and pinned his hands behind his back. Donatti ran over and placed his handcuffs around Pate's wrists. Virgil leaned in close and said, "You ever place your cane against my person again I'll show you the other end of it. I've got the resume, sir, believe me."

"Release my husband this instant," Amanda shouted. "For God's sake, Jonesy, he's disabled. You've got a crippled man on the ground in handcuffs on his own property. What's the matter with you? I demand to know what's going on here," she said. Why are all these police officers here?" She stomped her foot, her hands balled into fists at her side as she spoke.

Virgil reached into his pocket, pulled out the search warrant and handed it to her. "We have a warrant to search the premises, Amanda." Then to Donatti: "Have your men take the file cabinets and everything in the desk drawers. You brought trucks and dollies?"

"We're good to go, boss," Donatti said.

"Get started then. Grab the computers, too. They probably have a central server somewhere. A closet, or a small office. Don't miss that."

Pate mumbled something Virgil couldn't quite catch. "What was that?"

"It's in the basement," he said. "The door at the end of the hall."

Virgil looked at him for a moment without responding. Then Pate lifted his head and smiled. "I've nothing to hide, Detective. Nothing at all. You'll see. Then you and I, well, we'll talk again, I suspect."

Virgil ignored him and nodded to Donatti, who motioned for the other officers. They wheeled the dollies in and moved toward the offices. Tears were running down Amanda's cheeks. She held the warrant in her hand, down by her side. "Read the warrant, Amanda. It gives us permission to search and seize anything in this building. Your house as well."

Her head snapped up, the whites of her eyes veined with red streaks at the corners. "What? My house? You're going to search my house?"

"Not going to, Amanda. Are. We've got a team there right now as well."

"You bastard. If you think I'm going to let you get away with this you're mistaken," she said, her finger pointed like she was admonishing a child. "I'll have your badge for this, Virgil Jones. You watch and see. You think we don't have any influence in this town?"

Samuel Pate looked at his wife and said, "Amanda, go home. Please, you're not helping."

"But Samuel, can't you see what they're trying to do to us? We can't just let—"

"Amanda, I said go home. Keep your wits about you and get to the house and make sure they conduct their search in a respectful manner, then call Everett. Tell him what's happened and have him meet me downtown. Can you do that for me, Amanda? Detective, is she free to go?"

Virgil nodded. "Yes, but remain available. Do not leave the city."

When Amanda looked at him the veins on the sides of her neck bulged with anger. "This isn't over, Jonesy. Not even close."

Just then Sandy started shouting as she pulled the rest of the drapery off their support rods. "Hey, I need some help here. Someone get a fire extinguisher. Those burner cans are still going. The drapes are on fire. Jonesy? Jonesy, I need some help over here."

The burner cans from under the chafing dishes had spilled to the floor when Sandy tackled Amanda, but in the commotion that followed no one had noticed the smoldering drapery. Virgil helped Sandy yank the rest of the curtains down, then grabbed carafes of ice water from the tables and dumped them on the hot spots. A few of the people who were present to preview the Sunday broadcast and the rest of the wait staff picked up the smoldering curtains and pulled them outside and tossed them into a pile on the sidewalk.

Sandy pick up a chair, sat down and puffed out her cheeks. Her hands were shaking. "You okay?" Virgil asked.

"Yeah. Sorry. Fire sort of freaks me out."

"Yeah, me too. But I guess you knew that already."

She smiled at him. After a few seconds she said, "Well, all in all, I think that went just fine, don't you?"

"Yeah. Textbook," Virgil said.

VIRGIL'S PHONE RANG AND WHEN HE SAW IT WAS Cora's home number he thought, *Jesus, what now?*

"Good morning, Cora. How was your evening?"

"It was, mmm, productive. That about sums it up, I think."

"I'm not sure what you mean."

"I know. Listen, did you see everything you needed to over at that dilapidated church in Broad Ripple?"

"Yeah, pretty sure. Why?"

"Oh, no reason. I guess last night while you were sleeping and Elliott and I were...uh, well, while you were sleeping, it blew up and burned to the ground. I just got off the phone with the watch commander. Looks like there was some kind of explosion. He said it blew the steeple right off the top. It's lying in the alley behind the church. He said it reminds him of that Pan Am jet they blew out of the sky over Lockerbie. Remember that?"

"I'll get over there as soon as I can."

"Slow down, Slick. There's more. The firemen found a body inside the church. Unidentified female, but there was only one car in the lot and it's registered to Amy Frechette, so you can do the math on that. Crime scene is on the way to the Frechette residence as we speak. Didn't you tell me that's where Murton Wheeler lives?"

WHEN THEY PULLED UP TO MURTON AND AMY'S HOUSE, two crime scene techs were already there, waiting. Sandy hopped out of the truck and when she did both of the techs said something to her, first one, then the other. Virgil didn't hear any of it.

Sandy looked at them and shook her head. "Oh my God, how about we all just pull our dicks out and see whose is bigger?" She looked at each man individually for just a split second, then said, "I'd probably win. We may or may not need you boys. We'll let you know. Why don't you wait in your van? Go on now," she said, and gave them a little wave of her hand. Once they were gone, she looked at Virgil and said, "You want the front or the back?"

"Front I guess."

Virgil had to pop one of the small glass panes in the front door to gain entry, then went to the back and let Sandy inside. Amy Frechette's house was old, but in good shape. The walls were stucco instead of sheet-rocked, the ceiling was made of a biscuit colored stamped tin, and the walkways between rooms were all arched. The wall opposite the front door was covered from floor to ceiling with bookshelves, and each shelf was filled with row after row of both religious and psychology studies. For reasons he could not readily explain, Virgil expected to find a good selection of fiction novels, the utilitarian surroundings suggestive of an individual who lived through someone else's imagination, but that was not the case. Instead, what he found was book after book whose titles were reflective of someone who sought greater understanding of the people she served. Amy Frechette's home did not appear to be a place of sanctuary from her work, but instead it was a place of continued study of the work to which she devoted her life.

A hinged, two-photo frame sat at eye level on one of the shelves. One side of the frame held a sepia-toned picture of a young couple's profile as they looked at each other, the opposite side held a color photo, yellowed with age, of a young man dressed in jungle fatigues standing next to an airplane somewhere in the tropics. Her father perhaps. But it was a single photo next to the others that caught Virgil's eye and reminded him of Cora's comments about not being able to serve the state and his own personal agenda at the same time. The photo was one of him and Murton, taken just after they'd arrived home from basic training, before being shipped out to fight in the Gulf War. They stood side by side, their arms around each other, both of them smiling at the camera. Just off to the side, part of her face cut out of the frame of the photo, was Virgil's mother. She was looking at them and the flash of the camera caught the tears that ran down her cheek.

He left the photo untouched and continued to search the room. A February issue of Psychology Today was on the sofa, open to an article entitled, *A Field Guide to Narcissism*. Virgil wasted a few minutes scanning the article before deciding he was not narcissistic and tossed it back on the couch.

The kitchen was extremely small, a nook really, with only one florescent light bulb that hummed above the kitchen sink. The flickering light against the dark paneled walls reminded him of the times he'd spent as a child with his grandfather when he'd wake in the early morning to the smell of percolated coffee and toasted wheat bread before they'd go out to fish on his neighbor's pond.

They spent three hours searching Amy Frechette's residence—every drawer, all the closets, the attic, the crawl space and every inch in between turning up exactly nothing, though Virgil would have been the first to admit he didn't really expect to find a ledger in Murton's handwriting that detailed a master plan to kill Franklin Dugan. In the end, they'd made a hell of a mess but turned up no evidence whatsoever.

Virgil's cell phone buzzed and when he looked at the screen the number was not one he'd seen before. "Jones."

"You're not going to find anything," Murton said. "There's nothing there. There never was. I'm not the man you think I am, Jonesy."

"Murt, what the hell is going on? That was you in the cab, wasn't it? If you're not part of this, come in and we'll—"

He laughed without humor. "We'll what, figure everything out? Get me a lawyer? I don't think so, pal. We were going to be married, did you know that? Did she tell you that?"

"Murt..."

"I left to protect her, Jonesy. I told them she didn't know anything, that she was just a minister working with pre-school children. She was pregnant. We found out about a week ago. She died thinking I left her because she was pregnant. Jesus, what have I done?"

Virgil picked up the phone from the kitchen and dialed 911. "Murt, I'm sorry. Let me help you." He could hear the 911 operator in the background asking if someone needed assistance.

"You know, I always sort of had it in my head that you and I might hook back up one day, but I guess that ship has sailed. That's not on you, though. Hey, what's that we used to say? Pop 'em and drop 'em? That's exactly what I'm going to do. Tell your old man he's the best, will you? And don't bother trying to get a trace on this phone. It's one of those pre-paid specials. It's about to be road kill on the interstate. What a country, huh?"

Sandy came around the corner just as Murton broke the connection. "What's going on?" she said.

"I wish I knew."

CHAPTER NINETEEN

When Virgil arrived at his office Monday morning he discovered Amanda Pate sitting in one of the two chairs that front his desk. "Your assistant said I could wait in here."

"What do you want, Amanda?"

"What do I want? For God's sake, Jonesy, I want my husband released from that rat hole you've put him in. He's been in there all weekend. What were you thinking?"

Virgil looked at his watch. "Arraignment is in two hours. He can bond out afterwards."

"Bond out? Have you lost your mind? I want the charges against him dropped and I want him released this instant."

"That's not going to happen, Amanda. It's time to get a grip on reality, here. Samuel is being held for assault on a police officer."

"Oh, bullshit, Jonesy. That is pure and utter bullshit,

and you know it. You're holding him because you think he's somehow mixed up in Franklin's death, and that just isn't true. God, you piss me off."

"If it's not true, then convince him to talk to me so I can clear him and move on, otherwise, he's our number one suspect."

"Our attorney has advised us—"

Virgil waved her off. "Yes, yes, your attorney has advised you not to speak with the police or answer any of our questions. That's what attorneys do, Amanda. But the hard reality of the situation is this: The truth eventually comes out, and when it does, it's one of two ways. Either a suspect talks to us and we clear their story, or we move forward with charges and the whole thing goes to trial. Which would you prefer?"

She rose from the chair, her face and neck red with anger. "You're wrong," she said. "Those aren't the only two choices."

"I'm afraid that's the way I see it, Amanda. If you or Samuel change your mind and want to get on the record, let me know. Otherwise, we will be moving forward on the case with the evidence we've accumulated from both your home and your offices."

"What evidence? There is no evidence."

"We're building our case, Amanda. I'm afraid that's all I can tell you. If I were you, I'd advise Samuel that it's time to get in front of this thing before it's too late. Capital murder in the State of Indiana carries the death penalty. With a full confession, the D.A. might be willing to accept a plea deal of life without the possibility of parole, but I may be speaking out of turn here. I can check with him if you'd like."

She pointed her finger at him, the fear and rage evident when she spoke. "Fuck you, Jonesy. Fuck you times two, you son of a bitch."

"Good bye, Amanda. Next time you want to speak with me, make an appointment."

A few minutes later, when he looked out his office window at the street below, Virgil saw Amanda as she crossed the street toward the courthouse. The morning traffic was heavy and when she walked out into the street and stopped halfway across, she forced the vehicles around her to swerve or stop completely. She turned and looked up at Virgil in the window and shook her head, staring at him until he moved away.

In a way, Virgil almost felt sorry for her.

AN HOUR OR SO LATER VIRGIL WAS STILL AT HIS DESK when Agent Gibson knocked on the doorjamb and walked into his office. He sat down without being asked, bit into the bottom corner of his lip then raised his eyebrows at Virgil. "So maybe we got off on the wrong foot."

"Heard you tried to brace the governor. How'd that work out for you?"

"Hey, I'm trying here. You want my help, or not?"

Good question, Virgil thought. "What exactly do you want, Agent Gibson?"

"Bottom line? I want you to drop the charges against Pate. His arraignment is less than an hour from now."

"You asked me if I wanted your help. How exactly does my dropping charges against Pate help me?"

"Look, Detective. You've managed to drop a turd in the punch bowl and now I'm the one who has to clean it up. We've been monitoring Pate's activities for months trying to put our case together. If I can be blunt, you're getting in the way. This assault charge you've got hanging over him is going to hurt our chances and while you're doing that, I have to wonder, Detective, is it helping your case at all? Is it putting you any closer to solving the murders you're working on?"

"Nice speech, but you still haven't answered my question."

"How sure are you of Pate's involvement in Dugan's death?"

"He's our primary suspect."

"Based on what?"

When Virgil didn't answer, Gibson went on. "Okay, here it is. I work out of the Houston office, but I guess you know that. It's the Texas Department of Insurance that's under investigation by our office. For fraud. Pate torched his church in Houston and when the company who underwrote his policy started making waves about writing the check, the Texas DOI got involved and Pate walked away with a wad of cash before the building had stopped smoldering."

"So what?" Virgil said. "File charges on the Commissioner of the Texas DOI."

"We did. But his lawyer cut a hell of a deal and now the commissioner is part of witness protection."

"Witness protection? What for?"

Gibson half laughed at the questions. "You Midwestern guys are something, you know that?

"What exactly is that supposed to mean?"

"Let me put it this way," he said. "You think the Catholic priests are the only ones tweaking the twangers on little boys?"

"How about you take the corn dog out of your mouth and tell me the whole story?"

"Hey, great choice of words. When we took the commissioner down for fraud we discovered his personal computer was full of pictures of little kids with no clothes on. He cut a deal and put us onto Pate, who the commissioner says was supplying the photos. Our analysts compared the background of the photos to ones we could find of Pate's church before he torched it. We think they match up. In any event, the commissioner says Pate blackmailed him and had him lean on the insurance company to write the check or he'd start to squeal about the photos."

"You're saying Samuel Pate is a pedophile?"

"You tell me," Gibson said. "I read your report on that

dilapidated church he bought for five million bucks. What was he going to do with it? Knock it down and build a learning center for pre-school kids or something like that? But let me guess, when you searched the Pate complex and his home you didn't find one scrap of evidence that ties him to your case or mine. And in the meantime, that old broken down building, the one that wasn't included in your search warrant burns to a crisp along with any evidence that may or may not have been material to your case, let alone mine." He stood from his chair and turned to leave. "Someone is leading you around by your nose, Detective. Take the corn dog out of my mouth. I love it."

VIRGIL WALKED OVER TO CORA'S OFFICE TO FILL HER IN on the conversations with Amanda Pate and Agent Gibson. She sat quietly and listened, but when he got to the part of Pate's alleged involvement as a pedophile, her expression looked like that of a passenger staring out the window of an airliner at thirty thousand feet as they watched the rivets pop one at a time from the wing of a plane.

"What is it?"

"So you're saying we've got a suspected murderer and pedophile in custody and Gibson wants us to let him skate?"

"He's going to get out anyway," Virgil said. "Besides, I think Gibson may be right. Someone is pulling our strings behind the curtain. I just don't know who it is, or why. But I don't think it has anything to do with Pate."

Cora looked at him for a moment, then said something that made Virgil think they were having two different conversations. "Is there something you'd like to tell me regarding the nature of your relationship with Detective Small?"

When he didn't answer her right away, she said, "I see. What about Wheeler? What did Gibson tell you about him? You did ask, didn't you?"

"Not exactly."

"Your personal life is interfering with your job, Jonesy. Clean it up."

"I'm not sure I understand what you're saying, Cora."

"I think you do," she said, then stared at the paperwork on her desk until Virgil got up and walked out.

THE CONVERSATION WITH CORA LEFT VIRGIL CONFUSED and angry. He ate lunch by himself in a small diner near his office and by the time he was finished, he'd concluded that Cora was probably right. He was romantically involved with a co-worker, and his lifelong friend, Murton Wheeler, was somehow connected—at least on the periphery—with a serial murder investigation, and as the chief investigative officer of the State of Indiana he'd put no more effort into his apprehension than he would a Sunday jaywalker late for morning Mass. Virgil finished his sandwich, paid the tab, and got ready to leave when something occurred to him. Gibson was right. Somebody was pulling his strings and Virgil realized he'd been in possession of a large part of the answer all along. Maybe not the entire answer, but a pretty damn big piece. And more importantly, he knew what he had to do next.

He walked out to his truck and just as he reached the driver's door he heard the footsteps coming hard from behind. Virgil turned in time to see a club being swung at his head and he tried to bring his right arm up to block the blow, but the attacker made just enough contact to knock him off balance and he fell face first into the pavement. Before he could move or get up he was hit again, this time in the back of the head, and that's the last thing Virgil remembered until he woke some time later, a thick blindfold across his eyes, his body bound with rope across a vertical steel support structure with his arms out from his sides and tied to a cross member as if he were being crucified.

He tried to pull free, but knew it was pointless. He had virtually no feeling left in his arms or legs, and no idea how long he'd been unconscious and tied up.

Virgil let his head hang down, his chin against his chest. Heard himself whisper Sandy's name.

CHAPTER TWENTY

Often, with little care or attention, a seedling of a wish will take root and grow across a windswept garden of unspoken dreams. It will set ever deeper into the mind, its root structure wide and strong over the darkness of the psyche where it dares to exist as a hushed and secret desire. The subconscious will nurture this desire and feed it until it grows from a seedling of desire into a stalk of hope. And when that happens, a flower of dark faith is born, its root base entrenched deep into the hardpan of who we are, one where a dry and unfed hunger is concealed from the killing frost of conscious thought.

Brian Goodwell lived in the light of such darkness, his mind forced to conjure the images from his faded memories. Were it not for his hearing, his sense of smell, his ability to taste, or touch, Brian Goodwell thought he might go mad. Wondered sometimes if he hadn't already and no one had ever bothered to tell him.

Brian shared his life and his love with his wife, Tess, whom he had not seen in over eleven years. They had been married for only a year and a half when the doctor discovered Brian suffered from Retinoblastoma, a cancer of the retina. Both eyes were affected. When Tess came home from work that night Brian followed her around the house, trying to memorize every curve of her body, the angle of her jaw, the slight gap in her front teeth, the color of her hair, the shape of her hands, and the dimples in her cheeks when she smiled. They made love that night before Brian shared the news with Tess, and when he did, Tess took his face in her hands and studied it as if it were she who was about to go blind.

The doctor had said that surgical removal of both of Brian's eyes would be the most effective treatment option. If left untreated, the tumors would travel up the optic nerve to the brain and death would soon follow. They sought a second, third, and fourth opinion. Tess wanted to keep trying. She would have sought a ninety-ninth opinion had there been time. It was her insurance from her employer that would cover the tests and ultimately, the procedure to remove her husband's eyes. Tess worked as a hotel property district manager, her pay was good and the benefits, including their insurance coverage, were among the best available. From a financial perspective, the procedure to remove Brian's eyes would be painless.

From a physical and emotional perspective, the procedure would be devastating.

The night before the surgery Brian and Tess stayed up all night. They turned on every light in the house, as if the flow of electrons through copper wire could beat back the arrival of Brian's long and permanent night. With less than an hour before sunrise they walked back through the house once again and one by one began to extinguish the lights. "I want to go one more time from the darkness into the light," he had said to Tess.

They sat on lawn chairs in their back yard and held hands in the false dawn of the day, and when the sun snuck over the horizon, Brian looked around the back yard. "I was going to put our garden right over there," he said as he pointed with his chin. "Flowers and vegetables, and both red and green peppers, tomatoes, green beans. It was going to be beautiful."

"It will be beautiful," Tess had said. "You can still do it. I'll help you."

"You'll have to help me with everything. Everything, Tess. I can't ask that of you. I won't."

"Brian, don't. Please don't do this now. We'll figure everything out. One step at a time. I promise. It will all be okay. You'll see."

Brian buried his face in his hands for a moment, and then stood.

"Brian, I'm sorry, baby. I didn't mean that. It's a figure of speech."

"I don't feel like I'm losing my sight, Tess. I feel like I'm losing my mind."

Now, a little over eleven years later, Brian Goodwell grasped the handrail and walked down the three steps of his back door and into the yard. Seven steps forward, then a ninety-degree turn to the right, then nine steps more. The edge of his garden. He dropped down to his knees, and then felt carefully on both sides to make sure he was lined up properly with the neat rows of vegetables. His garden was getting better and better each year. Tess had told him so.

The first few years had been a disaster. He would sometimes pull the flowers and vegetables by mistake and leave the weeds to grow and prosper. The first year, out of stubbornness, he refused to allow Tess to help him, and the net result of his garden that year had been six green beans, two smashed tomatoes, and one red pepper. But his sense of touch and smell had gotten better over the years and he now knew his way around the garden like the back of his hand.

At the beginning of his second season, Tess confessed to him that she had gone to the market and seeded his garden with produce picked from the aisle instead of the ground. Brian confessed to her that he knew she had done so because he liked to eat the tomatoes raw and had, one afternoon, bitten into one that had a sticker on the side.

But now Brian moved expertly along, feeling first for the stalks and stems of his labor before he pulled any weeds that tried to rise around the plants. When he worked in his garden, he thought only of Tess. It was Tess who had helped him through the last eleven years. It was Tess who remained true to him, who taught him how to be self-sufficient, who did not pity him, who not only told him, but showed him how much of a man he still was, blind or not. Brian loved Tess more than he thought humanly possible.

He'd run his hands across her face, his fingers barely touching the surface of her skin. Every night when she came home from work he would greet her the same way. First a kiss, then he'd get to look at her beauty with his hands. At first, right after the surgery, this worked well for him. He would picture her face in his mind as he ran his hands across her delicate features. But over the years, the picture of her began to fade to what it was now, a dim shadow of a memory, like an under-developed photograph, a ghost of an image. He sometimes thought he'd give his own life to see his wife's face just one more time. In death he could look down upon her every day.

So Brian spent his days in the garden of his mind with a secret wish that grew unchecked, rooted deep in an unfulfilled desire that he cultivated into a depressive hope of death where he could free himself and Tess from the burden he had placed on them both.

When the Sids pulled the trigger, Brian got his wish.

———

WHEN CONSCIOUSNESS CAME IT WAS IN PROGRESSIVE,

laborious steps. Virgil couldn't see because of the blind-fold, but he knew he was naked.

Naked in every sense of the word. His guns, badge, clothes, and boots were all somewhere, but they weren't on him. His shoulders ached from supporting the weight of his body and he could no longer feel any sensation in his hands, the bindings on his wrists tight against the cold steel. Virgil found that if he stood on his toes he could relieve the pain in his shoulders for a short time, but then his legs would begin to tremble and buckle under the strain and he'd once again fall against the weight of himself, his body its own burden.

The footsteps echoed off the walls, their sound drawing close until he could sense someone standing close. An odd mixture of cigar smoke and just a hint of cologne...and Virgil thought, *money*. When he heard him start to move away, he said, "Who are you?"

The question stopped the man for just a moment, but then he continued to walk away, his footsteps growing faint until he could barely hear them. Virgil counted ten steps in all before he heard a door open and a voice say, "He's awake."

Ten steps. Thirty feet to a door. Tied to a steel beam and cross section in a wide-open space indoors. A ware-house? He tried to think how to turn the situation around, but his options were limited, if not downright non-existent. Two sets of footsteps approached this time, and when they were near enough Virgil tried again.

"Listen to me. I'm a cop. I don't know what you're

doing, or what you've got planned here, but I want you to know it's not too late to throw it into park and just walk away."

"You hear that," a voice to his left said. "It's not too late. What do you think? Should we just walk away?"

A laugh came from the right. Virgil felt himself swallow and hoped the two men did not notice. *Keep trying.* "Look, sometimes things happen and before you know it you're on a certain path and it looks like there's no room to turn around or go back so you just keep going forward no matter how bad forward may seem, but I'm here to tell you, it's not too late. Listen to me when I tell you that. You had me out before I saw your faces. I'm blindfolded now. That means I don't know who you are or what your agenda is, and I don't care. Cut me loose and walk away. I can't identify you, so no harm will come to you, I guarantee it."

"Take his blindfold off. He's supposed to see it coming."

"You don't want to do that," Virgil shouted. "Do not remove my blindfold." But he felt a hand on the back of his head and then the cloth that covered his eyes was removed. The two men who had followed Murton into the bar the other night, the same two men who worked security for Samuel Pate stood before him, their faces void of any emotion. "You shouldn't have done that," Virgil said. "You've just complicated the situation."

The two men looked at each other. "Get a load of this guy," the taller one said. "We've just complicated the situation." He turned and looked at Virgil. "It's your situation that's complicated, Hoss. It's about to get worse, too."

Virgil saw he was in a large room that looked like an abandoned warehouse. A solitary light fixture hung low on its cord over a small card table with two chairs. On top of the table were a rubber mallet, a roll of duct tape, a handheld stun gun, a pair of tin snips, an electric chain saw, and a small digital camera. The shorter of the two men saw him looking at the table and said, "We're supposed to get pictures along the way. Seems a little excessive to me, but people like this, you gotta do what you're told. Nothing personal, you understand."

A quiver ran through Virgil's jaw and he was surprised and ashamed at his inability to control its movement. But something else was happening along the way, and when it did, his breathing became more regular and his heart began to slow. If he was at his end, if this was his time, Virgil vowed to himself that he would go with as much courage as he could muster. His regrets were few, though significant. When he closed his eyes he saw Sandy and how they were just beginning their journey, a journey she would have to continue without him. He saw a faceless child and though he could not tell if it were a boy or a girl, he knew it was his and Sandy's. The thought of how he would never know a child's love or the joys of being a grandparent in the later season of his life filled Virgil with a sense of loss greater than he'd ever known. Then he saw his dad and Virgil suddenly realized that any pain he was about to endure would be immeasurable compared to the pain his father would suffer at the loss of his only son. When he spoke again his voice was strong, and for a moment showed no fear.

"No matter what happens to me here, I've got people in my life who won't rest until this is squared. Do you hear me? Whatever you think would happen to you if you walk away now is nothing compared to what it will be if you don't. You won't be caught and convicted. You'll be hunted like animals and someone, somewhere will flip your switch. You won't even see it coming. Samuel Pate isn't worth what you're doing here, don't you see that?"

The taller of the two men walked over and picked up the roll of duct tape from the table. He took the cloth they had used to blindfold him and forced it into Virgil's mouth, then tore a foot-long piece of tape from the roll and placed it over the cloth. "Samuel Pate? You think this is about Ol' Sermon Sam?" He looked at the shorter man and said, "You hear that?"

The shorter man shook his head. "Come on, let's get going, already," he said. "I don't want to be here all night." He then stepped closer and pressed the stun gun against the side of Virgil's ribcage and pulled the trigger.

THE SHOCK OF THE STUN GUN LOCKED HIS BODY IN A rigid arc against the restraints and caused Virgil's bowels and bladder to let go, the air rife with the odor of waste. He felt his heart stammer in his chest and the shock roared through his body like a double-header locomotive steaming through an electrical storm in the middle of the night. Both men jumped back away from Virgil's incontinence and the short man said, "Ah, Christ, look at that. Why don't we just park one in his squash and be done with it?"

"You know why," the tall man said. "We're supposed to do it slow, make it last. He's supposed to suffer before he gets it. Now grab that hose over by the wall and rinse him down. I ain't gonna work standing in his shit."

Virgil was numb from the shock they had just given him and when the water hit he couldn't tell if it was hot or cold. The short man sprayed the fecal matter and urine from the floor while the tall man took pictures, the flash of the camera momentarily lighting the darkened corners of the room.

The short man dropped the hose then picked up the mallet and beat Virgil repeatedly across both thighs, his stomach and chest. One of the blows struck him square on the shin of his leg and the bone cracked like a dead twig yanked from the branch of a tree. He tried to cry out but the rag held in his mouth by the duct tape prevented all but the smallest of sounds from escaping his throat. The tall man shocked him repeatedly with the stun gun and it took no time at all before Virgil lost all control of his body. His heart beat in an irregular fashion from the electrical charge and he was unable to draw even the most ragged of breaths through his nose. His nostrils flared wide as he tried to find his dying purchase of air.

His body hung limp now, his head low on his chest, its weight more than he could manage. His eyes watered without shame and in his quest for air Virgil had swallowed part of the rag and it now blocked his airway completely.

The tall man took another picture then ripped the tape from Virgil's mouth and pulled out the rag. A mixture of blood and drool ran down his chin and dripped across the flat of his stomach before it hit the floor and Virgil knew he was bleeding on the inside. The pain was unbearable, but with the rag out of his mouth he was able to get enough air to remain conscious. Virgil looked at the tall man once again and when he did he saw something behind him that gave him hope, not just for himself, but for all the things he thought he might never experience.

HE GATHERED WHAT LITTLE REMAINING STRENGTH HE possessed and lifted his head to speak. "Murton Wheeler is going to square this."

"I doubt it. Undercover fed's have a way of falling off the map sometimes. We're going to take care of him just like you. Your time here is up, Bub. Like I said, nothing personal, but you went and rattled the wrong cage."

Virgil felt his chest getting heavy and knew he was drowning in his own blood. He spit more blood from his mouth and lifted his head for what he was sure would be the last time. "I know where he is. Wheeler."

The short man had moved over to where the tall man stood and they were now standing side by side, no more than a foot away. "Okay, I'll bite, tough guy. It'll save us the trouble of finding him. Where is he?"

"Right behind you," Murton said. When he raised his arms in front of him, Virgil saw he held two chrome plated semi-automatic thumb busters, one in each hand. The light reflected off the .45's polished finishes and danced around the enclosure like shards from a broken mirror. He pulled the triggers on both guns at the same time, his arms flying high with the recoil of the massive weapons. The two men flew backwards as if they had been tied to a catapult and yanked from the room. Murton ran past and Virgil saw his lips move but the gunshots had temporarily deafened him so he couldn't hear what he said. But he did hear two more shots behind him, one right after the other and when Murton walked back around in front of him, Virgil eventually heard him, though his words seemed slow and sluggish, like someone had pulled the power cord to an old LP record player, the music of his voice getting slower and deeper as the record spun to a stop.

"Don't you die on me, Jonesy. I'm going to get you out of here. Just like before, remember? Hang in there man. Joncsy? God damn it, Jonesy, don't you die, you hear me? Jonesy?"

In the distance Virgil thought he heard a siren, but he didn't know if it was real or imaginary. When Murton cut the ties that held him against the steel beam and lowered him to the floor, Virgil was sure he saw his mother. She stood behind them, her face radiant, the room somehow brighter with her presence. She shadowed Murton's efforts, her hands over the top of his as she directed his movements and though he tried to reach out to them both, Virgil was too weak to move his arms and once again he slipped away, uncertain of his fate, his body warm in the embrace of his past.

CHAPTER TWENTY-ONE

J enny Anderson needed something. Trouble was, she just didn't know what it might be. She was bored. Not in the moment I've-got-nothing-to-do-right-now kind of bored, but bored with her life. She had no children to care for, she and her husband Bob found out long ago they would never conceive a child —her anatomy, not his—but it never bothered them enough to look at radical methods of child bearing like having someone carry a child for them. That just didn't seem right. "Might as well adopt a kid," Bob had said one evening about ten years ago. So they talked about that— twenty minutes all told—before they decided they didn't want the fuss and bother of the paperwork, not to mention the expense.

She didn't work. No, Jenny was not a worker. She was a stay at home wife. Yawn. Had nothing against work, really. Work was a tool. You used it to earn income to provide for yourself and your family. The problem with work was, if it wasn't a career, a real love-what-you-do kind of thing, like a doctor, or lawyer, or in her husband Bob's case, Air Traffic Controller, what was the point? It's not like they needed the money. The economy sucked anyway. Let someone else trade their time for cash minus taxes, thank you.

Friends? Sure, there were a few, but nobody she'd take a bullet for. The truth of the matter was, Jenny was sort of stuck between good ol' Mr. Rock and Sir Hard Place. She liked her solitude, but it sometimes bored her right out of her goddamned gourd.

And why in the world had she just knighted Hard Place?

Jenny walked outside to the pool with only one thing on her mind, the one thing that kept her from losing her mind.

Sex.

Yes sir, if there was one thing that got Jenny through her days it was good old-fashioned sex. She'd knock one off with Bob before he left to play his video games at the airport, and usually hit him up at night before bed, but Bob was, what? Worn out? No, that wasn't it. Fact was, it wasn't about big Bob at all. It was about her. She just couldn't get enough. She'd had a few guys on the side from time to time—one had even been a co-worker of Bob's—but that had fizzled like all the rest when they found out how insatiable her desires were. So most days she did what she liked best. Herself. Then, not long ago, she discovered something that killed her boredom like a big ol can of Bore-B-Gone.

An audience.

She stuck her big toe in the water of their built-in pool, more of a ritual than a gauge of temperature. The gas heater kept the water at a perfect eighty-five degrees throughout the season. A glance at her wristwatch told her the time, and a slow, almost wicked smile tugged at the corners of her mouth. She undid the tie that held her robe closed and let it fall open, the front of her naked body exposed to the expanse of the back yard and the tree line beyond. When she was sure he was out there— she'd caught just a hint of movement at the corner of the tree line, she let the robe fall to the ground and stood nude, her body his to admire.

As K.C. and the boys would say, Jenny was puttin' on her boogie shoes.

THE SIDS WERE IN PLACE AND READY, JUNIOR WITH THE rifle at the edge of the tree line, Senior back near the van, covering the road in case anyone from the cell company showed up. It was unlikely, but it paid to be thorough. When the woman came out to sunbathe, Junior would take care of business and they'd be out of there.

Nothing to it.

JIMMY HAMILTON HAD A SITUATION. ONE OF THOSE genuine you've-got-to-be-kidding-me situations. His house—okay, his parent's house—sat on the other side of the access road from the Anderson's. A tree line, much thinner than the one on the Anderson's side separated his yard from the narrow gravel road. You could cross the road in two quick steps, nothing to it. He'd done it twice a day for the last month since school let out. Sometimes three. Both his parents worked, so he was alone during the days. Weekends sucked because Mr. Anderson was home, as were his own parents. But the weekdays were his. His and Mrs. Anderson's.

Jenny.

Jimmy was naked from the ankles up; the only clothing that covered anything at all on his body of sixteen years was a pair of New Balance sneakers. He had his back and butt pressed tight against the chain link fence that bordered the cell tower's base and it was starting to hurt. He cursed himself for the foolish, even perverted bravado he had displayed. His shorts were on the other side of the road, his side, where he'd left them before crossing over and into the thicker trees. He should have kept them with him, but over the last month he'd grown more and more daring as he looked for ways to increase his level of excitement.

The first time he'd seen her laying nude by the pool he was just out exploring the area, looking for a nice quiet place to spark a doob. He crossed the access road and ventured into the tree line, sat on a log and lit up. When he heard the music he walked a little deeper into the trees and that's when he saw her. She was completely naked, just floating around in the pool on a couple of those foam snakes, one under her arms and one under her knees. Jimmy dropped his doobie, then his shorts. It didn't take much, six or seven tugs before he came and when he did, he let out a moan that caused Mrs. Anderson to raise her head and look at the tree line.

Jimmy froze, an honest to God deer in the headlights freeze. He didn't know if he should run or not. But then something happened, something that made Jimmy hard again almost immediately. Mrs. Anderson got out of the pool, looked toward the trees, right where he was standing with his Johnson in his hand, and waved at him.

Jimmy had to hold onto a tree with his free hand to keep from falling over.

Over the next few weeks he watched Jenny swim, he watched her exercise, he watched her lie in the sun, he watched her masturbate, and once he watched her blow her husband when he came home early from work. That had been the best.

This was only the third time he had ventured over nude. The last two times he had actually stepped out from the tree line and into her backyard and when he did she immediately started pounding away at herself. When he took a few steps forward toward the pool though, she held up her hand, palm out indicating she wanted him to stop. He guessed it was because of his age.

He guessed right. The next time he showed up there

was a hand written note stuck in the branches of the tree he always leaned on. It wasn't addressed to him, but it was for him. It simply said: You're too young. I can't allow anything more. But please keep visiting me. I love to watch and be watched.

Jimmy couldn't believe it. Sure, he was disappointed that he couldn't have her; she was hot, hot, hot. Perfect, in fact. But the please keep visiting me part? He'd take that in a heartbeat. For now anyway. If he could keep her going for another two years, really only a year and a half, he would be old enough to cross the backyard and go all the way.

But right now, today, he had a problem. A genuine OMFG, shriveled up nut-sack sort of problem. He had no sooner begun to cross the road, naked as a jaybird as his grandma would have said, when he saw the white van creeping along through the turn. He just managed to duck behind the cell tower's shack—there wasn't enough time to turn around and dart to his side—as the van came around the bend in the road and made a U-turn right in front of the tower's perimeter fence. He couldn't go back and he couldn't go forward. For the moment, he was trapped.

Naked.

With a boner.

JUNIOR WAS CLOSE ENOUGH SHE COULD HEAR THE NAKED

bitch moaning someone's name. Johnny, or Joey, or something. Couldn't quite make it out. Not that it mattered. Jesus, she thought as she watched the woman masturbate. What was it with people these days? Every last one of them nuttier than a squirrel turd. She thought about parking one right in her biscuit.

Needed a death shot, though.

She took it, too.

JIMMY COULDN'T TAKE IT ANYMORE. HE WAS JUST about to say to hell with it and make a run for his side of the fence when he heard a rustle in the trees to his left. He saw someone moving through, just a shape in the shadows. Then, when she came out of the trees, he peeked around the corner of the fencing and saw her. A woman. A good-looking woman at that, and an older man. Not real old though. His dad's age, maybe. Mid to late fifties. The woman was carrying a rifle. When they got in the van and drove away, Jimmy realized he'd been holding his breath. He memorized the plate on the back of the van and wondered why the woman held a rifle? Was it hunting season? Jimmy didn't know anything about hunting laws, but surely no one would hunt in the suburbs, even ones as secluded as this.

What Jimmy did know about was nature's law. With his boner still long and strong, Jimmy headed for the edge of the Anderson's property line. And why not? The van was gone.

Plus, he hadn't heard a shot, so what was the problemo? Jimmy thought he'd spray some DNA and be on his way. He was aching for it.

The problemo was, when Jimmy saw Jenny's dead body and the puddle of blood that leaked from the hole in her head and into the pool, Jimmy sprayed some DNA all right, just not the kind he'd hoped. He vomited all over his New Balance sneakers, which coincidentally, did not live up to their name. He fell to the ground and tried to convince himself what he saw wasn't real. When he finally managed to stand, covered in puke and leaves and dirt, he started toward his own house. He walked at first, and then he started to run. Kept repeating the plate number of the van over and over in his head.

SID, SR. DROVE THEM OUT OF THE SUBURBS AND INTO town. Junior looked out the window and thought about her lover, Amanda. They had one more shot to take…this was the big one, and then it would be over. She and Amanda could be together at last. They already had their place picked out down in the Keys. With the money Amanda had siphoned off over the last few years, they'd be able to live comfortably, though not extravagantly. But that was all right. Anything to be together and out of Indiana.

"Are you listening to me?" Senior said. "How are we doing on time?"

The governor was holding a press conference to announce his intentions to run for reelection. The media would be there and the entire thing would be captured on television.

"We're doing good," Junior said.

"Keep your head in the game. We're almost through."

"Interesting choice of words," Junior said.

"Don't get all mystical on me now. This is it. After we pop fly boy we're outta here."

"You never did tell me where you're going."

Senior laughed a wicked little laugh. "I'm going to hell, darling. But I'll be going via Mexico. You and that crazy cunt still going to the Keys?"

Junior wished she'd never told him where they were going, but she had, so... "Yeah. Leaving tonight. And don't call her that. We're in love."

"That right? Well, that was something about Sermon Sam, though, huh?"

No shit, Junior thought. "Fuck Sermon Sam. Pedophile asshole." Then a minute or so later. "Maybe you'll see him there. In hell."

"No maybe about it," Senior said. "No maybe at all."

THE PRESS CONFERENCE WAS BEING HELD AT THE USS Indianapolis Memorial, near downtown, on the east side of the canal walk. The Sids parked their van at the back of the lot just north of a medical education building that gave them a clear shot of the podium where the governor would give his speech. The plan was simple. Take the shot, burn the van, then walk away. They had a getaway car parked in the lot, and Senior had the keys in his pocket. They turned into the lot and drove to the back.

They were right on time.

<hr>

INDIANAPOLIS METRO PATROL OFFICER JONATHON Cauliffer drove along Roanoke Street and turned his cruiser onto West North Street and then hung a left on Walnut. He was in the area where the governor was going to give his speech and if he took Walnut to the end, right where it met Ellsworth, he could sit in his squad car, eat his sandwich and watch the big guy give his speech. Another day on the job.

Except the traffic was heavy, and there was no real place to park, so Cauliffer turned around and hooked a left and went back north toward the parking lot adjacent to the education building. He'd be able to see just as well. Either way, he'd have his lunch.

<hr>

SENIOR HAD THE VAN BACKED IN AT THE REAR OF THE lot that gave him a clear view of the memorial and the area where the governor was going to speak. He moved to the back and slid the rear window of the van open just enough to allow the barrel of the rifle to slip through. The lot was virtually empty. They were good to go.

CAULIFFER TURNED INTO THE MOSTLY EMPTY LOT AND parked right next to the building. He unwrapped his sandwich, took a quick bite, and then set it down on the passenger seat. He unbuckled his seatbelt, turned the volume on his radio down, lowered the window on his squad car and settled in. He was on the last day of his tour before his three days off. Four hours to go. He couldn't wait.

THE GOVERNOR STEPPED UP TO THE PODIUM AND turned on his smile for the cameras. "I have a quick announcement to make, and then I'll take a few questions, if you have any, that is." The reporters all laughed politely. "Well, as you all probably already know, I am here today to announce my intentions to run for reelection for the office of governor for the great state of..."

SENIOR PUT THE CROSS HAIRS ON THE GOVERNOR'S

forehead. His finger had just started to pull the trigger when Junior spoke and everything changed. "City cop turning in. He's parking right next to the building."

Senior relaxed his finger. "Son of a bitch."

"Want me to take him?" Junior said. She reached under the seat and pulled the silenced pistol out. "I bet I could get him before he knew what's what. Just like that state boy."

"No, no, hold off. Let's see what he's doing."

"Looks to me like he's eating a sandwich."

"Maybe today's not the governor's day," Senior said.

"It has to be today. We don't have a choice."

Senior thought about it. It did have to be today. The cops would put it together before too long, and they did not want to be around when that happened. The governor had flown the plane, everyone knew that. But it was Rhonda Rhodes' husband, the on-scene fire department commander who wouldn't let anyone in the hotel after the crash. Elle Richardson's husband, the city cop had backed him up. Together they let Sara burn. Goodwin's wife, Tess, was the one who'd switched Sara's schedule to the night shift, otherwise she wouldn't have even been there that day. And Bob Anderson? He worked the tower that morning, so his hot little number of a wife, Jenny, well she had to go too. Now every single one of them would know what it felt like to Sid, Sr., what it still felt like every damned day of his life.

The weight of it all had been building for such a long time that Sid felt like he might bust. He laid the rifle down, turned and spoke, his voice as hollow as Junior had ever heard. He was always going to tell her, but he was also going to wait until after they were done with the governor. But now...

"There's something you should know, Sidney. About the governor."

"What?" she said. "I know everything there is to know."

"No, you don't."

"What else is there? He crashed his plane into the hotel and Mom burned to death," Junior said as she pointed to where the governor stood talking to the media. "Nobody went in to rescue her or anyone else, all while that son of a bitch floated down in his parachute and landed without a scratch." She shook her head. "Now pick up your gun, take the damned shot and I'll go take care of the cop." Junior reached for the door handle but Senior caught her arm and stopped her. The pressure of the situation was almost too much for Junior to take.

"*What?*"

"Listen to me," Senior said. He practically hissed it at her. "There's something you don't know. Something I should have told you a long time ago."

"Well, what the hell is it? We're out of time, here."

So Senior told her...

CAULIFFER FINISHED HIS SANDWICH AND FOR THE FIRST

time noticed the van at the back of the lot. It was white. He scrolled through his computer and checked the logs. There was something about a BOLO for a white van. There was a plate number too, he thought. He found the report and read through the details.

⸺

...AND WHEN JUNIOR HEARD THE WORDS, SHE SNAPPED. Her life had been a sham, everything she knew to be true, everything that made her who she was and what she had become was a lie. She didn't think, she didn't weigh her options, she just did what she thought anyone would do, something that she was very familiar and very comfortable with after all these years. She raised her gun and fired. Senior took one in the forehead.

Then two in the heart.

⸺

WHEN CAULIFFER SAW THAT THE MAKE AND MODEL OF the van matched the BOLO he picked up the microphone to call for backup, but then just as quickly set it back in its holder. Check the plate first, he thought. Lots of white vans in the city. He opened his door, got out, and brushed the crumbs from his uniform shirt. He was about half way across the lot when the side door of the van flew open and a woman jumped out with a gun.

He pulled his service revolver and yelled. "Police! Drop the weapon!"

The woman spun and fired a single shot at Cauliffer. The bullet hit the handheld radio clipped to his belt and when it did a shard from the plastic casing fragmented upward and sliced into Cauliffer's forehead, just above his left eye. He ducked, winced at the pain, and momentarily lost sight of the woman. He thought about running back to his squad car to call for help, but then he remembered that the governor was only a few hundred yards away.

And the woman with the gun was running that way.

Cauliffer started after her, one eye pinched shut and full of blood.

JUNIOR HEARD THE COP YELL FOR HER TO STOP, OR freeze or some such shit that the cops were always yelling. She spun around, fired once to slow the cop, and then ran toward the governor. She was still on autopilot, the thoughts of what her father had just told her spinning through her brain.

Her father.

She'd been lied to, abandoned, neglected, abused, and rejected her entire life. But it was all about to stop.

It was all about to end.

CAULIFFER WAS GAINING ON THE WOMAN, BUT IT wasn't going to be enough. He wanted to stop and take a shot, but with one eye full of blood he knew the chances of hitting his target were slim at best. And if he missed she'd be on top of the governor before he could do anything about it. His radio was useless, so Cauliffer did the only thing he could think to do, something that at the academy they told you never to do because of the danger to yourself or others. Cauliffer fired three warning shots into the air.

WHEN JUNIOR HEARD THE SHOTS BEHIND HER SHE turned to look back, and when she did she tripped in the grass and fell to the ground. The cop was about thirty yards back and coming hard. Junior knew then that the governor would live and she would not. There would be no comfortable and peaceful villa in the Keys with her lover, Amanda. There would be nothing except a jail cell and ultimately a needle in her vein. She scrambled to her feet and turned toward the cop.

WHEN THE GOVERNOR'S THREE-MAN PROTECTION detail heard the shots, two of them took the governor to the ground and held him there while the third ran toward the sounds of the gunfire. Most of the media people were on the ground as well, but one of the cameramen, a veteran from the war and no stranger to the sound of gunfire put his camera on his shoulder and followed the cop. He got the entire thing on tape.

CAULIFFER SAW HER FALL AND HE KEPT RUNNING UNTIL he saw her get up. He stopped, leveled his gun and yelled one more time for her to drop the weapon. He saw her start to bring the gun up, saw the crazy light in her eyes and pulled the trigger. The nine millimeter caught her center mass and Sidney Wells, Jr. dropped in a heap in the grass. Cauliffer ran over and secured her weapon, then sat down in the grass and tried to wipe the blood from his eye.

When it was over the governor and his protection detail pushed their way through the circle of cops and chaos. The governor walked up to Cauliffer and shook his hand. "Officer Cauliflower, you've saved my life."

Cauliffer shook the governor's hand. "It's, uh, Cauliffer, sir."

The governor reddened at his repeated gaff. "Yes, yes, of course. I keep getting that wrong, don't I?"

The cameraman got the entire exchange. It made the evening news and went viral on the Internet within hours.

Indiana Governor...Saved By Cauliflower.

"THAT'S ALL RIGHT, SIR," CAULIFFER SAID, AS HE WIPED more blood from his eyes.

"What the hell happened?"

"It was a woman. She was headed your way with a gun. She fired at me. I chased her here and when she tried to fire again I took the shot."

"A woman? Where is she?"

Cauliffer pointed to the other grouping of cops. "Right over there," he said.

The governor walked over and looked at the body of the woman on the ground. When he saw her face he turned away, then vomited all over his shoes.

That went viral as well.

CHAPTER TWENTY-TWO

Virgil swam in and out of consciousness, or imagined he did over a period of time that may have been a few minutes or a few days. People shimmered in and out of focus, fuzzy around the edges, like images on a big screen television with poor reception. When he was finally able to hold his eyes open and keep them focused, he found himself on his back in an uncomfortable bed in a darkened room. A tube was taped to his right arm that led to a needle poked into a vein on the back of his hand, held in place with more tape. His left leg was in a cast that extended from the tips of his toes to the bottom of his knee. As soon as he saw the cast the pain brought him fully awake.

"He's up," someone said. "Better get the doc."

A door opened and a shaft of light from the hall snuck into the room then faded away as the door hissed closed and clicked against the latch. Sandy leaned in close and brushed the hair off of Virgil's forehead. "Hey, tough guy," she said. "About time you woke up." Mason stood right behind her.

It was all coming back now, the attack, being tied to the steel girder, the beating, everything. Virgil wanted to ask a dozen different questions, but when he opened his mouth to speak, all that came out was: "Hurts."

Mason stepped forward. "Cora was here, Son. She stepped out to get the doctor. There's a button for the pain. Do you want me to press it?"

Virgil nodded and his dad pushed the button. After a few seconds, the morphine made its way through the IV and Virgil felt it beat the pain back, though not completely. He tried to sit up a little, and then wished he hadn't.

"Where am I? What happened?"

The door opened again and Cora came into the room, a doctor in tow. "You're at Methodist Hospital, Detective," the doctor said. He took a pen light from his pocket and checked Virgil's eyes. "If you had to rate your pain on a scale of one to ten, what would you say the number is?"

Virgil tried to blink the light away. "Uh, I don't know. Eight now, I guess. My dad just pushed a button."

The doctor inspected the IV line and adjusted the drip. "I upped the dose a little. You can push this button every seven minutes if you have to, and you'll probably have to for the next twenty-four hours or so. Did anyone tell you what we did?"

"He just woke up," Sandy said. "We haven't had a chance."

The doctor wrote something on a chart while he spoke. "You apparently took quite a thrashing. You've got a broken rib on your left side that punctured a lung. You lost quite a bit of blood and I don't mind telling you that you had us all a little worried there for a while. Your chest is taped and we've repaired the internal damage so you're going to be just fine, but you've got a nice scar on your belly that will make a great conversation starter at the beach. The discomfort you feel in your leg is what's going to be the worst of it. We had to pin it, so it's going to take a while to heal. You'll need physical therapy. The pain you're feeling now is from the surgeries, and it'll get better over the next few days, but you're going to be pretty sore for a while. That cast is going to drive you bonkers for about eight weeks. You'll know when the weather is about to change, too."

The morphine filled Virgil's brain like a convective fog over a pond. "Okay."

"Your leg is broken, Son," Mason said. "The surgery took almost four hours."

"We used an artificial bone graft material, along with a few pins and screws," the doctor said. "Had lots of success with it in the past, so you're going to be okay. There's always a slight chance of infection, but we got you cleaned out pretty good. I'll check on you in the morning. The nurses will be in to bother you every time you're about to fall asleep. Good night."

Virgil reached out and found the pain button and pushed it. Twice. He looked at Cora and motioned her over to the bed. "Where's my gun and badge?"

"We've got them, Jonesy. They were there, at the scene. Don't worry about it."

"Okay."

"Listen, Jonesy," Cora said. "I'm going to get out of here and let you rest. Sandy'll fill you in on everything. Donatti and Rosencrantz were here earlier while you were still out. They said to let you know they'd be back in the morning. The governor sends his best. I'll check on you tomorrow."

Virgil could feel the morphine flowing through his body as if his blood were being heated then recycled through his veins. "Okay."

After Cora left Sandy moved closer and stood at the edge of the bed. "My god, Virgil, you could have been killed."

He was drifting and there were still questions Virgil wanted to ask but he couldn't seem to get them out. "I heard the sirens, Sandy. I saw my mom, too. She was there. I think she was there with me the entire time."

Mason was sitting in a visitor's chair in the corner of the room, and when he heard what his son said he walked over to the side of the bed. "What was that, Virg? Say that again, will you?"

But the drugs pulled him back under before he could answer.

THE DOCTOR WAS RIGHT. THE NURSES DID COME IN every time he fell asleep. It got to the point where Virgil thought they were all sadists. The doctor ordered rest, but then they didn't let you get any. But the next time he woke on his own the light of the day peeked through the slats of the window blinds and he could hear the business end of patient care coming alive from the other side of the door. Sandy was curled in a ball on a recliner next to the window.

His leg still hurt like hell, but it was not as bad as the previous night. It was more isolated and not over his entire body like it had been before. He found the call button for the nurse and pressed it, and when she came into the room he asked her about switching to a pain pill instead of the IV drip. "It's making me pretty loopy," Virgil said.

"I'll have to clear it with the doctor," she said. "But between you and me, I don't think you're ready just yet. In the meantime, don't be a hero. Hit that pain button if you have to. Loopy ain't all bad, honey."

A short time later an orderly wheeled in a breakfast tray and set the cart next to the bed. All the in and out woke Sandy. She stretched, yawned, walked over to the bed, and leaned in and kissed Virgil, hard, on the lips.

"You should have gone home last night," he said.

"Would you have?"

"No."

"So, okay then."

His leg was throbbing now, the pain worse as he became fully awake. "I was thinking about last night. The way you called me Virgil."

The door opened and Rosencrantz and Donatti walked in. "Of course she called you Virgil. That's your name, isn't it?" He looked over at Donatti. "Isn't that his name?"

Donatti nodded. "Yep. Hey Small, what's shaking? Did you know his middle name is Francis?"

"About time you woke up," Rosencrantz said as he lifted the lid on the food tray. "What's for breakfast?" He put the lid back down. "Wow, are they trying to cure you or kill you?"

"You know, you don't get jack for workmen's comp in Indiana," Donatti said. "I think you're faking."

"Yeah, definitely faking," Rosencrantz said.

"Hey, is it true you can predict when it's going to rain, now?" Donatti said. "I heard TV 8 is looking for a new weatherman."

"I'll bet they're giving you some good shit for the pain. Can I have some?" Rosencrantz said.

Virgil looked at Sandy with a 'help me' expression on his face, but when she held her hands up in a 'what can you do?' gesture, he did the only logical thing he could think of...he pressed the pain button again.

THAT MADE THE ROOM SPIN, LIKE HE WAS CAUGHT IN A vortex. Rosencrantz and Donatti were standing under the television, their heads tilted up toward the set, watching something on the screen. A few minutes later when the rush of the morphine tapered off, Virgil looked at Sandy and motioned for her to lean in closer. "Did you hear what I was saying before Mutt and Jeff walked in?"

"Yes, I did," she said. "But it wasn't last night. That was five days ago, Virgil."

Rosencrantz turned his head and said, "What was last night?"

Virgil ignored him, but Sandy turned her head and said, "We're talking about something else. Last night was nothing."

"You know how many times I've heard a woman tell me that?" Donatti said. Sandy shot him a look and then turned her attention back to Virgil.

"What are you talking about?" Virgil said. "What do you mean it was five days ago?"

Sandy had her hand on his leg. "You've sort of been in and out over the last few days."

"What?" Virgil didn't believe it. "What day is this?"

"It's Friday," Sandy said.

Donatti looked over at Sandy and said, "Hey, am I Mutt or Jeff? I think I'm Jeff. I'm Jeff, right?"

The door opened and a nurse came in and told Virgil the doctor had given the okay for Oxycontin instead of the morphine drip for the pain but the Oxycontin would probably, in her words, bind him up some. "Not much worse than the morphine, though."

"That's all right," Rosencrantz said. "He's full of shit anyway."

Virgil thought if the food in here didn't kill him, the cop humor probably would. When he looked at Sandy she mouthed a silent *I love you* and he felt his eyes water at the edges.

It became quiet in the room for a minute, then Rosencrantz looked at Donatti and said, "I kinda like the way she calls him Virgil, don't you?"

Sandy shook her head, then stood and said, "Hey guys, I think we need to let Virgil get his rest. What do you say?"

"Yeah," Donatti said. "She's right. Virgil's tired."

Rosencrantz turned and gave him a little finger wave. "Okay, bye, Virgil. We'll see you tomorrow."

Sandy waved them out. "I'll catch up with you guys later," she said.

When they were out of the room, Virgil pulled himself up in the bed a little. He could feel the tape around his ribcage. "See what you've started," he said.

"I'll talk to them," Sandy said.

"Ah geez, don't do that."

"Well what do you want me to do?"

The Oxycontin was working already—Virgil could feel the buzz—but he was not drowsy like he'd been with the morphine drip. The pain was still present, but it was in the background, like it was hiding inside a closet.

"It feels like...like everything is moving too fast. I was tied up and beaten and it feels like it all happened just this morning."

"We don't have to talk about this now, you know."

"I think I need to."

Sandy sat on the edge of the bed and put her hand in his. "Are you sure you're up for it?"

"I'm not really sure. I think there might be a lot I don't remember. In fact, most of it is blank right now, that part of it, I mean. I remember eating lunch at the diner, then nothing until I woke up tied to the post or beam or whatever it was."

"And when you woke up?"

He closed his eyes and told Sandy what he remembered about the beatings and the torture with the stun gun, seeing Murton and how he killed the two men, and then how he saw his mother. When he opened his eyes tears were running down Sandy's cheeks and when he reached up to wipe them away she took his hand in both of hers and held it tight against her face. She then kissed the tips of his fingers and held his hand in her lap. Virgil thought she might ask about his mom, but she shifted the direction of the conversation.

"We've got an ID on the men. Their names were Collins and Hicks."

"What about Murton? Where is he?"

"That's a little more complicated," she said.

"I'll bet."

"I might be able to help you with that," Agent Gibson

said. He was standing in the doorway, leaning against the frame. He pushed himself upright with his shoulder and said, "May I come in?"

Virgil nodded to Gibson and he walked further into the room. He looked at Sandy and said, "Would you mind if I spoke with Detective Jones in private?"

"That's not necessary," Virgil said.

"It's okay, Virgil," Sandy said. "I've got work to do. A lot has happened. I'll check back on you later and fill you in then. Get some rest." She leaned down and kissed him on the lips, then turned and stared at Gibson, her expression a challenge for him to comment on their private life. But he just nodded at her and after she walked out he looked at Virgil and said, "How are you feeling?"

"I've been better."

"I checked your records. Saw you were in the sandbox."

"That's a term only a soldier would use."

He pulled a chair close to the bed then sat down, a pocket of air held in the side of his mouth. "So maybe I was there."

"In what capacity?"

He chuckled at the question before he answered. "Let's just say I wasn't dressed in camouflage and humping a pack. But that was a long time ago, wasn't it? Right now you're wondering about Murton Wheeler."

"I've been wondering about Murton Wheeler for a long time."

"So like I said, I can probably help you with that."

Virgil thought for a moment before he spoke. "That day on the street, outside the bank...the bomb scare...the first time we met? You told me Murton was part of an ongoing investigation. You made it sound like *he* was the one being investigated."

"Did I? I don't recall. It depends on your perspective, I guess."

"So he's with the G?"

"Something like that."

"What does that mean?"

"I'll let him explain it. Believe me when I tell you though, Detective, he's paid a tremendous price for his country. I personally owe him a debt I'll never be able to repay, but that's another story. From what I gather, that puts you and me in the same boat."

"Where is he?"

"Out in the hall, waiting to come in," Gibson said.

MURTON WALKED INTO THE ROOM AND STOOD ABOUT halfway between the door and the bed. Virgil pushed the button on the control panel attached to the rail and elevated the bed into a sitting position. They stared at each other for a minute, neither one of them sure of what to say. It might have been the pain medicine, or it might have been the nervous tension, but Virgil felt the corner of his mouth turn upwards, then before he knew it they were both smiling.

"You're a fed?"

"Well, I was," he said. "But not anymore. I put in my papers this morning."

"Why?"

He laughed without humor. "Which why are you asking me about? The why did I disappear? Or the why didn't I tell you what was really happening in my life? Or the why I had to let everyone, including you, your parents, and even my girlfriend think I was a criminal and a convicted felon?"

"I'm sorry about Amy."

Murton stayed quiet for a long time before he spoke. "We buried her yesterday. Her mom slapped me in the face at the service. She thought her death was my fault. You know what? She was right, but for all the wrong reasons. After the service I told her who I was, who I really was and she didn't believe me. So I pulled out my badge and handed it to her and you know what she did? She fainted. Just like that. I thought I killed her. I've been under too long Jonesy. I had to get out. I let my job get in the way of my girlfriend's well being and it cost her and my unborn child their lives."

"Ah, Murt, I'm sorry. I don't know what else to say. Goddamn. I've been an asshole. I'm so sorry, man."

They sat there with that for a while, slowly coming to terms that they'd spent the first half of their lives together as best friends and brothers, and the last half under a flag of deception that drove them apart.

"Well, at least Pate got his, huh?" Murton said.

"What? What do you mean?"

"You're kidding, right? You mean no one told you?"

"Told me what, Murt? No one's told me anything."

"Ah, that's beautiful, man. After everything that's happened, I get to tell you. Guess you haven't been watching the news. Pate's dead, Jonesy. Yesterday morning at the taping of his show. Except it wasn't just a taping. Because of everything that's happened, he convinced the network to run a live special. The place was packed. He stood up there on the pulpit and confessed all of it. He had tears running down his cheeks and everything. It was like every other preacher you've ever seen on TV when they bare their soul and confess their sins, except ol' Sermon Sam outdid them all."

"What do you mean?"

"After he confessed to burning his church in Houston, and taking responsibility for the deaths of Franklin Dugan, and Amy, and trafficking in child pornography, he stuck a gun in his mouth and blew the back of his head all over the choir. All on live TV."

"You said with everything that's been happening. What else did I miss?"

"Plenty. A city cop who now has the unfortunate nickname of Cauliflower shot your sniper to death and saved the governor as well."

"*What?*"

"Say, I don't mean to change the subject, but I've got to tell you something else," he said. "When I was cutting you down, I could hear your mom's voice. In my head, I mean. It's like she was telling me exactly what to do. Can you believe that, man?"

———————

VIRGIL WAS STILL PROCESSING WHAT MURTON HAD told him when a physical therapist came in the room and explained that it was necessary to get up and move around. Murton said good-bye, explaining that he had six or seven reams of paperwork to complete and would look in on him later. Then, before he left, he walked over to the bed and kissed Virgil on his forehead. "Never stopped lovin' you, brother," he said. Virgil's lips trembled, but he couldn't get any words out. "You're welcome," Murton said, then ruffled the top of Virgil's head like they were kids again and walked out the door.

The physical therapist watched the exchange in silence. She was a short sassy brunette who looked like she should be working for an ice cream parlor or maybe a pet supply store.

"You can't see it, but there's a rubber knob on the bottom of your cast, right under the heel of your foot. Like the stopper on the end of these crutches," she said, holding up one of the crutches. "When you're moving around, I want you to keep as much weight off of your leg as possible. But, if you have to put any weight on it, keep it on the knob. That's what it's for. That, and to make sure you don't slip and fall. She tried a smile on so Virgil tried one right back at her, and when his scar lit up, she momentarily jerked the crutch across the front of her body, like a shield. "Uh, anyway," she said, "here, let me help you. Swing your legs off the side of the bed, but don't try to stand, yet."

"Just give me a minute, will you?" Virgil said. He gathered himself together and sat upright on the side of the bed and with the therapist's help managed to stand mostly on his good leg, the broken one held at an odd angle at the knee to prevent it from touching the floor.

"Good, good. That's good," she said. "Now straighten your knee and let the knob on the bottom of your cast rest on the floor, but don't put any weight on it. I just want you to get a feel for where it is down there." Virgil did what she asked, but when he did, the pain flared and the room spun. The therapist grabbed his arm and eased him back down on the bed. "I said not to put any weight on it."

Virgil nodded, his breath whistling through his teeth. "I didn't."

"Well, maybe you did a little. Do you want me to see about getting you a wheelchair?"

"No, I do not want a wheelchair."

"All right, then, come on, let's try again. It only gets better from here."

"I can believe that." He gripped the handle of the crutches, the therapist standing next to him like a gymnastics spotter. He leaned forward, put the weight on his good leg and pulled himself up.

"All right. Now, let's try moving around the room a

little. You look like a pretty strong guy. Just remember, the key to using crutches is in the forearms, not your armpits, okay? Keep your leg bent, and use both crutches at the same time. Step with your good leg, then follow with your arms, okay?"

"Okay, okay," he said, hating her already. But after a few minutes of her help and some painful practice, he had to admit, she had him moving around fairly well.

She handed him some kind of waiver stating that she had demonstrated the proper use of the crutches and asked him to sign at the bottom. Her parting words were, "Remember, if you stumble and think you're going to fall, and you probably will, just let your body go limp. Don't try to save yourself. Just relax and go ahead and let yourself go. You're more likely to re-injure if you try to save yourself than if you just go ahead and let it happen."

For some reason, her statement made Virgil think about his relationships with his dad, Murton, and Sandy.

———

A FEW HOURS LATER, ONE OF THE NURSES CAME IN AND told him his ticket out would be to show the doctor he could get around on his own, and that was all the motivation Virgil F. Jones required. He picked up the crutches and made his way toward the door, leaning against the jamb for a few minutes until the hall was mostly clear before venturing out. It wasn't too bad, the moving around, but the physical therapist was right; the key was to keep the weight off the leg. He went up and down the hall a few times, stopping to rest only once at the opposite end of the corridor. The hardest part really was holding his leg in the air, bent at the knee, and it didn't take long before the burn in his thigh was a little too much. There was a couch at the end of the hallway next to the elevators, so Virgil decided to sit and watch the business end of the hospital for a while.

As soon as he sat down he knew it was a mistake. The couch was lower than he thought—going down was not too bad—but once seated he knew he wouldn't be able to get back up without help. The nurses' station was at the other end of the hall, so he'd have to either yell for help or wait until someone happened by who could help him.

Smooth, Jonesy, he thought. He closed his eyes for a while and when he opened them back up his dad was sitting next to him and the look on Mason's face told Virgil they were thinking the same thing. "This place will kill you, you know that?" Mason said. "You remember your Uncle Bob?"

"No, not really. I might remember the name, but that's about it."

Mason nodded. "Yeah, I'm not surprised. You were pretty young when he died. He was your mother's uncle, your great uncle. He was a mortician. Had his own funeral home up in Kokomo. After he passed, his family sold out to a conglomerate, but I was talking to him one time, this was years ago, before you were even born I think, and you know what he told me? He told me that in the funeral home industry, they call it death care. I always thought that was the damnedest thing, death care.

"I'd sit up here with your mother, just one floor above this one while they pumped that poison into her veins trying to kill the cancer, and in the end all they did was make the last few months of her life more miserable than they already were. Every time we'd come in here I'd think about that conversation with Uncle Bob. They might call this health care, Virg, but it's really all the same thing sometimes." Then, like the concept of a segue was foreign to him, he finished with, "So, when they letting you out?"

"Tomorrow, I think. Want to help me back to my room?"

"You bet," Mason said. "You bet I do."

They took their time going down the hall. "Delroy and Robert are going back to Jamaica for a week, so I'm going to close the bar to sand down and refinish the bar top." When Virgil said he'd stop by to help if he could, Mason laughed and told him not to worry about it.

When they finally made it back to the room, they stood next to the bed for a moment, and Virgil looked at his dad and said, "I can't explain it, Dad, but it was her. She was standing right behind him and her hands were over the top of his. She helped him untie me and get me down. She was smiling at me, Dad. What do you think of that?"

"You were bleeding out from the inside, Virg. The doctors said you had about two and a half minutes left by the time they got you here. The mind can play tricks on you when you're in that kind of shape."

"I've been in that bad of shape before, you know."

"I know. You saw what you saw. Was it real to you?"

"Yeah, it was."

He opened his mouth to say something, but no words came out. Then he did something he hadn't done in almost forty years, an act that brought tears to his eyes.

He helped his son to bed.

A SHORT WHILE LATER THE NURSE CAME IN AND VIRGIL thought the nature of the conversation that followed must have made her think he might be suffering from brain damage.

"Do you believe in ghosts?" he asked her.

She had her hand on his wrist, checking his pulse. She held up a finger in a wait a minute gesture then said, "Sorry, I was counting. What was that you just asked me?"

"Never mind," Virgil said, but then he asked her something else. "I keep hearing this muffled little happy birthday tune. Is anyone else hearing it, or is it just me?"

The nurse laughed. "That's from the maternity ward. It's one floor below us. Every time a baby is born the new father gets to push a button behind the nurses' station and it plays the first few notes of happy birthday over the loudspeaker on that floor. You can hear it on this floor because they're right below us." She wrapped the blood pressure cuff around his arm just above the elbow and pumped the bulb, the needle on the indicator bouncing back and forth. He waited until she was done before he spoke again.

"I was wondering. Is there any way that I could move one floor up?"

"What?" the nurse asked. Why would you want to do that? That's the cancer ward."

"I know," Virgil said. She stared at him, a look of confusion on her face, and then walked out of the room.

CHAPTER TWENTY-THREE

The next morning when he woke, Virgil wiggled his toes a little and the pain pulled him from the clutches of sleep like a demented tour guide with a cruel agenda. His mouth tasted like at some point in the night he'd sworn off hospital food and eaten his pillow instead. And he had to pee.

Sandy showed up, said hello, then went to check with the nurses' station to see when the doctor might stop by to release Virgil and when she came back into the room, she told him that the nurse said the doctor was going to be delayed. "He got called into an emergency surgery."

"Ah man. Any idea how long?"

Sandy shook her head. "They didn't know. Listen, I talked to your dad this morning. I'm going to go pick him up and we're going to get your truck from the station and get it back to your house. I'll be back to take you home after I drop him off. That okay?"

"Sure," Virgil said. "Grab my case notes from my desk will you?"

"Virgil..."

"What? I'm just going to be sitting around. Might as well do the paperwork. By the way, how'd my truck get back to the station?"

"Rosie drove it over there and put it in the lot."

"Oh man, you let Rosie drive my truck?"

"Yeah, why?"

"Have you ever seen his car?"

"You worry too much, Jonesy. Hey, you're going home today. Treat me right and maybe I'll dress up in a little nurse's uniform for you, make you forget all about the paperwork. You know, show you what a real sponge bath is like." She winked at him. "See you in an hour or so, boyfriend."

Boyfriend. He liked that.

———————

LATER THAT SAME AFTERNOON SANDY WAS BACK AND the doctor came in with a list of instructions for his release. The nurse who was with him scheduled an appointment for a follow-up visit the next week and after another hour and a half of preparations and paperwork, Virgil was informed he was free to go. Forty-five minutes later they were back at Virgil's place.

Sandy turned on the lights and generally woke the

place up while Virgil settled onto the couch and tried to get comfortable. "What can I get you?" she asked.

The time had gotten away from him and the ride from the hospital had taken its toll. "I'm getting behind on the pain. I could use a couple of pills."

She brought him the medicine then slipped her hand into Virgil's and said, "So, what's next?"

"Is that a big question, or a little one?"

"What do you think?" she said.

"I think it's a big one."

"You'd probably be right," Sandy said. "If it were a little one, I'd say something like, 'how about a pizza?' And then you'd say, 'sure, what do you like?' And I'd say—"

"Okay, I get it. The truth of it is, I don't know what's next. But you know what?"

"What?"

"I don't want to know. I know where we've been, I know where we are, and I know what I want. You're here...we're here, and we're together. That's what matters to me right now."

Sandy pulled her feet up under her and laid her head on Virgil's shoulder. After a few minutes, she lifted her head and said, "You know, for a while, you're going to need someone here to help you."

"Yeah, I was kind of thinking the same thing."

They sat there with that for a little while, then Sandy said, "You could ask Donatti."

"That won't work. He's married, remember? His wife won't let him come over anymore."

"Well, what about Rosie?"

"Naw, he'd just drink all my beer. Plus, he's kind of a slob. I've got a certain standard I like to maintain around here."

"Hmm. Guess you're out of luck, then," Sandy said.

"Yeah. I guess so. Too bad there isn't someone, you know, who could sort of move in for a while and keep an eye on things. Help me around. Like that."

"Yeah, that is too bad," Sandy said.

"Just about anyone would do, really."

"You know, I'm pretty busy and everything," Sandy said. "But if I moved some stuff around on my schedule, I bet I could do it. And look, I don't want to seem too forward or anything, because I'm not really that kind of girl, but I went ahead and put a bag together thinking you might want me to stay for a few days or something."

"You put a bag together, huh?"

"Yep."

"Is it a big bag?"

"Well, it's big enough that I've got options."

"A girl's gotta have options."

"Yep, options are good."

Virgil tried to look serious. "Well, the closet is pretty full. I guess I could give you a drawer."

"Really? A drawer? You mean I'd get my very own drawer?"

"Well sure. That's just the kind of guy I am."

Sandy grabbed his pants at the top by his waist and

bunched them up in her fist. "I've got your drawers, mister."

And with that, Virgil forgot all about his past, both the distant and the recent and for a while, even the pain in his leg. It all melted away against the warmth of a place where no one is judged, where the mind, body, spirit, and soul are all one and the same.

WHEN HE WOKE THE NEXT MORNING, VIRGIL WAS alone in bed, the throbbing of his leg in time with the beat of his heart. Sandy came in a few minutes later carrying a tray with coffee and juice, her robe open in front of her body, its edges barely covering the swell of her breasts.

"How you feeling, cowboy?" She set the tray down on the night table next to the bed and leaned over and kissed him good morning.

Virgil looked at her in the robe, the curve of her hips, the little space between the tops of her thighs when she stood with her legs together, the dangled jewel of her belly ring, her hair tangled from sleep. He took her hand and guided it to his stomach, then gently pushed her further down. "This is how I'm feeling," he said. "Since you asked, and all."

And then the morning was mostly gone too.

LATER, AFTER THEY'D BOTH GOTTEN CLEANED UP AND dressed for the day, they sat across from each other at the kitchen table, Virgil's leg propped up under a pillow on the chair next to him. It felt good to have it elevated for a while, but then it'd start to bark at him and he'd have to set it down on the floor. Then that would become uncomfortable too, so he'd prop it back up again. The back and forth was driving him nuts.

"Wait till it starts itching," Sandy said. "That'll drive you mad. Listen, I need to talk to you about something."

Uh-oh.

"Yesterday, when I went to your office to get the case notes you wanted I ran into Cora. We had an interesting conversation."

"Is this about us?"

"Yeah, it is," Sandy said. "I know we didn't have a chance to talk about it—what she said to you a few days ago on the phone, but she laid it out pretty clear for me. We have to choose."

"I'm sorry. I'll talk to her."

She reached across the table and took his hand. "Let me finish, okay. It's not all bad. You probably don't know this, but about six years ago, and every year since, I've been trying to get on with the Indiana Law Enforcement Academy over in Plainville."

"Is that right?"

"Yeah. And guess who greased the wheels for me."

"Who?"

"The governor."

"What? You asked the governor to help you?"

"Well, I sort of mentioned it in passing."

"Sandy, he's a pretty powerful guy. Are you sure you want to get in bed with him?"

"You're the only one I'm getting into bed with, Virgil."

"You know what I mean. So I take it there's an opening at the Academy?"

"Yep. Director of Training. He says it's mine if I want it."

"Just like that?"

"Well, he said they'd have to keep the posting up, let others apply, all that business, but other than maintaining appearances, yeah, it's mine. I just have to say the word."

"What kind of timeline are we talking about?"

"The current director leaves in thirty days. They'd want me in time for that."

Virgil took his leg from the chair and placed it back on the floor. Things were moving faster than he thought they would. He and Sandy had something though. Something strong. Still, could he ask her to leave her current position for something completely new and different just so they could be together as a couple? It didn't seem fair.

Then, as if she could read his mind, she said, "It's just a job, Virgil. I know it might feel like things are moving pretty quick right now, but you and I both know that's nobody's business but our own. If I have to take this job so we can be together without the headache of hiding our relationship or dealing with someone else's bullshit bureaucracy, then that's what I think I should do. I won't do it unless you say you want me to, but I hope you do."

Virgil nodded, and the words were out of his mouth almost before he realized it. "I do."

"Say that again, would you?"

He smiled at her. "I do."

"I like the way that sounds. Big words though for a guy that only gives a girl one drawer."

"Yeah, well, about that. I was kidding about the closet. It's mostly empty."

"Yeah, I know. I looked."

"So there's probably something I should tell you," Virgil said. "I knew you applied for the job."

"What? How?"

"Well, I know quite a few people over at the Academy, and when they saw your paperwork come through one of them called me. I think you wasted a favor with the governor. From what they told me, unless you blew the interview or something, they were going to hire you anyway."

"Virgil..."

CHAPTER TWENTY-FOUR

The next day, late in the morning Virgil was back at the kitchen table, his case notes and files spread out around him. He'd tried working at his desk, but there were two problems: one, there was not enough desk space for everything he wanted to look at, and two, he just couldn't get comfortable. There wasn't a good way to prop his leg up. Sandy helped him move everything to the kitchen, then kissed him goodbye before she left to go downtown and hammer out the details of her new position with the academy.

Two hours later and halfway through his reports the phone rang. He followed the ringing and saw the phone on the end table in the other room. Should have thought about that. The machine was turned off, and by the time he got the crutches under him and over to the phone the ringing had stopped. He brought up the caller ID, saw who it was, and punched the number back in.

"Marion County Prosecutor's Office. How may I direct your call?"

"Hi, Detective Virgil Jones, for Preston Elliott, please."

"One moment, Detective, I'll see if he's in."

Virgil started to tell the receptionist that he knew Elliott was in because he'd just missed his call, but she had already clicked off. But then she clicked right back on, again. "I'm sorry, did I cut you off? I think you were saying something."

"No, no, that's fine. I was just saying I just missed his call, is all."

"Very well, sir. One moment."

Virgil thought he could hear her eyes rolling on the other end of the phone. A few seconds later, the line clicked again and Elliott picked up. "Jonesy, thanks for calling back."

"Sorry I didn't get to the phone. Takes me a little longer to get around than I'm used to. How are you, Preston?"

"I'm doing well. The question is, how are you?"

"Pretty good," Virgil said, wincing at his own bad grammar. "Behind on my paperwork, though. I'm guessing that's why you're calling?"

"I knew there was a reason they called you detective. We want to get everything filed and get this one off the books. How much time do you need for your reports, you being crippled and all?"

Instead of answering, Virgil said, "How many times

have you watched the tape?"

"The one where Pate takes the back of his head off, or the one with the governor tossing his lunch?"

"The one with Pate," Virgil said, hoping the sarcasm was not as obvious as it sounded in his head.

"Only twice, unless you count the nightmares I've been having."

"Anything jump out at you."

"Like what?"

"That's what I'm asking you, Preston. Anything at all?"

"Nothing other than the obvious," Elliott said. "He cried a river, admitted he was not only a sexual deviant but a pedophile as well, admitted torching his Houston church and then, well, I guess you know the rest of it. He punched his own ticket. Case closed."

"Yeah, I guess we've seen the same tape, then."

"What is it, Jonesy?" Some impatience.

"It's not what he admitted. It's what he didn't."

"What do you mean?"

"Why pack every seat in the house, go on TV and confess your sins then pop yourself without telling it all?"

"You're speaking of the fact that he didn't mention his connection with the Senior and Junior Wells?"

"You got it. But not only didn't he confess, he didn't even mention them. These two nut jobs are driving around the city taking people out with a sniper rifle, and we know they're connected, Pate and the Wells. It just doesn't make sense to me."

"Hey, who knows what these psychopaths are thinking? It was obvious he was going to go out on his own terms. Maybe he just got ahead of himself and popped his top before he said everything he wanted to say. I could sort of see that happening."

"I don't know. Seems off to me."

"Hey, at their heart, suicides are cowards, right? Maybe he just didn't have the stones to admit it."

"But he had the balls to put a gun in his mouth and pull the trigger?"

"Do you have any physical evidence that puts him at the scene of any of the other murders?"

"No."

"But we do have forensics that puts Wells and his daughter there, am I right?"

"And they're both dead. So if Pate was pulling their strings, why not just admit it, along with everything else?"

"You know what? I don't know. But it's case closed, Jonesy. Send me your reports so I can get on with my life, will you?"

"I'll have Detective Small bring them over to you tomorrow."

"Hey," Elliott said. "How is Sandy? I'm hearing a rumor that you two are some kind of an item. What's the skinny on that?"

"So long, Preston."

Virgil carried the phone back to the kitchen table and as soon as he sat down it rang again.

"Hey good lookin'. What's cookin'?" Sandy said.

"Nothing much. Just doing the paper. You finished down there already?"

"Nope. That's why I'm calling. I'm going to be here a little longer than I thought."

"Well, how long?" Virgil said, instantly regretting the tone in his voice.

"What's the matter, Jonesy?"

"Ah, nothing. I didn't mean to snap at you. These pills, they help with the pain, but they make me sort of cranky or something. I'm sorry. What I really want is for you to be here, at our place."

"Maybe you should call the doctor, see if there's something else he could give you."

"It'll be all right," he said, then told her of the conversation he'd just had with Preston Elliott. "It seems like a hell of a loose end to me."

"Yeah, I can see that. But I think I agree with what Elliott said. Guys like that have got a screw loose somewhere. They're completely unpredictable. Maybe he left that part out on purpose." Then, she added, "About the pain, it'll get better. You're in the hard part, right now, this period of a few days after surgery. They say that's always the worst. But you'll get through it. Look at what we've got ahead of us, Virgil. It's all going to work out beautifully. Hey, you know what I'm excited about?"

"What?"

"Excited and a little scared too."

"What?"

"Getting to know your dad. I don't have any precon-ceived notions about it or anything, but in the back of my mind I've got this idea that he'll be able to help me fill a gap I've been carrying around with me for a long time."

"You know what? I'm sure my dad would want that, but he's not the easiest guy in the world to get along with sometimes. He doesn't really open himself up that way. At least not with me."

"It's probably hard for him too. You're his child, Virgil. No matter how old you are, or how grown up you are, you'll always be his child."

"I think in many ways, my dad could give you what you're looking for. All I'm saying is he's the kind of guy that gives on his own terms and not necessarily the needs of others. I just don't want to see you get hurt because of an expectation you might have that he's not willing to fulfill."

"Your father could never hurt me, Jonesy."

"You're probably right."

"Probably, he says. Hey, did you hear yourself a minute ago? You said 'our place?'"

───────────

THEY SAID GOODBYE TO EACH OTHER AND AS SOON AS he set the phone down, it rang yet again. *Christ.*

"Hey Bud, I was wondering if I could borrow your

truck today. I've got to run over to the lumber store and buy a few pieces of board for the bar top. Don't think I can fit them in my car."

"Sure thing, Dad. Door's open, just come on in."

Twenty minutes later he heard the front door open, then close. "That you, Dad? I'm in the kitchen."

Mason came around the corner just as Virgil was moving away from the sink. "Hi, Virg. Looks like you're moving around pretty well."

"Yeah, I'm starting to get the hang of these things," Virgil said, as he wiggled a crutch in the air. "Still hurts pretty good, especially in the mornings."

"I'll bet. I put my car next to the garage, out of the way. Sure you don't mind letting me use the truck?"

"Naw, it's fine. But listen, how about I go with you? This just sitting around the house is driving me nuts. Sandy's downtown and I could sure use a change of scenery. I'll sit at the bar and keep you company while you work."

Mason looked at his son, the skepticism clear upon his face. "You sure you're up to it? I'd hate to get all the way over there then have to turn around and bring you back."

Virgil let out a sigh. "I just need to get out, Dad, okay? Sandy will be done in a couple of hours or so. I'll leave her a message and she can probably swing by and bring me back here."

"Okay, if you're sure."

"I'm sure, Dad. Let's go, huh?"

"You bet. Hey, I'll pull the truck around to the front.

Shorter walk, right? You want some help getting out there?"

"Yeah, maybe."

THEY RODE TOGETHER IN SILENCE FOR A FEW MILES, A familiar routine. After the stop at the lumber store— Virgil waited in the truck—they headed for the bar. "Which boards need to be replaced?"

"The ones on both ends that butt up against the cross-members, just above the sinks? They're fine on top, but they're getting soft underneath. All the water that splashes up there is taking a toll. I thought since I was going to sand and refinish the top, now would be the time to swap them out."

"Yeah, probably right," Virgil said. "So, uh, how's things with you and Carol?"

Mason shifted his eyes from the road without turning his head. "Okay, I guess," he said. "Why?"

Virgil shook his head. "What do you mean, why? I was just asking. Making conversation, you know?"

"You pissed at me or something?" Mason said.

"No...I'm sorry. It's these damn pain pills they've got me on. They're messing with my head. I'm snapping at everyone."

Mason nodded. "You'll be okay, Virg." After that, neither of them spoke for the rest of the ride over to the bar.

Way to go, Virgil thought.

MASON BROUGHT THE BOARDS IN FROM THE BACK OF the truck while Virgil hobbled over to the jukebox and put some music on, then hobbled back to the bar and sat on one of the stools and let his leg hang down below the brass railing underneath. It felt good to get the weight off of it. He looked at the clock above the back of the bar and checked the time, thought *close enough*, and took a couple more pills.

Mason placed the boards on top of the bar and set about prying the old ones from their mount while Virgil took a sanding block and began to work the area in front of where he was seated, father and son communicating the way men often do, not with words, but by working together.

LATER, WHILE THEY WERE TAKING A BREAK, VIRGIL picked up the phone and called Sandy to let her know where he was and to see if she'd pick him up. "You boys having fun?" she asked.

"Oh yeah. Nothing better than bar upkeep. Think you could swing by and pick me up when you're finished?"

"Sure," Sandy said. "But I thought I'd stop and pick up

something to eat. You think maybe the three of us could have dinner tonight?"

"Hold on. I'll check." He pulled the phone away from his ear and said, "Hey Dad, Sandy wants to cook for the three of us tonight. What do you say?"

Mason wiped the sweat from his brow. "Ah, geez Virg, I don't know…"

Virgil put the phone back to his ear, his eyes still on his dad. "He says he'd love to." He listened for another minute, then said goodbye and set the phone down.

"Don't be such a stick in the mud. She wants to cook for you."

Mason let out a sigh, then went back to work.

Virgil did too.

WHEN SANDY GOT TO THE BAR SHE WALKED IN, SMILED and kissed him hello. "Thought you were going to the store," Virgil said.

"I was going to, but I thought I'd stop by here first and see what sounded good to you guys. Any suggestions? Hi Mason."

"Hi little darling," Mason said. "You know how to make a meatloaf?"

"I sure do," Sandy said. "As a matter of fact, I've got a meatloaf recipe that'll make you love me forever."

Mason laughed. "Won't need a recipe for that. All you've got to do is take care of my baby boy, here."

Virgil thought, *huh*...and felt the love in his words.

SANDY EXCUSED HERSELF TO THE LADIES ROOM. "THAT'S one you don't let get away, Virg."

"I know, Dad. I know. This one's going to work. Meant to be, you know?"

"That I do," Mason said. He was marking a series of cut lines on the boards with a carpenter's pencil. He didn't look up when he spoke, but it didn't stop the words. "You know, Virg, you and I, sometimes it sort of seems like neither one of us has the right thing to say to each other. You ever feel like that?"

"Yeah, I guess sometimes I do, Dad."

Mason put the old board on top of the new one and traced the cut points out. "My dad, your grandfather, he wasn't much of a talker. I used to get mad at him when I was a kid because he wouldn't say anything except to correct me when I did something wrong. It wasn't until you were born that I finally figured out how much he loved me. Wasn't until he died that I figured out how much I loved him, faults and all."

They sat with that for a minute and during the silence Sandy came back out and stood next to Virgil. Then, as if she could sense the conversation: "I'm not interrupting anything, am I?"

Neither of the men had a chance to answer. The front door of the bar opened and someone stepped inside, just past the entryway. Mason looked up and said, "Bar's closed for renovations. Be open again next week."

Virgil heard his father say they were closed, but when he turned to look at whoever was at the door his foot slipped a little on the brass railing and got caught between the rail and the bar. He cursed, then gently tried to twist his leg back into position. Just as he did, he heard his father say the last word that would ever come out of his mouth.

"Gun!"

Virgil turned his head toward the sound of his father's voice, saw Sandy reach for her weapon, then felt himself being pulled to the floor.

SANDY GRABBED THE BACK OF VIRGIL'S SHIRT COLLAR and pulled him to the ground. She yelled something, her words lost over the sounds of gunfire. Sandy fired twice, but Amanda Pate managed to get one shot off.

And one was enough.

VIRGIL COULDN'T HEAR ANYTHING, THE SOUND OF THE gunshots booming in his ears. The cordite from the spent shells assaulted his nostrils like someone had stuffed fire ants in his nose. He turned on the ground and the pain in his leg made the room swim out of focus for a moment, but he saw Sandy kick a gun from Amanda's dead hand. She was yelling something—Virgil didn't know what—but when their eyes locked and she saw he was okay, she ran right past him to the other side of the bar. Virgil tried to get up, but his leg was caught in the railing, the cast wedged in tight. He finally managed to pull it free and when he did, he felt something pull loose and a wave of pain turned everything gray, like an old black and white film.

Sandy was shouting from the other side of the bar. "No, no, no." Her shouts were high-pitched. Almost screams.

"Sandy?"

"Virgil, I need you back here. You better hurry."

Virgil hopped and slid along the bar, trailing his bad leg behind him. When he turned the corner he saw Sandy covered in Mason's blood, his head in her lap. The bullet had caught him squarely in the chest at the bottom of his rib cage. The color had drained from his face, and blood ran from both corners of his mouth. Sandy had one arm wrapped around his body, holding him in place, her other hand pressed tight over the gaping wound in his chest. His blood burst between her fingers with every beat of his heart, and from the time it took Virgil to move from the end of the bar to where they lay, Mason had lost more blood than Virgil thought the human body capable of containing.

He already had his cell phone out. He punched in 9-1-1, shouted their location into the phone then let it slip from his hand. He got down by his father's side and put his hand on top of the wound as well. "Hang in there, Dad. You're going to be all right. You're going to make it. Help's on the way, you hear me?"

Mason reached out and grabbed his son's wrist. He tried to say something, but when he did, he choked on the blood that ran from his mouth and no words ever came. He took Virgil's hand and held it to his heart, then placed Sandy's hand there as well. Virgil watched him stare at Sandy, then saw his eyes go out of focus and felt the silence in his chest.

Virgil looked at Sandy and knew she grieved in ways he could not know. For her, it was summer again from a time long ago and this was yet another goodbye of a father figure she would never have the chance to know or love.

After a while, Virgil slid sideways and sat down next to her and ran his fingers through his father's hair. They stayed there like that until the police and the medics arrived, neither of them saying a word.

EPILOGUE

The sun was out, suspended high in the miracle of another day where everything felt fresh and destined to live forever. Virgil walked with a cane, a handmade hickory stick Sandy bought for him after the doctor had removed his cast and said he could go without the crutches. As they walked across the still-wet grass of an overnight rain, the tip of the cane sank into the ground in various spots and Sandy had to hold Virgil's arm to help steady him along.

It had been eight weeks since Mason died.

In the end, Virgil had decided that his father's death could only be attributed to a certain sense of bad luck and a failure of imagination on his part. Amanda Pate had pulled the strings on her husband for years as she lived with and hid from his desires, all while she served an agenda of her own. The police were able to piece together certain facts, Amanda Pate and Sidney Wells, Jr. being lovers, chief among them. When that fell into place, eventually the rest did too.

The fire that killed Amy Frechette, Murton's girl-friend, was traced back to Collins and Hicks by forensics and the hard work of the Arson squad. It was ultimately decided that it was nothing more than a way to draw Murton out into the open and it probably worked better than either Collins or Hicks would have liked. It took a number of weeks, but Virgil was finally able to put the final piece of the puzzle in place, and when he did, he almost wished he'd left it alone.

He called the governor on a Sunday morning at home and asked to meet him at his office.

The governor resisted the idea of a meeting.

Virgil insisted.

When he walked into his office the governor was seated at his desk, a glass of scotch in his hand. It was only ten-thirty in the morning. Virgil limped in and sat down in one of the chairs in front of his desk without speaking.

The governor watched him for a few minutes, then unlocked the center drawer of his desk and pulled out a brown expandable file folder. He removed the elastic string from the flap and pulled out a number of different photographs and arranged them on his desk. Virgil couldn't see the person in the photos, but then again, he didn't need to. "I should have known you would figure it out," the governor said. "Who else knows?"

"Sandy, and probably Murton Wheeler, though he

hasn't come right out and said so. But no one else that I'm aware of. My gut tells me you've probably confided in Bradley Pearson though."

"Your gut tells you true. That makes five people in the entire world who know, Jonesy. You, Sandy, Murton, me, and my aid, Bradley Pearson."

"Your wife doesn't even know?"

The governor took a sip of scotch then shook his head. "No, she does not. We were never able to conceive and I thought the cruelty of it all, the fact that I had a child by another woman, would break us apart. So no, I never told her. How did you put it together?"

"Murton had a lot to do with it." Virgil reached into his pocket and pulled out a copy of the birth certificate that had been in the safe deposit box and handed it to the governor. "He gave me this. Amanda Pate had the original before Murton got hold of it. How she got it, I don't know. I guess we'll never know."

The governor passed a stack of pictures over and Virgil leafed through them. They were all pictures of Sidney Wells, Jr. at various ages in her life. And then he told his story.

"Her name was Sara Wells. One night I stayed at the hotel where she worked. It was as simple as that. She was stuck in a bad marriage, I was stuck in a bad hotel, and when we met in the bar, I'm telling you, Jonesy, it was magic. She stayed with me that night and we met every chance we got for the next year and a half."

"And when you found out she was pregnant?"

"I'm not sure I understand your question. Is it my honor you're asking about?"

"I'm asking you what happened next."

The governor looked at nothing. "She told me she knew the baby was mine. She said she knew it to be true because Sid had been to the doctor. He had a low count or something. I asked her to divorce Sid so she could marry me, and she told me she would. My God, Jonesy, we were happy. That's where we were when everything changed.

"My call sign that day was Voodoo. You know what's funny? I remember almost every single detail of that day except the one that matters. The one where I picked up the phone and filed my flight plan. I had the option of going to Indy or Ft. Wayne first. For some reason I picked Indy. If I'd have picked Ft. Wayne..." He let it hang there.

"She might still be alive today?"

The governor pointed his finger at me. "Wrong. She *would* still be alive. I'd probably be flying for the airlines and we'd have a ton of kids. Instead, the woman I loved and my only child are dead because of me."

"Governor..."

He held up his hand. What he said next didn't surprise him, but it made Virgil's stomach turn just the same. "I'm sorry about your father, Jonesy. I really am. But what's done is done. I see no criminal involvement on my part in this matter. The Pates and the Wells are gone. I'll consider the matter closed as soon as I have my daughter

Sidney's original birth certificate. You do have that, don't you?"

Virgil did indeed have it. It was in his pocket.

He had two choices.

One, give the birth certificate to the governor and be complicit in hiding his secret, one that would all but destroy his political career if it ever came out, or two, include the birth certificate in the official file, and let the governor fend for himself.

Virgil stared at him for a long time.

The governor stared right back.

"You put me on Pate right out of the gate," Virgil said. "Why?"

"That was Bradley's doing, though I agreed to it. We knew he was being looked at by the FBI, but they were dragging their feet."

"I don't think that's entirely accurate. In fact, with all due respect, it's flat out wrong."

"It's neither right nor wrong, Jonesy. It's politics. How long do you think I would have lasted in my campaign against Sermon Sam once everyone found out that the woman I was sleeping with, the woman who just happened to be married to that idiot Wells was at work and in the hotel the morning I punched out of that plane? Not very long, I can tell you that."

"And what about the shootings?"

The governor took another drink of his scotch. "What about them? Sidney Wells was a psychopath. He was trying to destroy me by murdering family members of anyone and everyone he thought was even remotely responsible for the crash that day. He knew all along I was Sidney, Jr.'s father. If Pate's wife and my daughter were having some sort of illicit affair as you allege, then they must have put the plan together. Who knows?"

Virgil picked up a few more of the pictures and looked through them, but he didn't try too hard to hide the contempt in his voice. "And who cares, right?" After a few minutes he reached into his pocket and gave the governor the document.

When the governor addressed him by his formal title, Virgil knew he'd made the wrong choice.

"Thank you, Detective Jones. That will be all."

Virgil gave the governor a chance to correct himself. "Are you sure about that, Sir?"

When he looked away and didn't answer, Virgil pulled himself from the chair and limped out of his office.

SANDY TOUCHED HIS ARM AND PULLED VIRGIL OUT OF his thoughts. "Hey, you with me, big guy?" she said. They were next to the edge of the pond behind the house and when Virgil looked out across the water he saw it wrinkle in spots, the Bluegill hungry, nicking at the surface.

"Why did you want to come out here?"

Just then, a landscape truck pulling a backhoe on a lowboy trailer turned off the road and came up the drive. They lost sight of it for a moment when it went around the side of the house, then reappeared and stopped next to the out building where Virgil kept his lawn equipment.

"You're about to find out," Sandy said. "We wanted to do something for you...Murton, Delroy, and me. "

Murton hopped out of the truck, backed the tractor from the trailer and drove over to where they stood, about ten yards from the edge of the pond. He lowered the bucket on the backhoe and scooped out a pile of soil then placed it carefully in a mound a few feet away from the hole. He repeated the process two more times, then turned the tractor around, winked at Virgil like he may have just noticed his presence and drove back to the truck. When he returned the next time Delroy rode along with him. There was a Weeping Willow tree in the bucket of the tractor, its root ball enclosed with burlap and twine. Murton lowered the bucket next to the hole opposite the pile of dirt, shut down the engine and climbed from the operator's seat, a small package in his hands.

"Hey Jonesy. Sandy," he said, as he handed Virgil the package.

It was wrapped in plain white paper, the kind a butcher would use at a meat market, and tied across both ends with brown string that knotted in the middle. The paper wrapping was stiff, but the contents of the package soft and pliable. Virgil let a question form on his face.

"It's the shirt your dad was wearing at the bar when he was shot," Murton said. "I'm sorry I wasn't there for you, Virg. I spent a year undercover with the Pate's and never once looked at Amanda. I could have prevented the whole damn thing."

Sandy walked over and wrapped her arms around Murton.

"It's all right," Virgil said. "It's time to let go of the past, Murt."

Virgil held the package against his chest, his father's blood wasted and dry under a wrap of string and paper. He looked at Sandy. "He was telling me he loved me," Virgil said. "In the bar, when you came out of the bathroom. He didn't say the words, but that's what he was telling me."

Murton walked over to the tractor and pulled a shovel from the side rack and stood next to the hole. Virgil got down on his knees and placed his father's bloodied shirt at the bottom of the pit, then stood back and watched as Sandy and Murton and Delroy wrestled the willow tree into the hole and filled the remaining space from the pile of dirt.

"Willow trees use more water than just about any other tree," Murton said to no one. "I don't know how I know that."

Delroy put his hand on Virgil's chest. "The ground water will soak tru the paper and into dat shirt, mon. Your father's blood, it will flow tru dat tree just like it do your own heart, Virgil Jones." It was the first time Virgil had ever heard Delroy say his full name.

"It might not be much, but we had to do something," Murton said.

Sandy sat down in the grass next to the tree, and after a few minutes, the rest of them did too. Sandy took Virgil's hand. "I'm sorry, baby," she said. If I had been just a little quicker...."

He cut her off. "We agreed we weren't going to have this discussion anymore."

The shine in her eyes sparkled a turquoise blue, the un-felled tears caught in her lashes. "I can't help it, Virgil. I can't get these thoughts out of my head. My father died saving your life, and I keep thinking that surely there must be some reason things turned out this way. I was supposed to save your dad, Virgil. But I didn't. Don't you see that?"

"No, I don't. Amanda was after me. When dad yelled out, he took a bullet that was meant for me, and one that probably would have hit you. He not only saved my life, but he saved yours as well."

"And how am I supposed to live with that, Virgil?"

"The same way I have all these years. The same way I'm still learning how to."

"I don't know how to do that."

"I'll teach you," he said. "We'll do it together."

THAT NIGHT, AFTER SANDY WAS ASLEEP, VIRGIL WALKED outside and stood on his back deck and wondered if maybe their roles weren't reversed, if maybe he was the one being taught and led, not just by Sandy, but by those people who'd held a place in his life and still rented pieces of his heart as tenants in perpetuity.

Sleep did not come easy. His leg was hurting more at a time when it should have been getting better. He took a couple of pain pills then watched the moon journey across the sky, its reflection set deep in the sheen of the black-watered pond at the back of his house. The sound of the wind as it hissed through the leaves of his father's willow tree and the dull echo of semi tires as they snapped over the expansion joints out on the four-lane surrounded and comforted him, grounded him in some way.

A pair of headlights swung through the side yard and for a moment Virgil could have sworn he saw someone standing beneath his father's willow tree. But the lights swept past then abruptly cut off. Someone in the drive. Virgil looked out at the tree for a long moment, then limped around to the front of his house and found Rosencrantz leaning against the side of his car. "It's a little late, Rosie. Everything okay?"

Rosencrantz had a toe-in-the-dirt look on his face and a piece of paper in his hand. "Yeah. I'm sorry about this, Jonesy, I really am. Never mind. I'll just go. I shouldn't have come out here."

"It's okay. I'm not sleeping much these days anyway. What is it?"

"I know we're already short-handed with your medical leave and all, but something's come up and I was sort of hoping you'd sign off on some vacation time for me."

"Ah, man. Now really isn't the best time, Rosie. You know that."

"Yeah, yeah, I know. But like I said, something has come up."

Virgil noticed a small bag that sat on the roof of Rosencrantz's car. "What's in the bag?"

"You remember Margery, right? From the bank?"

Virgil let his eyelids droop. "Yeah, the name rings a bell."

"Well, she cashed it all in. The stocks, the bonds, the 401K, all of it. She's set for life, man. She bought a place in Jamaica right on seven mile beach...based on your recommendation, is what she said."

"We had a brief conversation about it a couple of months ago."

"Well whatever you said stuck, because she's headed down there tomorrow, and she wants me to tag along for a few weeks. If I'm being honest with you, I'm sort of into it."

"A few weeks?"

"Come on, Jonesy. What do you say?"

"You still haven't answered me. What's in the bag?"

"My luggage."

"Excuse me?"

Rosencrantz reached into the bag and pulled out the skimpiest Speedo bathing suit Virgil had ever seen. "She said this was all I'd need. At first it sort of scared me, but now I'm thinking what the hell, you only live once, right?"

"Rosie..."

"I tried it on. You ought to see it. The damn thing's so small I feel like I should get a wax or something. What do you think?"

Virgil held up his hands in surrender. "Ah, no no no. I don't want to hear it. Just give me the form. Where do I sign? Where do I sign...?"

And the story continues...
Virgil and the gang are back in State of Betrayal!

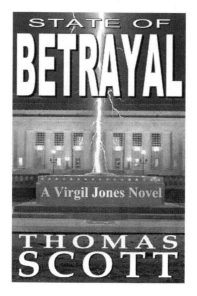

*State of Betrayal - Book 2 of the Virgil Jones Mystery
Thriller Series*

Twenty years ago a man named James Pope was shot to death in front of his twin children, Nicholas and Nichole, by a rookie cop named Virgil Jones. Now, as young adults, the Pope twins are looking for revenge against the man they hold responsible for the death of their father.

But when Nicholas Pope goes missing and his apartment is found covered in blood, Nichole turns to the only person she can think of to help her, the one person who could never turn her away: Virgil Jones.

You've felt the Anger...
Now it's time to experience the Betrayal!

Please turn the page for an exciting preview of
book #2 of the Virgil Jones Series:
State of Betrayal

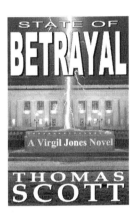

CHAPTER ONE

It was the season of baked asphalt, dry hardpan backyards, and boiled over tempers that flared red long after the sun would journey below the horizon. So much change for so many—that summer of heat and Boots—though Virgil Jones knew full well the one name they would never call him again, *Boot*, was a part of his past now...a past where the heat barreled on, an oppressive undertow that became the undoing of so many, the death of an unfortunate few.

Virgil was on patrol driving south on U.S. 31 about halfway between Kokomo and Indianapolis. He had the air conditioner set to maximum and that kept the temperature in his cruiser at eighty degrees, give or take. A heat wave had stalled out over the middle of the country a few days ago and if you were outside for more than five minutes, even in the shade, the humidity landed on you like a water balloon tossed from a second-story balcony. It

was so bad you could see the air. The blacktop a half-mile
out shimmered in the heat and Virgil thought it looked as
though at any moment he might drive headlong into a
pool of mercury.

His shift was scheduled to end in less than half an
hour and he was only a mile away from the convenience
store when he got the radio call of two males engaged in a
verbal argument that threatened to turn into something
much worse. He hit the switch for the light bar, then
punched the gas pedal and when he did, the Police Interceptor engine in his Crown Victoria responded with ease.
Traffic in the immediate area was light and he ran his
speed up to over one hundred miles per hour, the tires
gliding across the greasy, heat-soaked asphalt. He would
be on scene in less than forty seconds. If he would have
glanced at himself just then in the rear-view mirror he'd
have seen the smile on his face.

The convenience store sat along an access road just off
the highway. The entrance was at the far end of the lot
and Virgil was forced to drive past the store along the
perimeter road before he could turn back into the parking
area. The cause of the altercation was clear. Two vehicles
—one a clean, dark blue, mid-sized sedan, the other a dull
red and rusted pickup—sat nose to tail, the rear bumper
of the pickup firmly embedded into the headlight of the
sedan. Two white males stood just to the side of the
damaged vehicles. Virgil tried not to draw any conclusions
as to which vehicle belonged to each driver, but it seemed
obvious. One of the men wore a pair of cutoff jeans and a

sleeveless shirt, the other a business suit. There were two small children in the cab of the pickup, their hands and faces pressed against the rear window, their expressions a mixture of both fear and familiarity. A small crowd had gathered around the front door of the convenience store but no one was making any sort of attempt to curtail a situation that was rapidly escalating out of control. The men, both red faced and angry pointed their fingers at each other but their words were lost to the road noise and air-conditioning of Virgil's squad car.

Then, in an instant, everything spun out of control when business suit shoved sleeveless in the chest and knocked him to the ground before walking away. Virgil burped his siren to get their attention, but at the same time sleeveless jumped up, reached into the bed of his pickup and pulled out a piece of steel rebar. He hesitated for just a moment but the look on his face left little doubt about his intentions or his state of mind. Business suit faced Virgil as he approached, his back to his adversary, unaware of what was about to take place against his person and even though Virgil pointed at him and hit the siren again as a warning it had no effect.

Virgil braked to a stop just as sleeveless swung the rebar and hit business suit across the backs of his thighs. The suit dropped to his knees and his jaw unhinged with shock and pain. Virgil jumped out of the car, un-holstered his weapon and pointed it at sleeveless. "Drop the bar. Do it now. No, no, don't even think about it. Just drop it."

Sleeveless looked at him, but he was too far gone by

then, the flat of his eyes a sign of what was to come. He raised the piece of rebar high above his head, his yellow teeth bared, the tendons of his tattooed arms as tight as leaf springs and when he stood up on his toes and started to swing the bar again he left Virgil no choice at all. He fired two shots and they both hit their target. Sleeveless was dead before he hit the ground.

Virgil wasn't smiling anymore.

That was twenty years ago and it was the only time he'd ever fired his weapon as a police officer. It was also his first day out of training—no longer a Boot—riding solo as an Indiana State Trooper.

THE MAN VIRGIL SHOT AND KILLED WAS NAMED JAMES Pope. The two children in the truck with him were his five year-old twins, a boy, Nicholas, and his sister, Nichole. James Pope had just abducted his children from his ex-wife's house only minutes before the altercation in the parking lot that led to his death. Virgil never knew what happened to the twins after that day, but he did get a thank-you card in the mail from their mother a few weeks after the shooting. Virgil had hopes that the children would somehow grow up trouble-free, even though they had witnessed the death of their father at the hands of a police officer. When the thank-you card arrived in the mail from their mother, Virgil's hope died just as quick as James Pope did. It's one thing to be glad you're rid of someone. But it's something else entirely when you carry such hatred in your heart that you send a note of thanks to the man who killed your ex-husband. Virgil thought the Pope twins were in for a rough ride.

He threw the note in the trash and got on with his life.

CHAPTER TWO

Nicholas Pope sat in the darkness of his office, his face illuminated by the dim glow of his computer monitor. Pope was a programmer for the state's lottery, though the job description was something of a sore spot for him. He was not a programmer. Programmers were about one step up from the I.T. guy who kept Excel from crashing every time someone tried to recover a missing file. No, Pope was a coder and a damned good one at that. The distinction was important to him. Programmers and coders did share some similarities—Nicky would grant you that—but it was a bit like comparing a couple of house painters with artists like Renoir, or Monet. They all used paints and brushes, but that was about as far as anyone could extend the comparison. Guys with names like Billie Bob and Monty D. painted houses, but they could hardly be called artists. They were simple laborers. Coders on the other hand, just like Renoir, or Monet, were true artists. One little splash of color here, one little bit of binary there and...well, it made all the difference, whether anyone else noticed or not.

So. Nicholas Pope was a coder who was, at the moment, working on a scheduled update for the algorithm that was the basis for the random number generator, or RNG, for the state's lottery system. Gone were the days of numbered Ping-Pong balls floating about on puffs of air until they popped into a tube on live TV. Everything was digital now, including how the winning numbers were picked. The lottery's RNG algorithm served two primary functions. The first was to pick a total of six numbers at random between 1 and 48 whenever someone bought a lottery ticket and used the 'quick pick' method instead of playing numbers they'd decided upon themselves. The second purpose of the RNG algorithm was to pick the six winning numbers every time there was a drawing and in the case of the state of Indiana, that was every Wednesday and Saturday.

The RNG algorithm was one of the most complex algorithms that Nicky had ever seen, layer after layer of intricate code that every now and again made someone wealthy beyond their wildest dreams. Nicky was fascinated with RNGs, especially the one he now had access to. The lottery used a true RNG, one that worked by capturing background ambient noise from a variety of ever-changing sources—street traffic, wind, aircraft flying overhead, footsteps and voices in the hallways—

then converted those noises into a pattern. Once the pattern was established, it was output and converted into a string code that the system used as the key—or seed—that ran the algorithm. If the key kept changing, as it would with random ambient background noise, then the numbers would always be truly random. Even if they did happen to repeat—though that had never happened and as far as Nicky could tell, never would—they were still random by definition and that's what mattered.

Near the end of his shift, Nicky made note of his place in the program and began to back his way out of the layers of code that converted the noise into its sequential string. He was almost out when he found what he was looking for. Found it by dumb luck. It was right there and had been all along. He'd simply missed it going in. It was hidden, but not all that well. It was, he thought, a little like hiding a tree in the forest.

He double-checked to make sure what he'd found was the right section and when he was sure, he pulled the thumb drive from his pocket and uploaded his own little bit of binary code into the sequential string generator section of the program. He wasn't worried about being traced by the security measures the lottery had in place. He'd been logged in the entire time under his boss's user-name and password, two little items he'd copied from her phone over eight weeks ago after a particularly feisty night of drinking and well...feistiness. He logged out of the terminal and once clear of the building he took out

his cell and called his twin sister, Nichole. "We're in," he
said.

"You're sure?" she asked him.

"Oh yeah, no doubt about it."

"Will it work?"

"Of course it will work. I designed it. Hey, Sis?"

"Yeah?"

"We're doing it aren't we? After all this time, we're
going to make them pay."

"You bet your ass they're going to pay, baby brother.
They're going to pay big time."

"Hey, a minute and a half hardly makes me your baby
brother."

"Be careful, Nicky. Sometimes I think you don't
realize what we're up against here."

"No worries, Sis. I'll see you in an hour."

They still had some work to do, but they were almost
ready. Almost there.

NICHOLE WENT TO HER FRIDGE, PULLED OUT TWO BUDS
—the liquid kind—and handed one to her brother. "What
about Pearson? Maybe we should let that go."

"Little late for that. Besides, the plan is already in
place. Pearson is going to pay for what he did to our
family."

Their plan had evolved over the years. It started out as
nothing more than a childhood fantasy—a way to get

even with Pearson for the altercation he started that eventually led to their father's death by an Indiana State Trooper. Shortly after the Pope twins turned seventeen their mother died and that was when they began to understand a few things, the biggest of which was that they were on their own. They had no other family so they made a promise to themselves; they would take care of each other no matter what came their way.

And that's what they did. Nichole had proven herself to be quite a little thief, a talent she discovered in short order after their mother died. They had to eat, after all. She became a master shoplifter, which, Nichole discovered, required a good deal of acting. You couldn't look suspicious if you were about to steal something, no matter how big or small said something might be. You had to *act* normal. You had to *act* like you belonged where you were, doing whatever it was you were doing. Nichole discovered she was good at it...the acting. She could act like a punk or a princess...a young socialite, or a homeless teen. Her biggest score had been their most elaborate one to date, not counting what they were doing now. She went to the mall, stole the most expensive dress she could find—with matching shoes, of course—then went to one of the more exclusive college graduation parties in nearby Carmel, Indiana. Nicky had hacked into the guest list, added her name and once she was inside she used the list of probable passwords Nicky had given her and cracked the safe hidden in the parents bedroom closet. That score alone netted them almost fifty grand, mostly in cash and Canadian Maple Leaf coins. The coins didn't have serial numbers, God bless you, Canada.

Of course that wouldn't have been possible if Nicky hadn't become such an expert coder and hacker over the years, a skill he picked up on the Internet as he began to track Pearson's every move. It wasn't long before he'd found and built backdoors into virtually every area of Pearson's digital life, from bank records, to utility bills, personal and professional email accounts, cell phone records and texts, employment records, the works. When Pearson became the governor's chief of staff, Nicky followed him—electronically speaking—right into the second most powerful position in the state.

And that's when things got interesting.

The Pope twins began to understand just how corrupt and manipulative Pearson really was. They had accumulated massive amounts of data on him. They had proof of bribery, falsification of official state records, evidence that demonstrated election fraud and extortion. The problem though wasn't in the acquisition of the data. The problem was what to do with it. They couldn't just hand it over to the cops and say, "See...here's a bad man. Arrest him please and, oh by the way, it's really all about payback for our father. You see..."

No, that wouldn't work. They'd be the ones locked up for theft, spying and whatever else the prosecution could think of. They understood that whatever they were going to do, they would have to do it themselves, just like they always had. Which wasn't to say they didn't have a little help along the way.

Nicky hacked his way into the credit agencies, created a dozen false identities—all with excellent credit—then bought passports and driver's licenses that would stand up to not only human inspection, but machine inspection as well. Those had cost them dearly, but they were worth every penny, or in this case, every Canadian Maple Leaf.

"What is it?" Nichole asked.

"I guess I just realized that if our plan doesn't work, it won't be long before I'm broke and alone in a foreign country."

"Don't worry, Nicky. Everything is going to work out just fine. The code is in place, we've got Pearson by the short hairs and we are all about to be richer than Jesus H. Christ himself. That is, if your little bit of code works."

"That little bit of code as you call it took me over two years to perfect."

"But what if your boss gets one of the other coders to dig around and root out your program?"

"They'd never find it."

"But how do you know? For sure, I mean."

Nicky sat down on the sofa. "It's sort of complicated, but the bottom line is this: They won't be able to find it because it's not in the main system. It's buried deep in a tiny subroutine that overrides the security measures at the point of sale. Remember, we don't want or even need control of the main system. Just the printer that generates the ticket."

"And that instruction comes from the configured play slip you gave me?"

"Yep. Go get it and I'll show you."

Nichole went to her bedroom, got the slip and handed it to her brother. "See here," he said as he pointed to the slip. Every play slip has five boards you can play. Most people don't play that many, but some do. Anyway, see how every board has forty-eight spaces?"

"Yeah. So what?"

"You're supposed to pick six numbers for each board that you want to play. Take a look at the slip. I've played six numbers on each board except the last one. On that one, I've played eight. Not just any eight either. I've got the system set up to bypass the security measures at the point of sale, no matter where that might be. When the bypass occurs, the program will compile, the code within the algorithm will run and the nifty little printer they've got behind every gas station and grocery store counter in the state will print out a post-dated ticket with any numbers we want, which in our case happens to be the six numbers on the last board."

"Jesus, Nicky, that's a lot of money we're talking about. I hope you're right."

It was a lot of money, if you consider just a shade over three hundred million dollars a lot of money. And who wouldn't? It was the single largest jackpot in the state's history. Week after week not one single person had hit all six numbers, then the momentum started to build. When the amount hit fifty million people started to notice.

When the amount rose to one hundred and fifty million, people started lining up at gas stations, grocery stores, mini-marts and anywhere else a lottery ticket could be purchased. When it hit a quarter of a billion, people started showing up from out of state, buying tickets instead of paying their bills. Then, when it went to three hundred million dollars, the almost unimaginable happened. One person hit all six numbers and won the single largest jackpot in the history of the Indiana lottery.

Except that person never came forward to claim the prize.

At first, the media coverage was almost nonstop. Who was the winner? Why hadn't they come forward? When would they claim the prize? But after a few days of speculation, the media got bored, the losers got pissed and the story began to fade away. There was some thought that the winner—the real winner—had lost the ticket. Or maybe they'd passed away, lost it to a house fire, or flood, or some other disaster. Theories of what happened to the ticket were almost as numerous as the jackpot amount, but no amount of supposition produced the winning ticket or its holder. Now, with less than two weeks left before the six-month deadline to claim the prize, the money, if left unclaimed, would quietly go back to the state, just like all other unclaimed payouts.

"Oh I'm right. In a matter of days you and I are going to be filthy rich, retired and trying to figure out how to spend the interest on hundreds of millions of dollars."

"It doesn't seem real."

Nicky laughed. "I know what you mean. But believe me, it will seem real enough when you check your account balances. Listen, I have to ask, just to make myself feel better...you know what to do with that play slip right?"

"I do."

"Tell me."

She rolled her eyes a little, then told him.

CHAPTER THREE

I f Virgil thought about it—and he often did—he'd have to admit the shooting of James Pope still haunted him. After it happened he was still young and foolish enough to believe that the past was just that and once free from its grasp he'd not worry over it or attempt to be the arbiter of events outside his own control. Except those types of certainties are a preserve best left to youth, a lesson Virgil thought he might never have to learn. Then before he knew it twenty years had sailed away and now this; a summer like no other, the pain a constant companion as it cut a swath through the jungle of his life, a trail laid bare as if it were his only choice, at once clear and true. It would be a harbinger of things to come, a combination of that moment from long ago and his life now, one he might be able to point to someday and say, *Ah, yes, that's when it turned. That's when it all changed. If only...*

A late-afternoon haze drifted across the sun but the air temperature held steady so adjustments to his line depth weren't necessary. The bobber was simple, made from the cork of an old wine bottle and it vibrated in the water if he held too much tension on the line. It reminded him of those old electric football games Virgil and his boyhood friend, Murton Wheeler, used to play when they were kids. They'd line up the little plastic players, hit the switch, then watch the tiny figurines vibrate their way across the surface of the game board. Virgil could still hear the buzzing sound the board made when they toggled the power button and turned it on.

He had a two-pound monofilament line tied directly to an eye-hook at the end of the cane pole. The pole was twelve feet in length and stained dark with age and the regular applications of Tung oil used to maintain its beauty and structural integrity. The pole was one of Virgil's most prized possessions. His grandfather had taught him to fish with it and then had given it to him as a gift just a few years before he died. Virgil had a shed full of fishing poles, ones made of boron, graphite, fiberglass or some other space-age composite, and they were all fine poles. Some were so flexible and tough you could literally tie them into a knot without damaging the rod, while others were so sensitive you could detect a deer fly if it landed on the tip. Virgil didn't know why he continued to buy them. His grandfather's cane pole was the only one he ever used. When he held the pole in his hands the way he'd been taught so long ago he felt a connection to his grandfather, as if the linear reality of time held no sway in his existence and he was back in control of himself and his own destiny, his path clear, his choices many.

Virgil knew, at least on some level, that he was a sight this Saturday afternoon. He wore a pair of green cotton gym shorts that hung to his knees, a Jamaican Red Stripe Beer utility cap angled low across his brow and a pair of brown leather half-top boots with no socks. He sat at the edge of his pond, cane pole in hand and tried to relax, mostly without any measure of success. The fish were not biting but he didn't really care. He set the pole in the grass next to his chair, reached into the cooler and took out his supplies. Among them, a plastic syringe with a screw tip on the end, a glass vial of a drug called Heparin, and an odd looking, round container made of a stiff rubbery material about the size of a baseball. The baseball-like container held a drug called Vancomycin, a powerful antibiotic medication that the doctor had referred to as their 'drug of last resort.'

The glass vial of Heparin was fitted with a threaded female connector that matched the male connector of the syringe on the table. He scrubbed his hands clean with a disposable alcohol wipe, then used another to cleanse the top of the Heparin vial and yet another to wipe the connector that was sutured and taped under his arm. The tube that penetrated his body was a Peripherally Inserted Central Catheter, or PICC Line for short. Once he had everything sterilized he filled the syringe from the

Heparin bottle with the required amount of the drug and injected it into the tube.

Heparin, the doctor had told Virgil, was an anti-coagulant drug that prevented the formation of blood clots and helped aid in the healing process of human tissue. In non-technical language, it greased the skids for the real medicine, the Vancomycin.

After injecting the Heparin, he hooked up the Vancomycin container. The delivery process of the Vancomycin would take about thirty minutes as the medicine flowed from the ball and into a vein through Virgil's heart before being distributed throughout his body.

Five months ago, while working a case as the lead investigator for the state's Major Crimes Unit, Virgil had been kidnapped, tortured and beaten almost to death. In the course of the beating his right leg was broken and required surgery to repair the damage. The surgery went well, or so he'd been told and he was up and around in no time at all. Except one day about eight weeks into the recovery process, he woke in the morning with a low-grade fever that did not seem to want to leave him alone no matter how many aspirin he took. He began to feel worse with each passing day until finally on the fifth morning Virgil's girlfriend, Sandy Small, found him unconscious on their bedroom floor. During the surgical procedure to fix his leg, Virgil had picked up a staph infection. The infection grew in his body where it eventually worked its way into his blood stream, a condition known as staphylococcal sepsis. He'd been taking the

Vancomycin twice a day for the last six weeks in an effort to kill the infection. This would be his last dose.

It had been a rough couple of months. During his previous investigation—right after his release from the hospital—the wife of one of the main suspects in his case killed Virgil's father, Mason. She was trying to shoot Virgil, but his father took the bullet instead.

The buzzing in Virgil's head was with him constantly. It had nothing to do with childhood memories and simpler times, nor did it have anything to do with the Heparin or the Vancomycin. It was because of the other drugs he was still taking. Oxycontin was one. He took two of the blue-colored thirty milligram tablets three times a day. Between doses, he'd toss back two or three Vicodin... both for the pain in his leg.

At least that's what he kept telling himself.

When he thought about the men who kidnapped and tried to kill him, Virgil thought they might yet succeed.

HE BROKE TWO OF THE VICODIN IN HALF AND swallowed them with a couple of sips of Dew. A few minutes later he felt the chemical rush hit his system the same way a shot of whiskey will burn the throat and warm the blood. He closed his eyes and let the feeling flow through his body and for a few minutes he felt confident and strong and happy and free. But he also knew the feeling wouldn't last, that soon the reality of his situation would once again wrap itself around him like a second skin, one in which he could not seem to find an edge. He thought if he could he'd peel it away until there was nothing left at all.

After twenty-five minutes or so, the Vancomycin container was empty, so Virgil unscrewed the connector and capped it off tight. He had an appointment later in the day to have the tube removed and a blood test to ensure the infection was gone.

When he pulled his fishing line from the pond he noticed that not only was the worm missing from the hook at the end of the line, but so too was his desire to fish. The late morning air was warm and still and when Virgil let his gaze settle on the bowed limbs of the willow tree planted next to the edge of the pond water he saw his father standing there, leaning against the trunk of the tree, his face partially hidden by the leafy, feather-veined fronds. He was shirtless under his bib-style bar apron tied off at his waist and he had a towel thrown over his left shoulder. Virgil could see the scar from the bullet wound at the bottom of his father's chest, the skin around the edges gnarled and puckered, yet somehow pink and fresh like that of a newborn baby.

They stared at each other for a long time, then Mason moved sideways just a bit. "I'm worried about you, Son," he said. When he spoke, the buzzing inside Virgil's head went quiet and the absence of the incessant sound was more of a surprise than the vision of his dead father. "You're hitting the meds pretty hard, don't you think?"

"Better living through chemistry," Virgil said, but regretted the words as soon as they left his mouth. The sarcasm didn't seem to bother Mason though; the look of both love and concern on his face remaining steady. "I'm sorry, Dad."

"It's alright, Bud. I remember you told me that day in the truck how the pills were making you cranky."

"That's not what I meant. Why do I think you know that?"

"It wasn't your fault."

"Wasn't it?"

"Of course not." Mason looked away for a moment and wrapped his hands around the trunk of the willow tree. "This is a beautiful thing you did here, Virg. It's more significant than you might imagine."

After Mason's death, the people who meant more to Virgil than anyone else in the world brought his father's bloodied shirt to his house along with the willow tree. Together they buried the shirt and planted the tree on top of it. "Thanks, Dad, but I'm not exactly sure what that means."

"It's okay, Son. You wouldn't. You learn things over here. It's sort of a timeless knowledge. I can't really explain it. The actual words don't exist."

"Can I ask you something?"

"Sure."

"I don't want you to take offense."

Mason smiled. "What is it, Son?"

"Why haven't I heard from my grandfather?"

"He's been here with you all morning, Virg. In fact, he spends most of his time with you."

"I've never seen him."

"It doesn't always work that way."

Virgil closed his eyes and shook his head. "I don't—"

"I have to go now, Virgil. You have people in your life who are going to need you."

"What do you mean?"

"I mean you've got to be shut of those pills. You're not thinking straight."

"I'm trying," Virgil said.

The smile left Mason's face and Virgil felt as much as he heard the words that came next. To Virgil, it felt as if they passed through him, like a pressure wave from a bomb blast. "*Try harder.*"

"Will you tell him I said hello?" Virgil asked.

"You can tell him yourself, Virg. He hears you. We all do." Then Mason looked toward the house and pointed with his chin. "Say, looks like you've got company." The look on his face almost mischievous. "Don't worry, Virgil. Everything is exactly how it should be."

"I don't understand, Dad."

"Maybe not yet, but you will. Good-bye for now, buddy."

"Wait, Dad, there's something else I need to know."

"Dad loves you, Virgil. We all do. Stay tuned."

From the time Virgil was old enough to remember, he and his father had acknowledged their love for each other in something of an unusual way. Mason spoke of himself in the third person. He would say, "Dad loves you," and because Virgil was still young enough that he'd not yet grasped the many nuances of the English language, he'd say, "Dad loves you too." Virgil had always considered it one of the best things about his own life—the fact that they both continued to express their love for each other in that particular way: 'Dad loves you...Dad loves you too.'

The footsteps came from behind and when Virgil turned in his chair he saw his boss, Cora LaRue, and the governor's chief of staff, Bradley Pearson, as they approached across the backyard. Virgil put the pill bottles in the pocket of his shorts and stood to greet them, his legs not quite as steady as he would have liked. The air was thick and heavy without any wind and the surface water of the pond as smooth and flat as a tabletop mirror, but when Virgil looked over at the willow tree where he'd just spoken with his dead father he saw a few of the branches sway as if someone had just brushed them aside.

The buzzing in his head was back and at that very moment Virgil knew in his heart he'd do anything to make it all go away.

Anything at all.

WHEN THE PEOPLE OF INDIANA ELECTED HEWITT (Mac) McConnell as governor, he answered their concerns over rising crime rates by forming the Major Crimes Unit. He appointed Cora LaRue as the administrator of the

division and together she and the governor chose Virgil as
lead detective for all investigative operations. Because of
the nature of politics though, Cora spent most of her
time dealing with Pearson instead of the governor. As a
result, Pearson—the state's biggest political operator—
often used this to his advantage in ways that were not
only unnecessary but also counterproductive. In short, it
was typical politics, which Virgil despised more than just
about anything. Cora never let her dislike of Pearson get
in the way of her job, though she never tried to hide her
feelings either. Pearson, on the other hand, operator that
he was, rarely let his emotions show. You could be a friend
one minute if it suited any particular agenda, or
conversely, if the need arose, you could be an enemy of
the state. The problem with people like Pearson, Virgil
knew, was that those two things were not often mutually
exclusive.

"Jonesy, how are you feeling?" Cora asked.

"I'm squeaking by," Virgil said. His words were slurred
and his tongue felt thick and unresponsive and he had to
look away from Cora when he spoke.

"We need to talk to you, Jonesy. I'm sorry about this, I
really am."

"Sorry about what?"

"Oh for Christ's sake, Cora, look at him," Pearson
said. "It's the right call. He's in no condition. No condition at all. He has tubes coming out of him and he sounds
like he's three sheets to the wind. How about we get this
over with and get back to work?"

"Hi, Bradley, always a pleasure," Virgil said. "I'm standing right here, you know. How about telling me what's going on?"

Pearson ran his hands across his forehead then up through his thinning hair. He pulled back so hard on his scalp that for a moment the outer corners of his eyes angled upward in a manner that gave him an effeminate look. He started to speak, but Cora cut him off.

"Jonesy, about an hour ago, on direct orders from the governor, you've been replaced as lead detective of the Major Crimes Unit." She paused to let her words sink in and Virgil saw her eyes slide away from his own. "Ron Miles has been appointed by the governor as your replacement."

Virgil sat back down in his lawn chair and looked out at the pond water. When he didn't respond, Pearson filled the silence. "Jesus Christ, Jones, what did you expect? Look at yourself. You're a goddamned mess. How many pills are you popping these days, anyway?"

"Why are you here, Bradley?"

"To make sure that there is no misunderstanding regarding your situation."

The drugs were still working on him and when Virgil spoke he took no care with his words or their intent. "How much of that is your doing? Never mind, you don't have to answer. We already know the answer to that question, don't we? So here's the deal Pearson...I think I want you to leave. In fact, I'm sure of it. Would you like me to show you to your car?"

"In your condition? I'd like to see you try," Pearson said. He stepped forward and when he did his foot came down on top of the cane pole and snapped it in half. Pearson jumped a little at the sound the cane made when it broke and when he did, Virgil knew he had not stepped on it with purpose. Pearson bent over to pick up the ruined pole, as if the act of lifting it in his hands could repair the damage. "Don't touch that," Virgil said, his voice no more than a whisper. "I really would like you to leave now."

Cora looked at Pearson, then back at Virgil. "Would you two please give it a rest?"

"This is my home, Cora." Virgil said. "I make the rules here. Not him and not you, either." When she didn't respond, Virgil said, "What?"

"There's something else."

"There always is, Cora. I just can't for the life of me imagine what it might be."

"Your replacement isn't temporary. They're not going to let you come back."

Virgil stood and faced her. "Say that again."

Cora took an involuntary step back, as if in fear. "The state. They're forcing you out."

"*What?* On what grounds?"

"The medical reports for one. You'll qualify for three-quarters disability. With your time on the job your pension will kick in right away. I've done the math and the truth is you'll be making more by walking away than if you stayed."

Virgil kept glancing over at the willow tree, as if something his father had said would somehow help him. He bent down to retrieve the broken cane pole and when he stood, the look on Cora's face seemed as sad and mixed as his own emotions.

"How bad is it?" she said.

"I don't know, Cora. Some things just can't be fixed."

She stepped close and placed her hand on the flat of Virgil's bare chest, her eyes inspecting the PICC line. "I'm not talking about the fishing pole, Jonesy."

"I know you're not. Neither am I."

Cora shook her head, then raised her chin, her voice taking on an official tone. "I'm sorry, Detective, but I'm going to have to ask you for your badge."

Virgil dropped the cane pole back in the grass at Pearson's feet, then reached into his pocket, pulled out his badge and skipped it across the surface of the pond. The badge made it about half way across before it settled and then sank in the murky depths.

"You want my badge? Go and get it." He turned to walk up to his house, but Cora didn't let it play.

"You break my heart sometimes, Jonesy. Do you know that?"

CHAPTER FOUR

R on Miles ducked under the crime-scene tape and stepped up to the apartment door, then stopped in his tracks. He peered inside, saw the crime scene techs—seven of them in all, the most he'd seen at one location in quite a while—caught Rosie's eye, then backed out. He didn't want to contaminate the area. *Shit load of blood,* he thought.

Ron had been around. Had spent most of his career as an Indianapolis Metro Homicide cop, so he was no stranger to crime scenes or blood, but still, hell of a way to start a new job, that much blood.

A FEW MINUTES LATER DETECTIVE TOM ROSENCRANTZ stepped out of the apartment wearing Tyvek coveralls, shoe protectors and latex gloves. There were bloodstains on his knees, the tops of his shoe protectors by his toes and the palms of his hands. He unzipped the suit, pulled the hood back and stripped out of the gear. One of the techs handed him a biohazard bag and he dropped everything inside and handed it back. "Jesus Christ, I've never seen that much blood without a body," he said to Miles. "You just get here?"

"Yeah. What do you mean without a body?"

"I mean, there's enough blood in there to do a remake of Stephen King's Carrie, but there's no body."

"Huh. How much blood are they saying?"

Rosencrantz looked over Ron's shoulder. "You get a new car?"

"Yep, just picked it up two days ago. The guys over at the motor pool set me up with the radios, lights and siren, the works."

Rosencrantz smiled at him. "Nice." The car was nice too. A brand new black over black Ford Fusion. "Get the Police Interceptor motor?"

"You mean engine. Motor is electric. Engine is internal combustion. And yeah, did I ever. Goddamn thing runs like a raped ape. All-wheel drive too." Miles glanced at the apartment. "So anyway, how much blood?"

"Here comes Mimi. I'll let her explain it. I guess it's sort of technical. Plus, that voice of hers..."

Miles puffed out his cheeks. "Tell me about it. She could be one of those phone sex broads. Half the time when she's talking to me I feel like I'm about to get busted for sexual harassment just for listening."

"Just half?" Rosencrantz made a rude noise with his lips. "You're doing better than me."

"They still have that, don't they? Those phone sex lines?"

"I'm sure I wouldn't know," Rosencrantz said, his face as flat and blank as a piece of slate.

MIMI PHILLIPS, THE LEAD CRIME SCENE TECHNICIAN, told them in no uncertain terms—all with a voice that sounded like a 30-second satellite radio spot for a porn flick—that whomever the blood belonged to, they were, without question, as dead as the Pope's dick. "Double entendre intended," she added.

"You're sure?" Miles asked.

Mimi reached into her pocket, then folded a stick of gum across her tongue. "No doubt about it," she said. "The human body—and these are just averages, mind you, depending on size and so on and so forth—holds about six quarts of blood. The loss of about forty percent or more of that volume will generally require immediate resuscitation. But what you have to remember is the amount of blood loss any one person can withstand is going to depend on their physical condition and cardio-vascular shape. Athletes, people who live in high altitudes and the elderly are examples of disparate groups that will have differing susceptibilities to blood loss.

"The amount of blood we're talking about for that to happen...it's about a two-liter sized bottle of soda pop. What you've got in there is at least twice that. If it all belongs to the same person, then, yeah, they're dead all right. Deader than..."

⸻

"How soon before you can tell us if it all belongs to the same person?" Miles asked.

Mimi bit the inside corner of her lower lip. "Hmm, belonged, I think is the word you want there. Not very long at all to type it out. Three days if you want to match the DNA from the personal effects and we rush the shit out of it. You do want the DNA, don't you?"

"Yes, we do," Miles said. "Rush the shit out of it."

Mimi turned to go back to work, then over her shoulder, "Hell of a way to start a new job, huh? Nice wheels though. Bet that baby scoots."

⸻

"You talk to him yet?" Rosencrantz asked.

"Who?"

He gave Miles a 'Don't try to bullshit me' look. "Who, my ass. Have you called him? Anything?"

"Cora asked me not to say anything until she and Pearson had a chance to go over to his place and tell him in person." Miles looked at his watch. "They're probably still there."

"Three things," Rosencrantz said. He ticked them off his fingers. "One, if you haven't figured this out yet, Pearson is a snake and now he's *your* snake. I'd get used to it, I were you *and* I'd watch my back. Two, Jonesy is not only a good guy, but he's our friend. At the very least you owe him a phone call and when I say at the very least, I mean exactly that. Three, it is my belief that there might be something else going on, politically speaking, that put him out and you in. You may want to spend some time with that, you being the crack investigator and all."

Miles reached up and flattened his grey hair with the palm of his hand. "I know about Pearson. This won't be my first interaction with the man. And, I am going to speak with Jonesy, but I thought it might be best to let things settle for a bit. Also, I'm not a political guy. I'm an investigator guy. They tell me to investigate, that's what I do."

Rosencrantz held his hands up, palms out. "Hey, I'm not giving you grief, Ron, But this little squad we've got here, our MCU, it's always been run a little...sideways, if you know what I mean."

"If you mean you make your own rules, keep the intel to yourselves and don't have too much oversight, then yeah, I've sort of noticed that. That might change too."

Rosie shook his head. "That's not what I meant. What you said is true, but it's more than that. You're suddenly one of the most powerful cops in the state with only two layers between you and the governor himself."

"And?"

"Have you asked yourself why they wanted *you* for the job?"

Miles was starting to get a little pissed. "You work for me, do I have that right?"

"Yep."

"Then how about you do that?"

"Leave the big thinking to you?"

Miles pointed a finger at Rosencrantz. "Now look..."

"Relax, Ron. I'm on your side. No disrespect intended, okay? You're one of the best investigators I've ever known. I just want you to think about the situation. Investigate the 'why me?' part of the equation, for your own sake if nothing else."

"And maybe for Jonesy too?"

"Why not?"

"Because based on what I've heard, I don't think it will do him any good at this point."

"Maybe it won't. But I've been a part of this group almost since its inception and if I've learned anything, it's this: We get the hard stuff, the political stuff, the good stuff, as Cora likes to call it. But nothing is ever quite what it looks like. Not when you're this close to the top. Never has been anyway. Not one single time."

Miles thought about that for a minute. "Maybe this one will be different."

Rosencrantz laughed without humor. "Did you happen to get a look at Jonesy's files yet? In particular, the one I told you about?"

"Yeah, I did. What about it?"

"Anything jump out at you?"

"It looked like a good shoot. The department, the union, the lawyers, hell even I.A. said it was a good shoot. Plus, it was over twenty years ago. I had to blow the dust off the paper just to see the ink."

"Did you know that was the one and only time Jonesy ever fired his weapon on the job?"

"That's not so unusual."

"You're right about that. But let me tell you two things that aren't in that report. One, did you notice that the guy who almost got his ticket punched by James Pope—the victim so to speak—wasn't listed in the report?"

"Yeah, I did notice that. Who was it?"

Rosencrantz turned his back to Miles for a moment and looked up at the apartment where the crime scene techs were working. When he turned back he said, "Someone with enough juice to get their name pulled from the paperwork. Know anyone like that?" Before Miles could answer, Rosie said something else that made Ron wonder if someone he thought he could trust hadn't already played him for a fool. "That apartment behind us? The one with all the blood? It belonged to a guy named

Nicholas Pope. He was only five or six years old when Jonesy shot his old man to death. He and his twin sister were there, at the shooting. They saw the whole thing. Now it looks like there's another dead Pope. Might just be a coincidence though."

Miles rubbed his temples with his right hand, then squinted through one eye at Rosencrantz. "Who did Jonesy save that day when he shot James Pope?"

"It's not in the report, but it's not exactly a secret, either. The man he saved was Bradley Pearson." Then, as if to hammer home his point, he added, "Just out of curiosity, when they hired you, who approached you first? Was it Cora, or Pearson?"

Miles let out a sigh. "It was Pearson."

Rosencrantz raised an eyebrow at him. "Might want to think about that. Or hell, maybe not. You might be right. What do I know? Maybe this one will be different."

NICHOLAS POPE'S APARTMENT COMPLEX HAD BEEN converted from an old-style traveler's motel. The conversion process had gone like this: The original owner of the motel went broke, which is something that will happen when you don't pay your income taxes. The new owner picked up the building at the subsequent tax sale, fired the housekeeping crew and erected a sign that said 'Studio Apartments For Rent - No References Required.'

The only actual requirement for occupancy was cash in advance every Friday by five or your personal belongings were tossed out on the lot and the locks were changed faster than you could get to the payday advance loan sharks and back. The building was a two-story, L-shaped structure with units on both the front and the rear. Nicholas Pope's unit was in the back on the second floor, about midpoint in the short section of the L. The building was old and its occupants generally fit into one of three categories: Poor, transient, or illegal. Most, Ron thought as he looked around the backside of the building, probably fit nicely into all three.

"You going to suit up, take a look?" Rosencrantz asked him.

"No. I think I'll get with the uniforms and coordinate with the background."

"Start with the woman in the unit right below Pope's. She's the one who made the call."

"She hear or see anything?"

"Not really. But one of the city uniforms said the blood dripped through her ceiling and landed right on a little statue of the Virgin Mary she keeps on her living room coffee table. She thought it was a miracle."

Miles shook his head. "Ah, Christ."

Rosencrantz winced. "Don't say that around her. She'll take your head off."

"How long before she figured it wasn't divine intervention?"

Rosencrantz thought for a few seconds. "You know, I'm not sure. Probably at least a half-day, based on what Mimi is telling us."

Then, just as Miles was about to go talk to the woman, a car turned the corner around the back side of the building going much too fast, its tires squealing in protest. The driver slammed on the brakes and locked up the wheels, but it was too late. The car slid into the side of Miles' brand new squad car with the sickening sound of crumpled sheet metal and broken glass. The driver jumped from her vehicle and half ran, half stumbled toward the stairs that led to Nicholas Pope's apartment. She began to scream, "My brother, my brother. Where's my brother?"

One of the uniforms caught her by the arm, but Nichole Pope was a little faster and a little stronger than the cop expected and when she tried to pull free, they got tangled up in each other and they both ended up on the ground in a heap.

Rosencrantz looked at Miles, then his car, then back at Miles. "Probably shouldn't have parked there. My car is out front, across the street. Welcome to the MCU, Ron."

—End of State of Betrayal Preview—

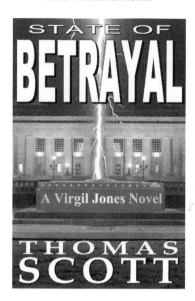

Book 2 of the Virgil Jones Mystery Thriller Series

GET YOUR COPY OF STATE OF BETRAYAL TODAY!

ALSO BY THOMAS SCOTT

The Virgil Jones Mystery Series in order:

State of Anger - Book 1

State of Betrayal - Book 2

State of Control - Book 3

State of Deception - Book 4

State of Exile - Book 5

State of Freedom - Book 6

State of Genesis - Book 7

State of Humanity - Book 8

And the story continues.

As Mason would say, "Stay tuned..."

Updates on future Virgil Jones novels available at:

ThomasScottBooks.com

ABOUT THE AUTHOR

Thomas Scott is the author of the Virgil Jones series of novels. He lives in northern Indiana with his lovely wife, Debra, his children, and his trusty sidekicks and writing buddies, Lucy, the cat, and Buster, the dog.

Thomas loves to read and is a self-proclaimed regular guy. He holds an Airline Transport Pilot Rating, is a former airline pilot, Chief Pilot, and Director of Flight Operations for a private corporation.

You may contact Thomas anytime via his website ThomasScottBooks.com where he personally answers every single email he receives. Be sure to sign up to be notified of the latest release information.

Also, if you enjoy the Virgil Jones series of books, leaving an honest review on Amazon.com helps others decide if a book is right for them. Just a sentence or two makes all the difference in the world.

For information on future books in the Virgil Jones series, or to connect with the author, please visit:

ThomasScottBooks.com

Made in the USA
Lexington, KY
28 November 2019

57812370R00226